Secrets Beneath the Saddle

A Martin Heir Novel
Sharolyn Richards

OTHER BOOKS BY SHAROLYN Richards

<u>Romantic Suspense Travel Series</u>
Arlington's Treasure
Betrayed in Taiwan

ACKNOWLEDGEMENTS

I HAVE LEARNED SO much writing this book. I want to express my appreciation to the editors at CookieLyn Publishing. They help me make my story so much better than I could do by myself. I am also so grateful to my fellow writing group members. Also, the book cover artist at LJP Creative did a fantastic job. So many people have come together to help create this book. Last, but definitely not least, I need to thank my husband and kids for supporting me through all the ups and downs and the busy times.

To my husband. For believing in me and supporting me and answering my horse questions.

CHAPTER 1

"I GOT IT TAKEN care of." Callum rubbed his eyes, fighting the guilt this conversation was bringing up. The dark alley was forbidding, and he couldn't think of why they had met here. Wouldn't have meeting at his house been just as secluded? Moisture rolled down the back of his neck, but Callum couldn't tell if it was from sweat or the drizzle of rain that was normal for this time of year in England. He pulled his coat tighter against him in an attempt to ward off the autumn chill.

"It will look like an accident?" Vin, Callum's cousin, asked.

"Yes." Callum swallowed the bile rising in his throat.

"And you're sure Emma will sell quickly?" Vin asked.

Callum nodded. "Why is this particular property so important to you?"

The question had plagued Callum since Vin had come to him with the plan and blackmailed him. Someone else had taken the punishment for Callum's wrongdoing, with the help of Vin, of course. He had wanted to go along with Vin no matter what. He owed him, after all, but the guilt had gotten so bad that he spent most nights drinking to help him forget. But this was different than theft. This was murder. Vin had already made it very clear that if Callum didn't do as he asked, he would 'find' incriminating evidence against Callum. Callum didn't want to spend time in jail and knew Vin could keep his name clear of this incident as long as everything went to plan, but he couldn't help his curiosity.

"Getting rid of the competition for you, of course!" Vin slapped him on the back.

Callum very much doubted Vin was doing this for him. Callum had to go along with what Vin wanted whether Vin told him his reasoning or not if he wanted to stay out of prison. He swiped at the moisture on his neck, grateful Vin wouldn't know he was sweating. All this talk of murder made him sick to his stomach.

Vin went on as if his statement cleared up everything. "I changed the will, so it says Emma is to run the estate and left the house to her. Thomas knows as well as you do,

Emma doesn't want the business." Vin's eyes darkened. "Since you failed to do your part and get into his good graces enough for him to leave it to you, we have to do things on our own timeline instead of waiting for the man to die naturally."

Callum swallowed hard. His control was slipping away. He just had to get ahead enough with his own horse training and breeding that he could move far away from Vin's influence. Maybe he would go to the continent, change his name and start a new life there. He had to stay on Vin's good side long enough to achieve that goal. He focused on the conversation at hand.

"Thomas Martin didn't put his own daughter in charge of running the estate?" Callum was beginning to think there were too many variables in this plan that could go wrong.

Vin snorted. "No. He put some kid in charge."

Callum could only think of one kid Thomas would put in his will but thought better than to mention it. If he did, he might have to stage a second 'accident.' It was bad enough that Emma Bailey, only daughter of Thomas Martin, could be in town again if she decided not to sell. He hated the woman.

"That's a big risk, Vin. You could lose your license."

"No one will be the wiser if you keep your tongue from wagging." Vin put his arm around Callum's shoulder and squeezed his shoulder hard—a signal that he should make sure that never happened. "And you're sure no one will know you changed the will?" Sweat coated Callum's hands, and he had to force himself not to wipe them on his trousers. "Thomas doesn't have a copy of the original will?"

"He does. I had to give him a copy of his will the way he wrote it, otherwise Thomas would know I was breaking the law before we had a chance to arrange for his accident."

"What if he gives a copy of his will to Emma before his... umm... accident?" Callum swallowed again to get rid of the lump in his throat.

"That's why it needs to happen quickly," Vin said. "We can't take that chance. You need to make sure he stores it somewhere. I'll make the suggestion. You make sure he dies before he is able to tell Emma where he put it. That will give you time to convince Emma to sell after his death." Vin raised his eyebrows.

"Emma doesn't want the business," Callum assured him. "She doesn't even want to live out here. She loves the city. She'll sell the moment I ask."

Callum was confident that part of the plan would work out.

Vin slapped him on the back again. The sound reverberated off the surrounding buildings. Callum winced and glanced around. The windows in the darkened buildings glared down at him. Callum had the distinct feeling that there were eyes witnessing their plan to ensure someone died. He was going to help at the estate later in the week. He would have to do it then, or he was going to go crazy.

CHAPTER 2

(6 MONTHS LATER)

The crowd around Macie made her head spin. Her brain felt fuzzy, and her legs ached from the long hours of sitting on a plane from Idaho to England. She was finally at Heathrow Airport. Though her purse was strapped securely around her shoulder, Macie clutched it against her chest. She didn't trust anyone around her not to steal her purse. She approached customs, fishing her passport out of her purse without letting go of it with the other hand. The attendant opened it and stamped the first spot.

Macie continued to follow the signs to baggage claim, hoping she wouldn't get lost, that her ride would be waiting for her, and that she hadn't made a huge mistake in taking a job as a nanny.

She had thought about it during her long flight. Her sister, Katie, had convinced her it would be a good idea to get away for a while. Macie figured Katie had her best interests at heart, but they had never been close. Why had she let her talk her into it? Macie had asked herself that question over and over.

Someone jostled her, bringing her out of her thoughts. She hunched her shoulders over to hide from the people pressing in on her from every side. Even though she was in England, a variety of languages echoed in the cacophony that was the norm for crowded places. Macie's breathing came out in ragged gasps, and she clutched her purse tighter. She took deep breaths. More people would speak English once she got out of the airport. It was an international airport after all. Her pep talk didn't help, and she continued to do her best to be invisible.

She found her bags and took he letter Mrs. Bailey had sent out of her backpack, if only to block out the chaos around her for a moment. Macie scanned the words. Mrs. Bailey hadn't said a specific time someone would pick her up, so Macie assumed it was at the time her flight had been scheduled to land. The plane had landed a bit late.

She closed her eyes and took three deep breaths before standing to find the passenger pickup. She could hear her father's voice. *"You don't need to go, you know."* She also heard the unspoken voice she read into his words. *"You've never been able to handle yourself away from us. What makes you think you can now?"*

Though Macie's father or mother would never say those things to her, she was sure they thought them.

The nanny job had a trial period of three months. If she didn't prove her worth in that amount of time, the contract very clearly stated she would have to pay her own way home. She had very little money, and the trial period provided room and board and only enough money to buy a ticket home. If she was sent home, she would have to admit to her parents she really was a failure.

Macie stiffened her spine. She would not fail. She couldn't. At twenty years old, Macie had barely managed to finish one abysmal year of college—an experience she would rather forget. Nannying three girls in a foreign country would hopefully break the cycle of her growing list of failures. She was not sure it was the best or easiest solution. She silently cursed Katie in her mind. Then she cursed herself. It was her own fault she was here. She could have pushed Katie's suggestions away, but for a moment of stupidity, she felt that watching kids again would prove she was capable and worthy of praise.

She wouldn't let herself panic. Never mind that she hadn't babysat in a long time. No matter how hard it got, Macie would not run to her family for help. Stupid pride got her into this mess; pride would get her out.

If her parents helped her get home, they would give her the familiar pitying look. They would say she was kind, and that was all that mattered. For once, she wanted to influence someone—do some good in the world—not just exist and cause trouble. She never meant to, but whenever she tried to do something, it always ended up wrong. Like the last time she babysat...but she wouldn't think about that, especially not on her way to nanny for three girls. Plus, that happened five years ago.

Maybe that was why Katie's suggestion had been so tempting. It was a way to redeem herself after that awful experience.

Macie followed the signs to the car pickup area of London Heathrow Airport, anxious to be on her way. Behind her, travelers pushed through the exit, their chatter excited and energetic.

She stood dismayed at the three loading zones. Was he already here? And if so, which zone was he in? Macie scoured each zone, searching for the stereotypical older gentleman holding a sign with her name and waiting to stow her luggage. Macie didn't see a single poster board.

Macie lugged her bags to the first zone and scanned the area but didn't see a poster, so she moved on to the second zone. She was already an hour past the time the driver would arrive.

Macie dragged her pile of suitcases to the third loading zone but stopped short as travelers crowded in front of her. What if she'd been duped? The thought brought tears to her eyes. But why would someone pay for her ticket here? It didn't make sense to pay money to get her here if the plan was to abandon her. More grisly scenarios entered her mind, but Macie forced them away. Her legs trembled, but she gritted her teeth. She would not show fear. Macie searched the line of cars in the third loading zone and still didn't see an eye-catching poster with her name.

She meandered back to the first loading zone, intent on walking the length of the loading zone to find her ride. Macie pressed her way down the line of cars in what she hoped was a confident stride. No one called out to her, and she didn't see even one Post-it note with her name on it.

A blond man leaning against a sleek black car caught her attention. He looked mid-twenties. He ran his hand through his shaggy hair, his muscles flexing slightly, and focused on his phone. She could almost feel the frustration flowing off him. She had a moment of sympathy, but then he lifted his eyes to scan the area, and she quickly put her head down and walked past him, embarrassed she had been caught staring. Macie stopped when she reached the end of the line and retraced her steps. Panic clutched her chest again, making it hard to breathe. Her first day, and she was already stranded.

"Hey, Miss. You need a ride somewhere?"

Macie jumped at the foreign voice, her thoughts and breathing both hard and uneven. Her heart hammered in her chest as she searched for who had spoken. A man stood next to a taxi—smiling expectantly. Macie wished she wasn't so out of her element, but her shaking legs and the tightness in her jaw gave her away.

Macie attempted to keep her voice steady. "No, thank you. I'm waiting for a ride."

She took a long shaky breath before backtracking down the long line of cars; some had been replaced by other vehicles as passengers were picked up. She passed the blond man and his sleek black car again.

His lips lifted slightly. Her heart stuttered with that small change in his demeanor from what she had witnessed before. His green eyes studied her in a way that made her feel vulnerable, so she glanced away, her cheeks heating at the thought that he saw her checking him out. She hurried forward, her hands clutching the handles of her bags so tightly her fingers tingled.

"Macie?"

Macie jumped and whirled around. The sound of her name in his English accent startled her almost as much as hearing her name at all.

"Macie Call?" he asked, his brows raised.

Macie nodded.

"Daniel Evans. I'm here to take you to Martin Estate." His accent wasn't so strong she couldn't understand him, but her heart stuttered before she caught onto what he had said.

Martin Estate? But her employer's name was Bailey, not Martin. "I'm sorry. You must be waiting for someone else. I'm going to nanny for the Baileys."

Daniel's jaw tightened. "The Baileys run the Martin Estate. Emma Bailey sent me to pick you up."

Macie's careful composure almost collapsed as a rush of relief swept through her, but she stiffened her spine and regained her presence of mind. This was no knight in shining armor. He let her pass him without calling out or holding up a sign with her name. No matter how much his accent was making her heart do funny things. She had to remember that he was not here to save her from her distress. Macie bit her lip to keep from snapping at him, since he might drive off without her.

"Mrs. Bailey said you would have a sign with my name."

Daniel nodded and unfolded a small piece of paper with Macie's name printed boldly in the center.

Macie's jaw dropped open. Blood rushed past her ears. "Why weren't you holding it up?"

Daniel shrugged and put the paper back in his pocket. "I figured I'd recognize an American."

If only she could wipe that smug look off his arrogant face. Macie clenched her fists and counted slowly to five, the way she had when her brothers annoyed her. She wanted to throttle the man. Though with him a full head taller than she was and sporting muscles Macie shouldn't be admiring, she wouldn't do much harm to him.

Daniel's countenance changed. "Sorry. I shouldn't tease you. I got distracted with business and was texting my colleague when you walked past, and I didn't notice you. I guess I should have had the sign up from the beginning."

Macie eyed him. He seemed sincere, but she couldn't be sure if he was just mollifying her.

"Let me get your bags." Daniel stepped toward her.

The indentation of Macie's grip were probably now permanently pressed into the handles of her bags, but she forced her grip loose.

"Are you not the normal chauffeur?" Macie stepped away and let Daniel put them in the car.

Daniel snorted. "No. I apologize if I caused you stress. I assumed she would fly you into Gatwick. It was dumb of me not to look at the agenda until I got to the airport."

Macie felt some of her anger subside. "Well, my flight was late, so I actually just landed."

He nodded, scooped up her first bag, and threw it in the trunk of the car. He stopped when he noticed her watching him.

"Did you require my assistance getting into the car?"

Macie's eyes stung with tears. She was at the end of her rope today and didn't need this stranger making fun of her ignorance. Macie jerked the car door open and sat stiffly in the passenger-side back seat, waiting for Daniel to load her other bag. She clutched her backpack to her chest and clung to her frustration, hoping it would keep her from crying in front of him.

No matter how much time it took to get from London to the Bailey's Estate, or Martin Estate—or whatever it was called—Macie was sure it would be a painfully long drive with only this man for company. When Daniel opened the door and sat in front of her, Macie glanced at what should have been the driver's seat. No steering wheel. *Oh… right… They drive on the other side of the road here.*

Daniel looked at her in the rearview mirror. His eyes glinted, and she swore he was secretly making fun of her.

Macie looked away.

She turned her attention to the fact that she was in a new country. When she was hired, Macie scoured the internet for every detail she could find about England, hoping she would have the chance to see some of its sights while she was here.

"So, do the Baileys travel a lot?" Macie asked Daniel, determined not to let her irritation show. Daniel would likely tattletale to Mrs. Bailey if Macie was rude. Macie watched the cars swerving around them on the road and was grateful she didn't have to drive.

Daniel shook his head. "Not a lot. They mostly stick close to home to run their horse training business."

"Horses?" Macie almost clapped, but Daniel would probably judge her. Macie had always wanted to learn to ride, but her parents didn't have time or interest in getting her lessons. She probably wouldn't have been any good anyway.

Daniel's lips twitched into the beginnings of a smile.

"Can you tell me what the estate is like?" Macie asked, hoping he would stop smirking at her.

"Lots of pastures and lots of horses to hurt little girls."

Macie crossed her arms over her chest, which was barely larger than a little girl's.

Daniel must have noticed her movement, a slight flush appeared on his neck. "Meaning your charges, of course."

He turned to look out the windshield so quickly Macie wasn't sure if he was being sarcastic or not. He was not being very welcoming, and Macie held on to her frustration to keep the tears at bay.

Macie leaned back in her seat and refused to look at Daniel. His words were polite enough, but every twitch of his lips implied he was making fun of her.

"How long will it take to get to the estate?" The sooner she could get out of this car, the better.

"It's a long way. About two hours."

Macie rolled her eyes. How English of him. Two hours, and she was less than half across Idaho.

Buildings raced past her window as Daniel circled yet another roundabout. She clutched her seatbelt as Daniel swerved through traffic and entered massive roundabouts with four lanes filled with cars. The big double-decker buses towering over their car seemed in danger of tipping.

Macie watched the city give way to trees and bushes lining the highway. She stared at the back of Daniel's head, trying to decide if she should continue to drag conversation from him.

She forced herself to let go of the seatbelt and closed her eyes, and eventually the jet lag caught up to her, and she fell asleep.

CHAPTER 3

DANIEL GLANCED INTO THE rearview mirror as he left the worst of the traffic. He couldn't understand why anyone would want to live in that city.

Macie was asleep. She must be knackered. He had never gone anywhere so didn't know what flying was like. Why was he even playing chauffeur when he had so much work to do? And the fact that Mrs. Bailey bought tickets that took Macie to Heathrow instead of Gatwick infuriated him. He knew it was his fault for assuming she'd bought tickets for the closer airport and not checking earlier. It was no wonder Macie looked ready to collapse with relief when she realized he was her ride. She was probably worried she was going to be stranded.

He looked at Macie's reflection. She was pretty. Her long, almost black hair was pulled into a braid. Her skin was a nice olive complexion. Her brown eyes were what had captivated him before he had realized she might be the nanny. He had seen her vulnerability, even though she had tried hard to hide it, but he was used to seeing vulnerability in his mother's eyes. He wouldn't miss it. She was young. He would guess twenty at the oldest. She would have her hands full with the girls.

Daniel didn't talk much to the nannies. He was too busy keeping up with Mrs. Bailey's demanding training schedule to make small talk. But the tears Macie had swiped away made him replay their short interaction.

He genuinely hadn't noticed her pass the first time and berated himself for getting distracted with his phone and not holding up the sign. He was only one man and could only do so much. No one else could do his job at the estate. Mrs. Bailey wanted him to train as many horses as they had when her father was alive and doing half of the training himself. It was an impossible expectation for one man.

Because of that, Mrs. Bailey was losing more money than she was making. She kept telling customers they could bring their horses before Daniel had the time to work with them, so they were paying to feed a horse they weren't making any immediate profit on.

Jack should have been the one to pick Macie up, but Mrs. Bailey—he couldn't seem to think of her as Emma even though he felt comfortable addressing her husband by his first name—had insisted that he needed to accompany her to some social event. So instead of picking up the nanny on his way home from London—which would have made more sense—Jack had arrived home just as Daniel was leaving. Daniel shook his head. Ridiculous. The hours he was losing picking up the new nanny heightened his stress with every passing minute.

He hoped Macie would last longer than the last two nannies. He didn't know what the girls did to scare them off, but not one of them lasted more than two weeks. Mrs. Bailey couldn't seem to find an English girl to come out to nanny. He didn't know how much she paid them, but Gladys, the cook and head eavesdropper of the estate said they barely made enough in the three months trial period to buy a return ticket. Gladys said they made probably half of minimum wage. No one in England would work for the price Mrs. Bailey offered. He didn't know why American girls agreed to it. Maybe the thrill of working in a new country outweighed any idea they were likely being taken advantage of.

He turned into the driveway. The sign above the gate read: Martin Estate. The gates hung on their hinges—a sign that the Baileys were not taking care of the house like Thomas would want. At least the brick wall that separated the entire front of the property from the road looked nice. The curtains in the office window drew back. The Baileys must have returned from their social event. He wanted to get to work and would prefer not talking to Mrs. Bailey for the rest of the day. If only he could get a job elsewhere and not have to speak to her for the rest of his life, but then what would become of his mother?

And what of his promise to his father? He didn't regret helping Mrs. Bailey's late father, Thomas Martin, but he did regret he wasn't able to set up a proper vet clinic at the estate because of his death. That had been Thomas Martin's plan, but now he couldn't even get the horse training done. He sighed. No use brooding about it now. He had to get out of the car before Mrs. Bailey came out.

He glanced at Macie in the back seat. She was awake, blinking. Fear flashed in her large brown eyes and she shot a look in his direction that almost convinced him to stay and help her find her way around, but he had his own job to do, and the less he was forced to talk to Mrs. Bailey, the better. Daniel didn't understand why Jack always bowed to her wishes when it came to matters of the business. She didn't know anything about it, not that she did much anywhere else in the house, either.

***

A bump jolted Macie awake. Daniel drove up a long driveway to a huge mansion. Macie couldn't help but stare. No wonder it was called an estate. Windows lined the side of the red brick house, suggesting the number of rooms in the mansion to be astronomical. Macie's jaw dropped. How many kids had she signed up to nanny again? She really hoped it wasn't twelve.

The large three-car garage attached to the left of the house was probably the size of her house at home. Her eyes flicked to the front door. Large half-circle stairs led to the wooden double front door. Two sidelight windows flanked the door, making it look even larger. Everything here was enormous, making Macie feel even smaller.

Daniel parked the car parallel to the imposing front steps. She sat stock still in the seat, unwilling to exit the car first. This couldn't really be the estate. It was a mansion. The pay she was receiving had not given her the impression she would be living in such luxury.

He turned and held her gaze for a moment, and she thought she saw a spark of sympathy flash in his eyes. He returned his attention to the house, and she was sure she had imagined it.

A thin, beautiful woman wearing a dress that rivaled any ballroom dress Macie had ever seen came bustling out the front door. Her dark brown hair was done up in an elegant chignon at the base of her neck. Macie guessed it was Mrs. Bailey. She was beautiful. Macie took in her own appearance. Her jeans and T-shirt made her feel very underdressed. Mrs. Bailey carried a baby in a pink day jumper on her hip, who bounced up and down with the woman's movement. The baby's tiny hands grabbed at the neckline of Mrs. Bailey's dress, even though Mrs. Bailey kept pulling her clothes out of the baby's grip.

Daniel opened his door and walked away as fast as Macie thought was possible without running without a backward glance. Apparently, his chauffeur duties were over. At least there was no mistaking Daniel as a doting gentleman. Macie climbed out of the car and slung her backpack over her shoulders.

She turned in a circle to take in her surroundings. A large brick wall separated the estate property from the road. The gate that closed off access to the property was open and appeared to be bent, but Macie couldn't tell for sure from where she stood. The front yard was lined in large trees, but she could see pastureland fenced off beyond the trees to her right and she could see the roof of a house through the trees to her left. Macie whirled around to face to house again as the tap of heels on cement reminded her she was here to do a job.

"Macie! Cheers!" The woman, her voice lower than Macie had expected from the thin woman, was shorter than even Macie's five and a half feet. Her accent was more lilting, like she was very careful about how she sounded and presented herself to strangers. "How was your trip? I'm Mrs. Emma Bailey, and this is Evelyn, one of your charges. I trust your trip went well." Mrs. Bailey swung Evelyn over to Macie.

Macie barely had hold of the baby before Mrs. Bailey dropped her arms. Evelyn's dimpled hands clutched Macie's shoulder for balance. Her feathery brown hair tickled Macie's cheek as she shifted her head to find her mother.

"I'm so glad you've come. I haven't been able to get a thing done since the last nanny left," Mrs. Bailey said. "I wish my London nanny had been willing to move out to the country with me. She was a gem."

Macie tried to listen to Mrs. Bailey's chatter, but Evelyn started squalling and reached for her mother. Before Macie could give the baby back, Mrs. Bailey headed toward the large mansion and glanced over her shoulder as if to ascertain Macie was following.

Macie tried to bounce Evelyn on her hip while balancing her bag over her shoulder, wondering when she would get her luggage out of the trunk. She jogged after Mrs. Bailey, struggling to keep Evelyn from nose-diving onto the driveway as the baby continued to squirm and reach for her mother. Macie wondered where they were going. The woman had come out the front door, but was leading her to the side of the house opposite the garage.

As they turned the corner of the mansion, the white and pink blossoms of fruit trees dancing in the breeze almost made her forget the nervousness rising in her chest. Daniel mentioned horse training. Macie took a moment to take in the surroundings here. Beyond the trees were rounded fenced-off areas. Macie figured that might be where some training took place. Macie tried to look beyond those. She could see the edge of a building the same color brick as the mansion. Mrs. Bailey stopped suddenly at a door positioned nearly center of the side of the mansion.

A man led a horse from the side of the back building. Daniel. Macie caught her breath. Even from this distance she could see the confidence in his stride. He wore a riding helmet. She looked away, embarrassed at the way she was gawking at him.

"Horsie!" Evelyn squealed and shifted the direction of her lunging. Macie smiled. Even the baby had a delightful accent.

Macie scanned the area but didn't see anyone else. "Is Daniel the only one working with the horses?" Macie couldn't keep the curiosity out of her voice. She found horses fascinating. Maybe it was the result of never being around them.

Mrs. Bailey eyed her. "Daniel has Nate's help. That's all he needs."

Macie's arms tightened slightly around Evelyn. She had no reason to know anything about the estate but couldn't help the familiar tightening of self-consciousness in her muscles.

"I have no idea what those horse boys do," Mrs. Bailey said.

Macie opened her mouth as Mrs. Bailey opened the side door, and Mrs. Bailey raised an eyebrow.

"So does Mr. Bailey run the estate?"

Mrs. Bailey visibly bristled but took a deep breath. "I run the estate. Jack works in London during the week, but you'll meet him tonight."

Macie tried to make sense of the woman's words. She didn't know what the horse boys did, but she ran the estate. It didn't make sense, even with her nonexistent experience in horses or running a business.

Mrs. Bailey led her inside. "This is the quickest way to your room. It's right next to the nursery, so you can take care of Evelyn if she needs anything in the middle of the night."

"Excuse me?" Macie was sure she misunderstood. Did Mrs. Bailey expect her to care for the children at all hours of the day?

"You said you'd care for the children, correct?"

Macie nodded.

"Part of that care happens in the middle of the night. Evelyn sleeps through the night, but if she gets sick, you will have to be on hand. That won't be a problem, will it?"

Macie shook her head.

"I need my sleep to have my wits about me so I can manage the business affairs, since Jack isn't around during the week to help." Mrs. Bailey's tone spoke volumes of her bitterness. Mrs. Bailey went on, forcing Macie to pay attention. "You understand. You're young. Young kids don't need as much sleep."

Macie forced her lips to stay frozen in a smile as she juggled the baby on her hip. She fought the heat creeping through her neck at her ignorance. Why had she been stupid enough not to realize that as a live-in nanny, she would be taking care of the children day and night? Maybe because in Mary Poppins, it didn't show her getting up in the middle of the night.

She clambered up the stairs behind Mrs. Bailey. Her thighs burned with the extra weight required to climb the steep stairs with a child in her arms. Macie wouldn't ruin her first day by saying she had always needed nine-plus hours of sleep if she was going to be the patient, fun nanny she planned on being. She shook her head. *Macie, you really are stupid. No wonder Mom and Dad thought you were a fool for taking this job.*

Her breaths came in short bursts when Macie reached the top of the stairs and Mrs. Bailey opened the door to a room. The crib in the room told Macie whose room this was.

Mrs. Bailey took Evelyn from Macie's arms and plunked her into the bed. Then she walked out and closed the door. "It's her nap time."

Macie glanced at her watch. "So, she naps at four in the afternoon?" Wasn't it a bit late if the baby went to bed early? She hoped she'd set her watch to the correct time. Maybe she misunderstood the flight attendant on the plane.

Mrs. Bailey pressed her lips into a straight line. "She takes a nap whenever I need a break. She has been so clingy. This is her third nap today." Mrs. Bailey paused as if thinking. "I don't think she slept the other two times, but I needed a break."

Macie fought to keep her mouth from falling open. Maybe she could get Evelyn established on a routine nap time. Macie had taken a child development class during her first of only two semesters at College of Southern Idaho. She remembered reading something about how kids thrived on order and routine.

"You have no other responsibilities besides watching the girls, so Evelyn will only need one nap under your care. You are to be with the girls at all times." Mrs. Bailey opened a door across the hall from the baby's room. Macie wondered briefly if that meant she was supposed to sit outside Evelyn's door with the older girls while she napped, but she quickly rejected the thought. Surely they could do something while she slept. Mrs. Bailey had said girls, but how many were there again? Macie knew it had been on the job announcement, but was so tired she couldn't think.

"Now," Mrs. Bailey said with a sigh. "Here is your room. You have a private washroom. The other girls have rooms farther down the hall. The master suite is in the other wing. We will have dinner in two hours. I've got to get out of this dress. You arrived before I could change after I returned from a charity function. You look knackered, so you may rest until dinner. Get the baby and join us then. Go down the stairs down the hall, and you will practically run into the dining hall. I'll send someone up with your luggage shortly."

Evelyn screamed from the other room. Macie looked to Mrs. Bailey, wondering if she should run in and grab the baby or something.

She waved her hand. "Don't worry, she'll fall asleep eventually."

Macie nodded, unable to form any questions, no matter how many tumbled around in her head. Mrs. Bailey started down the hall when one finally erupted. "Do I get any days off?"

It probably wasn't the best question to blurt out, having only been on site for fifteen minutes.

Mrs. Bailey turned to Macie with an expression that bordered between amusement, irritation, and incredulity. "Taking care of children is a full-time job. There are no breaks."

"But didn't Mary Poppins take a day off each month?" The words popped out before Macie could stop them.

Mrs. Bailey raised her eyebrows as if to say Mary Poppins was a fictional character, so her schedule had no bearing on what she asked of Macie.

Macie tightened her lips into a smile, nodded, and opened the door Mrs. Bailey indicated before she could make a bigger fool of herself.

Mrs. Bailey took two strides down the hall then turned around. Macie paused, dreading whatever would come next.

"Also," Mrs. Bailey said, looking over her shoulder, "you are never to use your phone when you are with the girls. They need your undivided attention, and I know how young people are with their phones. You should have your phone nearby even in the house, but you are not to be texting or playing games or other such nonsense. For safety reasons, of course, you should have your phone on your person when you go outside."

Macie nodded to let her know she understood and entered her room.

Macie shut the door and leaned against it before scanning the large room. It was evident the house was old, even though it had been updated. The arched ceilings pinnacled at a large chandelier. The bed was huge and had more pillows than she would ever know what to do with. Was she supposed to sleep with all of them? Or were they for decoration? Macie guessed the latter, but she wondered if she could ever put the pillows back as artfully as they were currently arranged. The walls were papered with a cream and pink floral pattern.

Macie explored the two doors inside the room, grateful for the distraction. The first door opened into a large closet; she didn't know how anyone owned enough clothes to fill the space. The other was an elegant bathroom with a claw-foot tub, a shower, and enough fluffy towels to shower five times a day and still have towels left over.

She would have flopped on the bed with a happy sigh if she hadn't just found out she wouldn't have any free time. Overwhelmed with everything and wishing she were stronger and able to either take all this in stride or advocate for herself better, Macie flung herself onto the coverlet and cried for a few minutes. If this were her only break, she would take advantage of it. She tried not to feel guilty as Evelyn's cries penetrated her door at an alarming volume, but after five more minutes, the cries quieted.

A knock sounded at Macie's door, so she hurried to dry her eyes. "Come in."

A black teenage boy entered, carrying her suitcases. The boy was probably as tall as Daniel, but his youthful face and lanky limbs made Macie guess he was closer to fifteen. He placed her bags next to her bed. The boy turned to leave.

"Wait." Macie wanted to talk to someone and hoped this boy would give her a better welcome than the other people she had encountered so far. Mrs. Bailey had been professional and curt. Macie wanted a friend. "What's your name?"

"Nate, Miss." He grinned, almost shyly. He sounded almost as dignified as a butler with his accent, even though he was young.

"Nate. You help Daniel with the horses?"

Nate looked surprised but nodded.

Macie reached out her hand. "I'm Macie."

He grinned and took Macie's hand. "I help out in the stables mostly, but you'll probably see me around in the house as well."

"It's nice to meet you." Macie smiled her first genuine smile since arriving in England. At least someone here was nice. She wasn't sure how she felt about Mrs. Bailey. She hadn't been what Macie would call welcoming.

Nate left. Macie sat on her bed, already feeling a little better. There might be people in this house she could confide in if more were like Nate. She didn't think she could confide in Mrs. Bailey and didn't think Daniel would want to be friends. She needed to unpack and take a nap as Mrs. Bailey had suggested. She obviously wasn't too concerned with her meeting the other children yet, so Macie wouldn't be, either.

Macie's fingers twitched as if begging to call her parents, but they tell her she was crazy for accepting a position with low pay, despite being offered room and board. She was starting to believe them.

She would show her parents—and herself—she could stick it out. She could prove to the Baileys she was the best nanny ever. She would prove she was as much a gem as the London nanny, even if she became a sleep-deprived crazy person.

CHAPTER 4

DANIEL RUBBED THE HORSE down. Riding had done wonders to his mood. Nate came in and started putting the tack away.

"The new nanny seems nice," Nate said.

Daniel grunted. He didn't want to talk about her. He didn't want to sour his improving mood with guilt.

Nate grinned. "She's pretty, too."

Daniel grunted again. Nate was goading him.

"She must be exhausted and a little lonely. She'd been crying when I took her bags up to her room."

Daniel paused in his strokes across the horse's flanks. "She was crying?"

"Yeah. She tried to hide it, but her eyes were red, and her eyelashes stuck together like they were wet."

Daniel hoped it was not because of him.

Nate shrugged. "Yeah. It seemed to help make Macie feel better when I talked to her. Mrs. Bailey isn't the most welcoming to the new nannies. She gives them Evelyn and leaves. At least that's what Mum says."

Another twinge of guilt. He hadn't been any better. He'd escaped as soon as he'd cut the engine.

"I think I'll like this nanny. She doesn't act like she thinks she's better than anyone else. Not like that last one." Nate made a face. "I think she was expecting to be part of the social events when she signed up." Nate shrugged. "Maybe she figured the girls got all fancied up and went to the social events with Mrs. Bailey." Nate paused, then laughed. "The first one seemed especially smitten by you."

Daniel rolled his eyes. There had been two nannies since Mrs. Bailey moved in, and they had both snubbed their noses at him. "Go on, Mate. Get to work."

Nate laughed and went off to do other chores.

It had been a long six months since Thomas had died and left the house and business to his daughter. Sometimes Daniel really missed him. He had been down to earth. Daniel was more knackered than ever with Mrs. Bailey in charge. Mrs. Bailey had moved in immediately. He didn't know why. She hadn't bothered to even visit here since she moved out ten years ago. Daniel had already been helping train by then. Thomas had had to go to London to visit them if he wanted to see his daughter and her family. Nate had said the girls tried to make the nanny's life miserable, but two weeks seemed really quick. Then Mrs. Bailey forced the maid, Daisy, to nanny and clean.

His first impulse was to wonder why Daisy put up with Mrs. Bailey's treatment. But he put up with it, so who was he to judge? If only he believed his mother would be okay without him. He could move away and start a vet clinic and his own breeding and training business. He had the experience to be successful, but he didn't have the money to get started.

Daniel put the horse he had been working with in his stall. He noticed an odd mark, a small white circle with a slash through it, on the stall next door. The horse in that stall was one the Baileys owned. Thomas bought him a year before he died in that riding accident. He would be ready to breed if he could ever convince the Bailey's to do so. Why didn't the Bailey's know that had been Thomas's plan?

Daniel studied the mark, wondering how it had gotten there. Nate had no reason to draw symbols on the stables. He swiped his thumb over the mark and found that it rubbed off easily, so he grabbed some water and a sponge and washed it off, distracted by thoughts of Thomas Martin.

He had been like a second father to him. Thomas had gone out to ride, and when he didn't return, Daniel went out to find him. He had found Thomas dead. Just like he his father. At least at Thomas's death he didn't have to see the grief of his daughter, as he worked through his own grief. He had watched his father's death change his mother, which had made the traumatic event of watching his father be thrown from the horse even worse. He hadn't told his mother he witnessed the event, scared that would make her withdraw even more.

Moments later, Nate's footsteps pounded against the floor as he turned the corner in the barn, excitement written on his face. "Mate, I think the Morris mare is going into labor."

Daniel followed Nate to check the mare. She wasn't so far along that the colt would be born in the next hour, but Nate was right; it would be tonight.

"I'll go get Jack after we prep the stall."

Jack liked watching the births as much as Daniel did. He was going to be pleased that he had had to come home early for whatever event his wife had dragged him to. He couldn't believe he worked in London during the week while his family lived here, but he was probably holding onto his job since his wife wanted to sell the place. Daniel was only grateful they hadn't sold yet, though he wasn't sure why.

***

When Macie woke up, she felt like she could sleep the rest of the night but knowing she couldn't. She shot off a text to her parents letting them know she had arrived safely, then she dialed her sister.

"Did you make it?" Katie asked as way of greeting.

"Yes, and I'm so tired."

"How do you like the kids?" Katie was one of the few people who acted interested in Macie's life, but she was six years older and hadn't been at home for most of Macie's teenage years. She had moved away right after graduating high school to be nanny for a year and had married someone she met there. Macie briefly wondered how she had time to date if being a nanny meant you never left the kids' sides, but decided against asking. She didn't want Katie telling her parents anything negative.

"I only met the baby. She is sweet. It's fun to hear their accents. I don't know if I'll ever get used to it."

"I'm sure you will. I just know you are going to love it. Just forget all about what happened with that other little boy. One mishap doesn't mean you are doomed to be a failure with kids forever. You do alright with my kids."

It was true, but Macie had only been with her kids while Katie was around. Katie had worked hard to convince Macie she should nanny. She told her it was the only way to get past what had happened with Tommy.

"How are the kids?" Macie asked in an attempt to keep her sister from digging any further. She was glad she had her sister to talk to, but she also knew she had to be careful of what she said, otherwise it would get back to her parents. She didn't want them thinking she needed rescuing.

Katie bubbled about Sophie taking her first steps and Jax starting kindergarten in the fall.

After listening to Katie talk for twenty minutes, she figured she should probably get ready for dinner.

"Katie. It's been great talking to you, but I have to go down to dinner to meet the rest of the kids."

"Okay. Keep your chin up. You can do this." And with that Katie hung up while yelling Jax's name.

Macie splashed water on her face and studied herself in the mirror. She stared into her own eyes and said quietly, "You can do this." Then she tried to ignore the taunting voice in the back of her head that said she had never finished anything she started.

Macie made her way down stairs. She was halfway down before she remembered Mrs. Bailey asked her to get the baby. Macie trudged back up to Evelyn's room and opened the door.

Evelyn sat up. Her hair was rumpled, which suggested she had slept the couple of hours Macie had. She scooted away from Macie as she approached, her brown eyes widening.

"It's okay, Evelyn," Macie assured her. "I'm going to take you to your mommy."

"Mummy?" Evelyn squeaked.

Macie put out her arms. Evelyn willingly stood up and came to her. At least that was something. She quickly changed her diaper.

Macie carried Evelyn into the dining hall, expecting Mrs. Bailey to take her as soon as they entered. Mrs. Bailey had changed from her formal wear, but her dress was still nicer than anything Macie owned.

Mrs. Bailey pointed to the high-chair. "Put her in there and spoon feed her the mashed potatoes and some cooked carrots. Feed her the carrots first, otherwise she won't eat them."

A tall man with blond hair stood and extended his hand. "I'm Jack Bailey."

Why was it that everyone sounded so sophisticated with their accent? Macie figured it was just an idea she picked up from watching movies.

Macie smiled at his friendly greeting. "It's nice to meet you, Mr. Bailey. I'm Macie."

Macie immediately flushed at the ridiculousness of her introduction. He would obviously already know her name.

"It's a pleasure to meet you."

Macie put Evelyn in the high-chair and pulled out a seat for herself next to Evelyn.

Mrs. Bailey pointed to the two girls sitting across the table from Mrs. Bailey. Macie wracked her brain to remember the ages she had been told, but came up empty.

"This is Charlotte," Mrs. Bailey said, gesturing to the older one.

She looked to be about nine or ten and sat ramrod straight in her chair. Her blonde hair cascaded down her back. Macie was impressed with its length. The chocolate color of her eyes seemed to make the glare she shot at Macie more impactful and Macie fought to keep eye contact with her. Her dark eyes were a startling contrast to the girls blonde hair. With the pale pink dress, Charlotte would have been quite beautiful... except for that glare.

"And that"—Mrs. Bailey pointed to the younger girl who Macie guessed to be about five or six—"is Audrey."

Audrey smiled, her blue eyes bright and open. Charlotte elbowed her and she lowered her eyes to her plate. Her dark brown hair fell in front of her face. Her hands played with the ribbon on her pink dress that matched her sister's. Macie felt underdressed in jeans and a ponytail. The two girls' appearances made it seem like they never did anything to mess up their hair or ruffle their clothes. She hoped they were only dressed up to meet her. She felt inadequate as it was, but she knew she wasn't up to the task of nannying the prim and proper.

"It's nice to meet you. I look forward to getting to know you better," Macie said, making her voice as nice and inviting as possible.

Macie sat down and put some carrots and potatoes on a little plate. She had never fed a baby before. Why was she even hired? Why had she even applied? She had put on her resume that she had taken a child development class but had obviously left out the fact that she hadn't babysat in five years. She had helped with her younger siblings, but they were able to feed themselves by the time she was asked to help with their care.

When am I going to eat? It felt like days since her last meal on the plane. Macie's stomach grumbled at the delicious smells wafting through the air. Macie stared at them a moment, wondering if she should cut the carrots. She figured it would be better to be safe than sorry, so she cut the orange circles in half. She thought that a baby as big as Evelyn would be able to feed herself with her hands at least, but Mrs. Bailey said to spoon feed Evelyn, so she wouldn't argue.

Macie forked a cooked carrot into Evelyn's mouth. The baby gagged.

"Oh." Macie jumped up, knocking her chair over.

Mrs. Bailey turned her shocked gaze on Macie. "What is it, dear?"

"Is she choking?"

Mr. Bailey laughed. "No. She just hates carrots."

Mrs. Bailey eyed her. "You do know what to do if she were choking, right?"

Macie's face flushed. "Yes."

She had taken CPR classes.

"Have you ever cared for a baby?"

Macie's eyes dropped to the floor and she shook her head. This was it. She was going to be shipped home.

The silence stretched so long that Macie finally glanced up. Mrs. Bailey looked like storm clouds were in her eyes, but as she opened her mouth to speak, Mr. Bailey put a hand on her shoulder.

"It will be fine. She seems capable enough. She just isn't used to Evelyn's antics when she wants to avoid eating a certain food."

Mrs. Bailey relaxed. Macie reached a trembling hand to her tea cup, wanting to do something other than face Mrs. Bailey's scrutiny. The tea touched her lips, but it was obvious salt had been added. She made a face, swallowed the foul tea, and set the cup down gracefully.

Charlotte snorted at the same time Mrs. Bailey asked. "Is something wrong?"

Macie pasted a smile on her face. "No. I just prefer some cream in my tea, is all." She turned and raised the one eyebrow Mrs. Bailey wouldn't see at Charlotte, silently communicating she was on to her.

Mrs. Bailey's expression went thoughtful. "If you do not prove you are able to take care of the children, you will go home. I'll be watching you very closely."

Macie nodded, grateful for the chance since she was obviously well below what was expected.

"So, Macie. Tell us about yourself." Mr. Bailey's friendly tone helped Macie relax.

"We already know a lot about her," Mrs. Bailey snapped. "She filled out the question-naire."

"Yes, but the girls didn't read it. They deserve to get to know their nanny."

Macie looked from Mr. Bailey to Mrs. Bailey, unsure if she should say anything. Mr. Bailey gave her an encouraging nod. Macie tried to think about what a child would want to know.

"Well, I'm from Idaho. I love the outdoors and hope we can spend a lot of time outside."

"It's always rainy," Charlotte blurted.

Macie decided not to respond to that. She was sure they had jackets, and if it was pouring they obviously wouldn't go outside, but it couldn't possibly be rainy every day.

"I like to play games," Macie went on. "I have a lot of experience entertaining my younger siblings, though they are older than you now."

Charlotte stared straight ahead, as if pretending Macie wasn't there.

Macie shrugged. "I look forward to getting to know you girls."

"Me too," Audrey said, quietly, but Charlotte elbowed her. "Ow."

"Girls," Mr. Bailey said. "Behave."

Macie turned her attention to feeding Evelyn.

Evelyn ate exactly five pieces of carrot before she refused to open her mouth. Her lips pressed together, and she tipped her head away from Macie. Macie gave up on the carrots and scooped a spoonful of mashed potatoes. Evelyn nearly dove onto the spoon. Macie pushed the carrots to the side of the plate and focused on the potatoes.

After a few minutes of silence while everyone but Macie ate, there was a knock on the dining room door, and it slowly opened. Daniel appeared. The light in his eyes grabbed her attention. That one change was enough to make Macie catch her breath at his appearance. She swallowed hard and reminded herself he wasn't exactly welcoming.

Mr. Bailey stood up, but Daniel spoke before he could ask anything. "Hartlett is in labor." His accent must have must have been stronger than Macie realized because Macie didn't understand what was going on.

"Really?" Mr. Bailey stood, his half eaten meal apparently forgotten.

Daniel nodded. "She hasn't expelled her fluid yet, but I think it might be within an hour. I figured you might want to come watch."

Macie's mind raced. She knew enough to know they were talking about someone having a baby. Was it Daniel's sister? Hartlett seemed a strange sort of name, but she was new in England. Maybe it was a popular name here. What she didn't understand was why Mr. Bailey would want to watch.

Mr. Bailey was out the door in a second. Mrs. Bailey frowned and stood. "I need to talk to Jack. I'll be back later."

Macie's stomach clenched at her tone. It was clear Mrs. Bailey hadn't forgotten Macie's moment of panic with Evelyn.

CHAPTER 5

MACIE LOOKED AT WHERE the girls were sitting, all staring at where their mother had disappeared. The oldest one glared at Macie. Macie sat up straighter, keeping her tone light and conversational, even though she felt exhausted.

"What's happening?" Macie asked.

"The horse is going to have a baby," Charlotte said, rolling her eyes. "Don't you know anything?" Her accent made her sarcasm sound even sharper.

Macie didn't know how she was supposed to know that Hartlet was a horse, but now it made a little more sense why Mr. Bailey would want to watch. "That's fun."

Charlotte rolled her eyes again.

Audrey grinned. "Yeah. I like that Mommy and Daddy house horses that have babies. But I don't get to see them."

Macie scooped some food on her plate and inhaled it before one of the girls demanded she do something and while Evelyn was happily grabbing food from the plate Macie had set on her tray.

Charlotte pointed at Evelyn. "Mum doesn't let her do that."

Macie stared at Charlotte a moment, trying to figure out what she was talking about. Mrs. Bailey didn't let Evelyn eat?

"Mum doesn't let her do that," Charlotte repeated in a tone Macie was sure meant she would tattle on Macie the first chance she got. "She's going to get all messy."

Apparently Evelyn wasn't allowed to play with her food. Macie didn't care. She needed to eat too. "It will be fine," Macie assured Charlotte. "I'll clean her up."

After Macie ate, she took Evelyn out of the high-chair. "I'm going to the kitchen to clean Evelyn up. You girls go get shoes on." Macie was going to get some fresh air while waiting for bedtime.

The Charlotte folded her arms and sat back in her chair, while Audrey squirmed.

Or just sit there. Macie didn't know how to make Charlotte do anything. Audre seemed to follow her sister's lead. She was in way over her head. *Am I supposed to physically drag them?* Macie took a deep breath, reminding herself she wanted to keep this job. A maid walked in and started collecting dishes. Macie followed the maid to wherever she was taking the dishes—which was hopefully the kitchen—leaving the girls to decide what they would do.

The sink was full of dishes, but Macie sidled her way over to turn on the tap to wash Evelyn off before she smeared more of her dinner all over her clothes.

"You must be the new nanny," a loud voice said from behind Macie. She whirled around and found herself staring at a large black woman in street clothes. At least she looked friendly with a bright smile on her face. Macie was sure she would never get used to the accents. It seemed to surprise her every time someone spoke.

"Umm, yeah. Sorry if I'm in your way. I wanted to wash Evelyn."

The woman took in Evelyn's food-smeared dress. "My goodness. What a mess she has made. Here... I'll wash those clothes and put them away before Emma finds out that she rubbed food all over them. She would think she needs to throw them away then take it out of your paycheck."

Macie stared at the woman with an open mouth. Her paycheck would barely give her enough money at the end of three months to pay her way back. She couldn't afford anything to be taken from it.

"Oh, I'm Gladys by the way. I'm the cook." She gestured for Evelyn so Macie handed her over. Gladys stood Evelyn on the floor and took off her dress, leaving her in a diaper. "Now take her up and bathe her to get the potatoes out of her hair. Next time clean her tray off and give her small pieces of bread before you eat or..." Gladys winked. "Eat first. That would be better. After you put the girls to bed tonight, come to the kitchen, and I'll give you a cuppa. You look like you could use one."

Macie had no idea what a cuppa was but nodded as Gladys bustled away to start the washer. Gladys seemed reasonable and even nice. Macie remembered Nate saying something about his mom being here. Was this her? She was grateful someone was willing to help her learn what she was supposed to do. Obviously that person wouldn't be her boss, which was odd. It was like Mrs. Bailey expected Macie to know everything without telling her the rules.

Macie went upstairs to give Evelyn her bath, postponing any fight that might happen with the girls about getting shoes on so they could go outside.

She dressed Evelyn and exited the bathroom, when she heard her name.

"Macie?"

It was Mrs. Bailey, so Macie hurried to the top of the wide staircase that gave her a full view of the entryway below.

Mrs. Bailey motioned to a tall, thin girl who looked to be about Macie's age—the maid. "Give Evelyn to Daisy. She will entertain the girls in the nursery while I speak to you."

The tone in Mrs. Bailey's voice caused Macie to pause before she shook herself and hurried down the stairs. Mrs. Bailey was sure to yell at her now that she knew she had never cared for a baby before. But Evelyn was fifteen months. Macie remembered that much now that she had had some sleep.

Once Macie handed off Evelyn, Mrs. Bailey motioned toward an open door next to the staircase. Macie tried to walk confidently into the room, but she could feel her legs shaking. She smiled as genuinely as her nerves would allow. Mrs. Bailey sat across a large dark desk from Macie, her lips pressed firmly together.

She picked up a piece of paper. "I had to follow Mr. Bailey to the barn to talk to him." Mrs. Bailey made a face. "I was under the impression you had experience caring for children. You even took classes in university."

"Yes, I did, and I have experience babysitting. I have several younger siblings I helped care for, but my mom never had me feed them. I'm sorry. I truly was afraid she was choking, and I panicked for a moment. It won't happen again. I am CPR certified. The stress of the day and traveling must have had me on edge." Macie clamped her mouth shut to stop her babbling; sure it would just show Mrs. Bailey how insecure she felt.

Mrs. Bailey's eyes showed doubt, but she nodded. "Very well. You will care for the girls. But as I said, if you do not meet my standards, you will go home. You were the only applicant, and I was getting desperate to get someone here. I should have been more patient." Mrs. Bailey wrote something on the paper as if unaware how painful her words were. "Charlotte is homeschooled, so you will have to do that. Daisy can show you what she has been learning, and you can start that on Monday."

Macie forced herself not to look shocked at the revelation. Why hadn't the job description mentioned that? She had no experience teaching children. In fact, Macie tried to think about what the job description had said. Katie had convinced her being a nanny would be fun. Macie hadn't been sure, but had agreed to try. Now she wasn't sure she agreed with Katie's definition of fun. Katie had loved her time nannying, but then she had also met her husband at the same time. Macie had wanted to get out of her parents' house. She had been pretty miserable after she failed two of her classes her second semester at CSI. Her parents hadn't said anything about her lack of work, but had put her to work at the house, cleaning and cooking, saying now she was an adult she had to pay her way somehow. She needed to save money to continue her schooling, but she also needed to figure out what she wanted to do in life before she tried that again.

Mrs. Bailey was looking at her curiously.

"Sorry. I was just thinking."

Mrs. Bailey raised an eyebrow.

"Yes, of course," Macie rushed to say, thinking Mrs. Bailey was looking for confirmation. Macie couldn't remember what the job description of this nanny job had said, but she didn't remember homeschooling being on the list. It was too late now. She would see this through. Even though a part of her trembled at having so much responsibility, Macie was determined to prove herself.

"Gladys will cook for them, but you will serve them and feed them. Act like a mother, except you don't have to do the cleaning and cooking." Mrs. Bailey smiled as if that should ease her mind. Macie supposed if she mimicked the attention her parents gave her siblings, that would be guide enough. She hoped.

"Have you always had a nanny?" Macie asked, unable to help her curiosity.

"After two months at home alone with Charlotte, I was going crazy. I immediately hired a nanny, and suddenly I had my life back. I could come and go as I pleased without a baby to tote around and pack for."

"Why did you have more?" The question slipped, and Macie clamped her hand over her mouth before muttering. "Sorry."

"Mr. Bailey wanted more." She shrugged. "It all works out if I have a nanny. If not, then I get grumpy." She turned away. "I just wish I were still in London with all the events where I could get out of the house and away from the kids."

Macie wasn't sure what to say, so she settled for a generic, "I'm sure there are lots of things to do in the city."

"And good nannies are easier to find." She paused. "My first and only nanny in London got married right before my father died, so she couldn't come with us. No one has measured up since."

Macie nodded to let her know she was listening and refrained from comment.

Mrs. Bailey eyed her for another too long moment before she sighed. "You may go. The girls should be in bed by eight o'clock. I will be heading to bed myself about that time."

Macie glanced at her watch. That gave her over an hour.

Macie found the girls in the nursery. As soon as Macie entered, the young woman Mrs. Bailey had sent with Evelyn to play with the girls rose and bobbed a curtsy. With the stress of meeting with Mrs. Bailey, Macie couldn't remember her name. She had short light brown hair that curled slightly under her chin, and her hair bobbed slightly with her movement. She went to rush past, but Macie put out her hand, hoping to stop her.

"What's your name, again?" Macie asked when she stopped, looking down, avoiding eye contact.

"Daisy, Miss."

Macie had the feeling she had gone back in time with the maid calling her Miss. Even Nate had done it.

Macie stared at her. Wasn't she one of them? Why was Daisy calling her Miss?

"It's Macie."

Daisy shook her head. "Mrs. Bailey says I need to address the nannies as Miss. I can only call Gladys by her first name."

"Why?" Macie was bemused. She assumed she was on equal footing with the others who worked in the house. She also wondered if she ever talking to Nate or Daniel since she hadn't mentioned them.

Daisy shrugged. "Caring for the girls is more important."

"Who has been watching the girls since the last nanny left?"

Daisy grimaced. "Me, but it is so hard to keep up with the house work and take care of them."

Macie felt a surge of sympathy. "Did Mrs. Bailey pay you extra?"

Daisy flushed but nodded. "A little. It's a good thing, too. I took this job because there wasn't much I could do."

"There's not a lot of work around here?" Macie asked.

Daisy raised her eyes to meet Macie's. "My mum is really sick, so I needed to take a job close by. I sleep here, which keeps the burden off them a little, but I am close enough if they need me. There wasn't much better options. This way I can send them money since I don't have to pay for rent or groceries."

Macie wanted to hug her. Her own eyes burned with tears on behalf of the girl. At least she had been paid extra for caring for the girls and cleaning.

"Well, please call me Macie. If you were the nanny, that puts us on equal footing."

Daisy smiled but shook her head. "I don't want to give Mrs. Bailey any reason to fire me."

Macie sighed, and Daisy rushed out the door. Macie turned to see Charlotte's icy glare trained on her. Audrey was smiling shyly, and Evelyn was busy playing with some toy dishes, banging them together.

"What do you want to do until bedtime?"

"You shouldn't be talking to the maid like she's your friend," Charlotte informed me.

"I'll talk to whoever I please however I want."

"I'll tell Mum. You'll be fired." Charlotte's face turned smug. Macie wondered if it would be even worse if Charlotte knew one slip up might send her packing.

Macie ignored the comment and turned her attention to Audrey. "Do you want to go outside?"

Audrey nodded vigorously. Charlotte rolled her eyes.

"You can stay inside and play in here if you prefer," Macie told Charlotte.

Charlotte smirked. Audrey tugged on Macie's sleeve. "You can't leave any of us alone except when we're asleep."

Macie did remember Mrs. Bailey saying something about that.

"She can run out to get us if she needed something." Macie couldn't believe that someone as big as Charlotte couldn't play by herself in the nursery.

Charlotte wicked grin grew bigger.

"She'll go to Mum," Audrey pointed out.

The implications struck Macie. How had she not seen it? Audrey obviously knew her sister well.

"I guess she has to come with us."

Charlotte folded her arms and stared at Macie, defiance written all over her face.

Audrey grabbed her sister's arm with both of her hands. "Please, Charlotte. We never get to play outside."

"It's cold." Charlotte didn't even look at her sister.

"We can wear our coats. It's almost May, and some flowers are blooming in the gardens."

The mention of flowers seemed to catch Charlotte's attention. She relaxed marginally before stiffening her spine. "Fine."

"Brilliant." Audrey's grin brightened, and she grabbed Macie's hand to pull her out the door.

Macie laughed at the English phrase and at Audrey's enthusiasm. "Hold on. I need to get Evelyn."

Macie scooped up Evelyn and followed Audrey to the mudroom next to the garage to get their jackets. Macie realized she didn't have her coat but decided she would be fine without it. She didn't want to take a detour to her room, now that she had convinced them to go outside.

After all the jackets were buttoned up, Macie took Audrey's and Evelyn's hands and walked slowly to accommodate for Evelyn's short steps.

The night air wasn't too cold, but Macie knew it would get chilly once the sun went down. At least it wasn't raining like Charlotte had suggested it did all the time. Macie stopped to take in the backyard. It was large, but not so large that it would take forever to mow the lawn. Macie wondered who did that. Hopefully not poor Daisy. She was obviously already overworked. Maybe it was Nate's job. The large barn at the back edge of the lawn grabbed her attention. It was huge and not like the picturesque barns in the West. It was the same color brick as the mansion. It was as long as the house and U-shaped with gravel in front of it. A long, lit walking area running down the middle of the barn let Macie see through to the green pastures beyond. Pastures also lined the left side of the lawn and curved around to the back of the barn. How many horses could fit in a barn that large? She looked for a sign that would tell her where in the barn the foal was being born but didn't see one. Macie let her eyes travel the length of the house. It was time to do some exploring. Colors dotted the flower gardens bordering the house. The only flowers Macie could identify for sure were the tulips, but she had never been one to pay attention to the plants.

Audrey sighed. "I love the flowers."

"They are pretty." Macie led the girls along the back of the mansion. She glanced behind her to be sure Charlotte was still with them.

Charlotte glared at her. "I won't run off."

"She would get in trouble," Audrey said.

Macie was sure she would also get in trouble. Mrs. Bailey was already convinced Macie was inadequate and would use any excuse to fire her, even if Charlotte hid from Macie on purpose. A lump rose in Macie's throat. A kid hiding was what had prevented her from babysitting through most of high school. From that moment on, Macie had tried hard to do things she would succeed at. But it seemed that was the starting point to all of her short life's failures. Macie shook her head, shutting out the memory.

They slowly walked the edge of the flower gardens. The mansion seemed even bigger walking along its entire length. What did the Baileys do with all this space? She had noticed at least five doors on the second floor, just on the side of the stairs that led to her room. There was a whole other wing past the stairs with who knew how many rooms. Her family of eight lived in a four bedroom house that was a quarter of the size of this mansion. And her two older siblings had been out of the house for some time. Her two younger twin brothers shared a room. Macie shared a room with her younger sister.

The orchard beckoned them forward, and they made their way to the grove. The blossoms waved gently in the cool breeze. Goosebumps spread over Macie's exposed skin. She picked up Evelyn, holding her close, relishing the warmth of the toddler's body. They walked to the edge of the orchard, and Macie breathed in deeply, filling her lungs with the sweet scent. The round corrals were not far from where they stood. At least that is what Macie thought they were called. She had watched westerns with her father after all. She took a couple of small involuntary steps toward the barn, as if by some magnetic pull, wanting to see the horses. A walking path lined the corrals and led to the edge of the barn. The path was lined with stones, presumably to keep the grass from growing into it. For being a farm, it looked very clean and orderly from the outside.

Macie turned to look at the house and recognized the door Mrs. Bailey had taken her into earlier. Inside the mansion, she had been completely turned around. She had never been good at directions. Really, all she was good at was staying invisible and out of the way—something she would need to change if she was in charge of three girls.

"Let's race to the barn."

A flash of interest sparked in Charlotte's expression before she went back to glaring. "Ladies don't run."

Since Charlotte didn't approve of running, it must be the barns that had caught her interest.

"Ready, set, go," Macie yelled, dashing off, with Evelyn squealing with pleasure and clinging to Macie's shirt.

Audrey passed Macie and reached the edge of the barn just before Macie. Audrey turned to beam up at Macie. "I win."

"You win." Macie turned to see Charlotte walking primly toward them along the gravel path. Macie tried to hide a smile. Charlotte seemed to be showing she was better than everyone else.

Macie heard soft words through the open doorway at the side of the barn. Curious, she slowly walked along the end of the barn to peek inside. She was immediately assaulted by the smell of manure and something else Macie couldn't identify. She tried to subtly block her nose so the smell wouldn't be so putrid.

What Macie assumed was the mother horse led her foal to a corner of a large stall near the open doorway. Next to the gate that separated the stall from the large hall in the barn, Daniel moved forward into the stall to clean up the soiled straw. Only his shoulders showed over the tall stall wooden sides. Macie watched his muscles flex and lengthen as he moved the bloodied straw away and Nate replaced it with fresh straw. They worked in perfect tandem. They didn't need to communicate. They each understood their job and got it done.

Macie wished she knew her job.

CHAPTER 6

MACIE SHOOK HER HEAD to get rid of the despondent thought. She took a step inside the barn. Audrey clung to Macie's leg, but Charlotte took a couple steps forward ahead of Macie, her eyes never leaving the horses.

Macie caught Daniel staring at her.

He looked quickly away, then shook his head as if disgusted by Macie's presence. Macie couldn't help the hurt that came over her. She tried to let it go. *Maybe you are reading him wrong.*

"What are you girls doing here?" Mr. Bailey stepped away from the stall. Macie hadn't even noticed him.

"We're showing Macie the flowers," Audrey announced.

Mr. Bailey's gaze lifted to meet Macie's. "You better get them to the house." Then he mouthed, "Mrs. Bailey."

Macie wasn't sure what Mrs. Bailey had to do with anything. Macie checked her watch. It wasn't eight o'clock yet. Macie nodded, wanting to at least be on Mr. Bailey's good side, and ushered the girls out the barn door. They made their way straight across the large expanse of lawn straight to the door at the back of the house near the garage. It wasn't the door they had come out of, but it was closer, and the chill in the air was starting to make Macie shiver.

Audrey and Charlotte gave her bemused expressions as she stepped to the door and grabbed the door handle.

"Come on," Macie muttered, not wanting to know what she was doing wrong this time.

They walked into the kitchen.

Gladys let out a startled, "Blimey!" and put her hand to her chest.

"Sorry," Macie apologized. "I thought this led into the mudroom." Then she tried to remember if there had even been a door to the mudroom or if it just went into the garage.

"It's no bother," Gladys said. "You just gave me a fright. Here, let me help you put their coats and shoes away." After they hung the coats, they returned to the kitchen.

"Do you girls want a biscuit?" Gladys asked.

A biscuit for bedtime snack? The girls nodded eagerly, and to Macie's surprise, Gladys gave them each what looked more like a cookie than a fluffy biscuit.

Macie took the offered cookie and sank gratefully into a chair near the kitchen table. She wondered if they would ever eat in there or if they always ate in the dining room. She liked the relaxed feel here.

When the cookies were gone, Gladys took Audrey and Charlotte's hands. "Come on girls. I'll tuck you into bed tonight and let Macie rock Evelyn."

"Will you tell us a story?" Audrey asked.

"You can't go to bed without a story." Glady shot Macie a pointed look.

Macie smiled her understanding. A story was part of the bedtime routine.

Macie grabbed Evelyn and followed Gladys through the maze of halls until they reached the grand staircase. Macie hoped she would get the hang of the house's layout sooner rather than later.

Macie found what looked like pajamas in Evelyn's room, then changed her diaper and her clothes.

Macie carefully lay Evelyn in her bed and was about to shut the door when a rustling stopped her. Macie turned around. Evelyn was standing in her crib. "Sing song?"

A song? Macie put her palm to her head. She had already forgotten a story as well. She couldn't see any books, so she figured she had to do one from memory.

"And a story?" Macie asked.

Evelyn clapped her hands. "Story."

Evelyn reached for Macie, so Macie picked her up and carried her to a rocking chair in the corner. She sat with Evelyn tucked into her arms with her blanket wrapped around her. Macie settled on the story of *The Three Little Pigs*, but the only song Macie could think of was *Rock-a-Bye Baby*. The story done, she started singing.

Macie rocked as she sang the song slow and low. Macie felt her own eyelids droop, so she stood slowly. Macie lay Evelyn in bed.

Gladys met her in the hall as she made her way to the stairs. "That's Charlotte's room," she said as they passed; she pointed to a door next to Macie's room. "That's Audrey's. You might want to keep an eye on their doors for a while. They try to sneak out when a new nanny comes."

"How many nannies have they had since they left London?"

"Only two, but they both only lasted about two weeks, then it was more than a month before a new one came."

"Poor Daisy," Macie muttered remembering that Daisy was the one doing the nannying in between.

Macie slumped to the floor, exhausted. "Thank you. I am so tired from the trip I thought bedtime would never come. We managed to distract ourselves outside and even saw the new colt for a second."

"The other nannies never got a chance to recover either before they were thrown in the thick of things. Mrs. Bailey has interesting ideas of what her responsibilities are as a boss."

Macie put her head in her hands. "And I'm already failing. The first sign I show I'm incompetent, she'll throw me out."

Gladys sat on the floor next to Macie and rested her hand on her shoulders. "It will all work out. It has been an adjustment for all of us since Thomas died six months ago."

"Thomas?" Macie asked.

"Mrs. Bailey's father. Mrs. Bailey only came after his death. She wanted to sell, but for some reason, she didn't. I haven't figured out why. I think Mr. Bailey likes the country even though Mrs. Bailey hates it... and it is Mr. Bailey who spends most of his time in London." Gladys shook her head. "How they ever got together, I'll never know."

"So you didn't know the nanny she had in London? She seems to hold her on a pedestal."

"No. They moved in without a nanny, then Mrs. Bailey hired the first nanny who applied."

Macie's hopes shrank a bit more. If Gladys had known the girl, maybe she could have shared all the wonderful things she did that would help Macie measure up.

"I'm probably saying too much," Gladys went on. "But you deserve to know since your success might depend on some of this knowledge. The Estate is slowly failing. Daniel does his best, and my boy helps him the best he can, but with Mrs. Bailey spending so much money, the estate can't keep up with her."

"Is your boy Nate?" Macie asked while mulled over this other information. If Mrs. Bailey really wanted to sell so she could move back to the city, then Macie wouldn't be here long anyway. And Mrs. Bailey wouldn't be able to afford to pay her if the estate failed. Macie could see Mrs. Bailey wasn't happy. So why did she stay?

"Yeah. Have you met him?" Gladys' voice brought Macie out of her thoughts.

Macie nodded. "He brought my bags to my room. He was really nice."

"I'm glad. If he didn't have good manners, I'd give him a sound scolding."

"He was very polite." Unlike Daniel.

"Good to know." Gladys thumped Macie on the back.

Gladys stood and offered her hand to help Macie. "You might as well sit in this sitting area while waiting for the girls to fall asleep." She led Macie to a sort of balcony that overlooked the entry hall. "Mrs. Bailey's room and suite and also the library and spare bedrooms are in that wing." She pointed to the other side of the balcony to a hall Macie hadn't been in yet.

Macie tried to force a smile, but couldn't muster it. It was all so overwhelming. She would never last the three months. She would be forced to ask her parents for help.

Gladys must have read her thoughts. "It takes time to figure out how to care for each child."

Macie put her head into her hands. "I don't know how to care for kids at all." Why had she let Katie talk her into this? Why had she thought that taking one child development class would qualify her for this job? Why did Mrs. Bailey agree? Mrs. Bailey probably thought she had more experience since Macie's resume listed experience in preschool classes where she took care of the kids with a teacher's supervision. That supervision had been the only thing that kept Macie sane during that class since her mind always went back to Tommy, only her second ever babysitting job, who managed to destroy her reputation and her confidence for the rest of her teenage years.

"Now don't you start feeling sorry for yourself." Gladys patted Macie's shoulder. "You can do it. All you have to do is win over those girls, and Mrs. Bailey will most likely follow suit."

Most likely...

Macie didn't like the sound of that. It meant if she didn't win over the girls, Charlotte especially, she could only be here a week and would have failed again.

Gladys quietly opened the doors to both of the girls' rooms and nodded. They were obviously asleep. Gladys gestured for Macie to follow her down the stairs. "Come get that cuppa."

***

Daniel was relieved when Macie left the barn. Having her watch him work was unnerving. He suddenly felt the need to analyze every movement he made. When he had caught her watching him, he shook his head to help him focus on the task at hand. After stealing another quick glance at her, he was confused at the hurt he saw in her eyes.

That couldn't all be because of him, could it? He thought about what Nate had told him. He had not been very welcoming. He wanted to blame stress, but he knew that wasn't the case.

She was pretty... pretty distracting. He couldn't afford distractions. He had already wasted most of his day thinking about her, wondering if she was okay. Nate said she had been crying. He thought he should apologize to her but hadn't been able to find the time. Or maybe he was avoiding.

She probably wouldn't be on the estate for long, but he couldn't *not* apologize, either. He wasn't about to go looking for her, though. He would just wait until he saw her again.

He was friends with Gladys and Nate, and he was as close to his mother as he could be given the circumstances. His heart hurt at the thought of his mother. Getting too close to people led to pain. But he could be kind.

Daniel shook his head to clear it. He had other problems to think about. The business was failing, and if he didn't convince the Baileys to add breeding to the services they offered—as Thomas Martin planned—the estate his father had worked so hard to help build would vanish. He would not let Thomas's hard work go to waste.

After he cleaned up, he hopped over the fence that separated his mom's property from the Bailey's. It was still weird to think of it as the Bailey's when for all his life he had known it as the Martin's. Even after six months, he couldn't get used to the change.

He opened the door softly, not wanting to wake his mother. It had been three years since his father died, but she was still in a slump. Her usual interests had all but disappeared. As he approached the house, he saw her sitting in the parlor, staring out toward the road, but her blank expression told him she wasn't seeing what was outside. She was living in memories. He hated seeing her like that. He missed his father very much and wanted to improve his relationship with his mother, but he couldn't do that if she wasn't really present. Was he such awful company that his mother preferred her memories to him?

Daniel raked his hand through his hair. He knew that wasn't the case. His mother tried to engage with him, and maybe she was giving her all, but the interactions lacked her previous vitality.

"Daniel?" His mother's voice echoed in the dark house.

He stepped into the parlor. The full moon lit his mother's features.

"Mum. Why are you sitting here in the dark?"

She whirled around, tears springing to her eyes. She ran to him and threw her arms around him. "Where were you?"

"Morris's mare went into labor. I sent you a text." Daniel's shock at seeing any emotion in his mother was overridden by guilt that she had been worrying about him.

"Oh. My phone is in the kitchen, and I didn't hear it. I was so worried you had gotten hurt." Her voice caught, and Daniel's guilt rose. She had been sitting in the parlor thinking her only son had been killed the same way his father had been.

Her relief seemed to drag her into a her usual depression. Her blue eyes turned listless again. The dullness in them cut at him more than her fears had.

"Did you eat dinner?" Daniel hadn't been home to make sure she ate. That was the one thing she usually didn't do if he didn't make her.

She shrugged, a sure sign the answer was no.

It was almost midnight. He wouldn't make her eat now. He would wait until breakfast. "Come on. Let's get to bed." Daniel wrapped his arms around her thin shoulders. "I'm sorry, Mum. I didn't mean for you to worry."

Daniel helped his mother find her phone and then led her up the stairs to her bedroom. Once he had his mother settled, he went to his own room and collapsed on the bed.

***

"What is taking so long?"

Callum held the phone away from his ear as Vin shouted at him.

"You said you could get Emma to sell within a week of Thomas's death. It's been six months."

"I felt sure she would. She hates the place, but Emma is digging her heels in. Emma is making the estate go bankrupt. I can't understand why she would choose that over selling."

"Can we help her along on that account?" Vin asked. "We need to up the ante. You said they own several horses."

Callum swallowed. "Yes, but I won't do anything to the horses."

"Getting cold feet, cousin?" Vin sneered. "With only the one man training there is no way they can keep on top of the expenses, especially if Emma is trying to make it fail."

Callum didn't say anything. He didn't think Emma was trying to make it fail, she just didn't understand the business. He'd helped Thomas on several occasions and hadn't seen Emma since high school. Daniel knew him and he couldn't sneak around the estate. What Daniel didn't know was he only helped Thomas to get in his good graces enough to set up a believable 'accident'. He still lost sleep over that fact.

"I'll call Emma," Vin said. "I'll ask to meet with her since I was her father's lawyer see what we can work out. Emma will inevitably let up if all their assets are gone."

"You think she will?" Callum asked.

"You tell me."

Callum didn't know how Vin would convince her to sell. There had to be some reason Emma was holding out. Callum knew Emma. She hated horses and the estate. Maybe if he talked to Jack, he could convince him it was the best option, for Emma's sake. Then he wouldn't have to do anything to hurt anyone else.

CHAPTER 7

MACIE GROANED WHEN EVELYN called out for her mother. Dim light made its way through the crack in her curtains. Macie wanted to sleep for a while longer, but she had a job to do.

Only the drive to prove she could take care of the girls convinced Macie to leave the warm confines of the comforter. She quickly dressed and pulled her hair into a ponytail.

Macie stumbled to Evelyn's room with her eyes half shut.

Evelyn's face contorted when Macie entered the room. "Mummy?"

Macie rushed to soothe her. "We'll see if we can find your mummy. Maybe she will be at breakfast."

Macie hoped Mrs. Bailey would be there. She needed to ask about rules for the children.

After Macie changed and dressed Evelyn, she quietly opened the girls' doors to find their rooms empty. She checked the dining room, but finding it empty, she made her way to the kitchen where she heard the girls' voices.

"Ah," Gladys said when Macie entered the room. "The girls just came down. I told them I was so proud they got ready by themselves." Gladys raised an eyebrow.

Macie caught the hint. "Yes. That was very good. I'm glad I have such big girls to help me learn the routine here."

Charlotte raised her chin. "I don't need you to help me, ever."

Gladys shook her spoon at Charlotte. "I better not hear one complaint from Macie, or I won't make the chocolate truffles you've been asking for."

Charlotte's nose rose a notch higher. "You're not the boss of me." She spared Macie a fleeting glance. "And neither is she."

Macie's mind raced through several possible remarks, but each of them felt like giving Charlotte what she wanted: a fight. And yelling at the children was most likely not going to win Macie any points. She looked at Audrey. The little girl stared at her bowl, avoiding eye contact.

Macie put Evelyn in a high chair. She guessed the girls only ate in the dining room when their parents were eating, too. Gladys set a bowl of what looked like oatmeal in front of her. She stirred to cool it and tested it on her own lips, as she had seen her mother do for her youngest brother, before feeding it to Evelyn. After she had given Evelyn a few bites, she set the bowl down next to hers and quickly added some sugar to the cereal before taking a bite. Her face puckered, and Charlotte snorted.

Again? Next time Macie would have to remember to taste sugar or salt before adding it to anything. She didn't want to end up putting sugar on her potatoes.

Macie fought not to glare at Charlotte.

"Charlotte. I will not stand for that kind of behavior in my kitchen," Gladys snapped.

Gladys switched the offending bowl for a new one as Macie fed Evelyn a few more bites, but Macie didn't miss the tongue Charlotte stuck out at Gladys's back.

"I understand you homeschool. Your mom said Daisy would show me what you are working on, even if it is Saturday." Macie tried to sound happy and excited, but the growing despair that she was so clearly out of her element caused her voice to be a notch higher at her overcompensation. "We'll play in the nursery until lunch."

Macie didn't want to spend the day cooped up in the house, but rain pelted the kitchen window. They finished eating and Macie got Evelyn out of the highchair.

"I would put Evelyn down for a nap at about two. Then find something outside to do with the older girls," Gladys murmured in Macie's ear. She glanced outside. "If the rain lets up."

"Um, where is the nursery again?" Macie was all turned around.

"Oh, right." Gladys led the way toward the front entry hall then down a corridor under the stairs to the room where Daisy waited for them. Macie thought maybe if they got bored in the nursery before lunch, they would wander the house just so she wouldn't get lost.

Macie thanked Gladys for her help and went into the room with Daisy.

"Miss Emma said to show you the homeschool routine before I started my daily chores. You won't be doing any learning today, but this way you'll be ready to start on Monday," Daisy said.

Daisy explained the schedule and what Charlotte was currently learning. "I've been teaching Audrey the alphabet as well. She is anxious to start, even though she doesn't start school until this September."

"Were you were homeschooling them, too?" Macie couldn't keep the shock out of her voice. She had assumed Daisy was just the messenger. Daisy was way more qualified than Macie if she could care for them and keep the house so clean. No wonder she said she was tired.

Daisy nodded and bobbed a curtsy before leaving the room. Macie found the gesture oddly amusing as she stood in her jeans and T-shirt, holding Evelyn. Macie wondered if she should have asked more questions.

"How old are you?" Macie asked Audrey.

"I'm five." She leaned forward as if telling Macie a secret. "I had a party last month."

She had just turned five. Macie felt another stab of sympathy for Daisy if she had to plan the party on top of all her other chores. She hoped Mrs. Bailey had paid her more than just "a little" over her regular salary.

Macie turned her attention to Charlotte. "And you?"

"I'm eight and a half." Charlotte jutted her chin out. Macie would have to convince Charlotte that wasn't a very attractive way to hold one's head.

"Her birthday is in the summer," Audrey supplied.

"And Momma will plan me a big birthday party."

"I'm sure I'll be able to help as well." Macie smiled, letting Charlotte know she really did want to help make her birthday the best it could be.

"Why don't you just go home and make things easier on all of us?" Charlotte spat.

Macie fought to keep the shock off her face. Charlotte was probably goading her and it wouldn't do to let her know her words affected her.

"Because I want to take care of you," Macie said.

Charlotte rolled her eyes. "No one wants to take care of us. People do it because they have to."

"Celeste wanted to take care of us. She was with us since you were a baby," Audrey pointed out.

Macie did her best to not look too interested in their conversation.

"She left as soon as she got married." Charlotte's voice held a bitterness that Macie thought she could understand. Macie had felt the same when her parents had left her to herself to give their attention to her other siblings, especially her rowdy twin brothers.

"Was Celeste your nanny in London?" Macie was sure she knew the answer but wanted to show them she cared.

A smile flitted across Charlotte's face before she fixed her features into a glare, but Audrey nodded.

"She was so nice. She took us on a lot of outings."

"What kinds of outings?"

"To parks mostly. She would let us feed the ducks." Audrey's enthusiasm was endearing, and Macie found she could connect with Audrey, but she didn't know what Charlotte liked. She had liked the idea of seeing the horses. Macie had noticed the flash of interest.

"So what kind of outings have your nannies here taken you on?"

Audrey's shoulders slumped. "None."

Charlotte's eyes flicked to Macie, then Charlotte put a book in front of her face. Macie wanted to reach out and give Charlotte a hug and let her know she knew what it felt like to be forgotten. It wasn't the same as not being wanted, but Macie felt she could understand. Charlotte had built up a wall to protect herself. In order to pull that wall down, Macie would have to prove she understood and cared.

***

Daniel dismounted the horse. Nate held onto its lead rope, then led the horse to the part of the barn they kept the horses they were training. Daniel stepped toward the horses the Bailey's owned. Pain shot through Daniel's leg as it gave way. He stumbled but caught his balance. He put a hand on his calf as pain radiated momentarily up his leg. This was the first time on that horse and it did its best to unsaddle Daniel. The brute crushed his leg against the corral fence, but Daniel showed the horse who was boss.

His steps became more sure, and he shook off the pain. It was time to work with Shadow. At least he knew this horse. Shadow was a fine thoroughbred, and Daniel guessed he would bring high stud prices. To prove his worth, he would have to race. It would be a year before he could race, but that wouldn't happen if Mrs. Bailey had anything to say about it.

Thomas Martin bought Shadow as a young colt. Daniel couldn't understand why Mrs. Bailey didn't follow through with any of what her father wanted. Thomas had known breeding would put their services at the top, and even paid for Daniel to become a vet so they wouldn't have that extra expense when breeding their own horses. Had Thomas not left any instructions for Mrs. Bailey in his will? Daniel would have to ask.

Shadow would be a great stud horse. Flash and Buck, two Cleveland bays, were also bought to breed. They weren't old enough, but he would do what he could to have them ready. Thomas Martin had been deliberate in the horses he bought for breeding, and Daniel was determined to continue what Thomas had started. He would have to bring the subject up with the Baileys that night.

Right now, he wanted to ride Shadow. It was always good to ride a better-trained horse, even a high spirited one like Shadow, after enduring a hard session with a green broke horse. After lunch he would check on the newborn colt.

CHAPTER 8

AFTER LUNCH, MACIE PUT Evelyn down for a nap, then turned to Charlotte and Audrey, grateful the rain had stopped. "How about we tour the stables?"

Charlotte's eyes sparked before she frowned and crinkled her nose. "The stables stink. Ladies don't spend time in the stables. They have tea parties and balls."

Macie suspected she was repeating what her mother had told her, but after all her time spent on the edge of things, she had learned to read people pretty well.

"Ladies also listen to their nannies," Macie retorted. It came out a bit sharper than she intended. She took a deep breath, reminding herself she needed to show she cared. Charlotte obviously did her best to get nannies to leave. Macie had a feeling it was because she wanted her mother's attention, and she got it however she could.

She led them to the door by the servant's staircase next to her room. That door was closer to the barns. If it was cold, they would return for their jackets, but the sun had brightened the sky while they were eating lunch. Macie hoped it would be warm enough to be outside. She had to remember she didn't know anything about the weather here in England.

Audrey pulled Macie down. "I tell her that, too, but she doesn't listen. She doesn't listen to anyone. Not even Mum."

Charlotte sniffed. "Mum doesn't care about us. If she did, she wouldn't pay someone else to watch us."

Macie's steps slowed. "Has your mom not watched you since the last nanny left." Macie knew Daisy had taken over a lot of the duties, but surely their mom spent some time with them. Macie had only been there a day. She hadn't had the opportunity to know if Mrs. Bailey took any time during the week to spend with the girls.

Charlotte rolled her eyes. "She has Daisy watch us, but she has us sit in the study or the library while she works when Daisy has to do the cleaning."

"After the first nanny left, Aunt Jessie sometimes watched us at her house." Audrey's face fell. "But then we had to stop, and Mum would yell if we asked."

Macie wondered how far away Aunt Jessie lived. Maybe they could visit her sometime soon. It might be a good way to show Charlotte she cared. She wouldn't leave them there, but a visit would be fun. It was obvious Audrey loved her. Macie grabbed Audrey's hand and pulled her out the side door. "Let's go see the baby horse."

A ghost of a smile flitted across Charlotte's face.

Audrey squealed and jumped up and down. "I didn't get a good look. Can we pet it?"

Macie shrugged. Would Daniel even let them in the barn?

Macie led them to the barn and approached the side where they had entered the night before. She wasn't sure if they would have moved it to another place, but it was a good place to start.

"Mr. Morris should be comin' by to get the mare and her baby tomorrow morning," a voice she couldn't place said as they neared the barn. "Mr. Bailey told me so this morning. Also said we should charge more per night."

"Probably. As long as it's cheaper than a vet would charge to make a house call." Though he hadn't said much to her the day before, Macie was almost positive it was Daniel. She stepped inside the barn.

Daniel spun around.

"What are you doing here?" Daniel's shocked expression battled his curt words.

"We wanted to see the horse born last night. I guess we came at a good time if it will be gone by tomorrow."

"Miss." Nate nodded at her.

Macie smiled, turning her attention to Nate. "How are you, Nate? Can we see the baby horse?"

Audrey looked up to Daniel, but when he scowled she turned her dimpled cheeks to Nate. "Please. I've never seen a baby up close."

"That's because your mum doesn't want you near the horses." Daniel was staring at Macie. So, it was a rule—a ludicrous one, since they lived on a horse estate. Macie's shoulders drooped.

"I guess we better go," Macie said. She couldn't do anything Mrs. Bailey wouldn't approve of.

Daniel's face softened when he looked at Audrey again. Her disappointment was evident in her trembling lip. "I guess it will be okay... if you're quick."

The compassion in Daniel's eyes as he led the girls over to the stall surprised Macie. She had already decided Daniel was arrogant and didn't do anything that made his life more difficult. Maybe he wasn't as selfish as she supposed. But staying mad was safer than showing vulnerability. Vulnerability was weakness. Weakness meant she was incapable.

Nate followed along next to them. Daniel stopped a short distance from the stall, but the girls moved forward to peer through the slats, Macie right on their heels with Evelyn in her arms. The white patch on the baby's forehead almost looked like a unicorn. She went to point it out to the girls, but then remembered Daniel was in the barn and stopped herself. She didn't want him thinking she was childish.

The baby hid behind the mother. Macie tried to determine whether it was a boy or girl, but couldn't get a good look, even though she felt heat blaze her cheeks for even trying. *It's just an animal*, Macie reminded herself.

"Is it a boy or a girl?" Luckily Audrey asked the question.

"A boy," Nate answered.

"He's so cute. I wish we could keep the babies. I want to learn to ride someday," Charlotte lamented.

Macie fought to keep the shock off her face. Maybe there was an old horse here that Charlotte could ride. Macie looked to Daniel, but he was already shaking his head, apparently anticipating her question.

"Most of the horses here are being trained and would not be fit for an eight-year-old to ride."

Macie nodded once, disappointment filling her. "I was hoping I could learn as well."

She hadn't meant to say it out loud but couldn't take it back now.

There was an awkward silence. Tension radiated between Macie and Daniel. Macie wondered if he was nervous in her presence.

Daniel cleared his throat. "Can I talk to you for a minute?"

Macie mouth fell open when she made eye contact with Daniel. His accent still made funny things happen to her heart. She nodded mutely.

Daniel gestured toward the opening they had entered through. Macie looked back at the girls. She couldn't leave them alone in the barn.

"Just back here a bit," Daniel whispered.

Macie followed Daniel to the front of the barn, keeping her eyes on the girls as she went.

Daniel removed his hat and ran his hand through his hair. "I'm sorry for my behavior yesterday. I was not very welcoming and teased you when you were stressed. For that, I apologize."

Daniel turned stiffly away. He actions seemed at odds with his words. He may be apologizing, but Macie didn't believe he meant them.

"Have I done something to offend you?" she asked to his retreating back.

He froze and looked over his shoulder, confusion evident in his eyes. "No." Then he turned and was gone.

Macie let out a huff. She shook off her irritation. It didn't matter. If the girls weren't supposed to be in the barns, then she wouldn't need to talk to him much, anyway.

Macie collected Audrey and Charlotte to play in the yard, hoping the few minutes they had spent there wouldn't send her packing home. Maybe she should have listened to her instinct and left right away.

***

Daniel led Shot, an Anglo-Arab horse, out of the last barn to take a ride. Macie walked with the girls to the center of the large backyard. He pushed away the guilt that surfaced again. He had apologized. He didn't need to feel guilty. He was busy; he didn't have time to talk and didn't owe her explanations or a tragic backstory.

The stab of guilt was probably for lying to Charlotte. She wouldn't know they owned eight horses, two of which would be perfectly fine for the girls to ride. He didn't want them getting ideas he could take them riding or give them lessons. If Mrs. Bailey found out, she would be furious.

Daniel rubbed his hand through his hair and went to the corral. Shot was a dream to ride, and Daniel often rode him in the fields beyond the Bailey's pastures.

He sighed. He obviously hadn't left Macie with a positive impression when he picked her up. He had apologized, but her question threw him. His delivery probably wasn't the best, but it had been awkward enough without rattling off explanations or doing something to let her know they could be friends. He didn't want more friends. He had already lost two people he was close to and didn't want to open his heart to more pain. Even though his mother was still with him, she was so closed off, still grieving his father. Her presence didn't bring any light to his life. It added to his burden. He had to make sure she ate just so she wouldn't starve herself. He couldn't lose her, too, and he didn't have the bandwidth to make more friends. Nate and Gladys were enough.

He tied Shot and ran in to double-check he had shut the tack room closet. The same white mark he had noticed the day before was on Gypsy's stall. He washed it away before returning to Shot.

Daniel used his time in the saddle to think about the case he would present to the Baileys. He made a mental note to mention Thomas Martin's wishes. Maybe Mrs. Bailey wasn't aware of them.

Chapter 9

DANIEL FLEXED AND RELAXED his hands several times, trying not to show his frustration. He stood in the study to talk some sense into Mrs. Bailey. Did she want this business to fail? Tonight was the perfect night to talk to them since Jack was home for the weekend. Daniel hoped he could talk some sense into his wife. Mrs. Bailey acted as though she wanted the estate to fail, though he couldn't figure out why she would let her father's legacy die. Callum had been willing to buy it from her, but Emma had refused. Why would Emma refuse to sell when she didn't want to help the estate thrive.

He glanced at Jack, who watched his wife warily, like he was afraid to overstep any bounds. Even though he had his job, the money the estate brought in would have been a nice bonus, except now they only made enough to cover expenses. Jack had admitted as much to Daniel when they were a week late paying him.

"Breeding as well as training horses would double our revenue. Your father bought two thoroughbreds and three Cleveland bays to breed," Daniel explained.

"I will not bring more of those beasts onto my property. They will create a mucky appearance. We will not breed." Mrs. Bailey shuddered.

Daniel fought to keep his face semi-neutral. She grew up around the horses for at least some of her life. It had been her father's livelihood. She was okay having people pay her to house and deliver horses and train them, but breeding went too far?

"Can you at least consider it?" Daniel hated his pleading tone.

"Absolutely not." Mrs. Bailey's voice rose in volume. "We will not add more expenses to our already floundering estate."

"But breeding could open new possibilities." Daniel wished the woman would see reason.

"It's exactly what Callum wanted to do." Mrs. Bailey huffed. "I will not have the beautiful pastures of my home turned into a mucky breeding enterprise."

"It's what *your father* wanted to do," Daniel countered.

"I don't believe it," Mrs. Bailey snapped.

"I don't know what Callum told you. He only came to help on occasion, so he wouldn't know what your father wanted," Daniel went on in an even voice. "We will only need to schedule the training clients more carefully. We tend to house more horses to train than we can actually get trained at one time, especially when only I can do the training. Nate is learning but isn't up to the task on his own yet."

"Then you need to be more efficient," Mrs. Bailey snapped. "We cannot afford to do less training. My father was able to handle it until the end."

Daniel took a deep breath, knowing his first impulsive response would end with him fired. Then where would that leave his mother? He breathed slowly through his nose to calm himself.

"Your father had help—mine and my father's. I have helped him my entire life until his unexpected death. He planned for this a long time, but wanted to wait until after I graduated—"

"I will not do anything Callum was planning," Mrs. Bailey said.

"We'll think about it." Jack's voice was soft.

Daniel turned to leave, knowing Jack was offering him a dignified exit. Just because Callum wanted to continue what her father wanted, Emma was against it. What did she have against Callum? He only helped for the last six months before Thomas died. How did he even know what Thomas had wanted?

***

Macie got to the bottom of the stairs and noticed Gladys standing just out of sight. The yelling from the study was so loud she heard what was being said at the top of the stairs where she'd been sitting in a little nook, making sure the girls stayed in bed. She had heard nearly every word—Mrs. Bailey's anyway. She didn't have time to question Gladys before Daniel burst through the door, storm clouds and defeat warring in his gray eyes. He shut the door behind him then stopped short when he noticed Macie and Gladys. His neck turned red, and he stalked past them.

"There's no way she'll keep me on for more than the three months, if I make it a week," Macie whispered. Mrs. Bailey clearly did not want to spend any more money than she had to. The contract had said after three months her pay would go up significantly, but dreams of a nice paycheck were now gone. What did Mr. Bailey do to make a living? They obviously had less money now than they had in London. Why did they stay?

Gladys placed a hand on her shoulder. "Macie. You don't have anything to prove to these people. They're hurting and dealing with that hurt the best they know how. You have nothing to do with that. You are just a part of the business."

Macie's shoulders slumped. Gladys's tone was kind, but her words hurt. Just part of the business. No one important. "Are you saying I don't have a chance?"

"My goodness, Macie. I'm not saying that at all. You're worth far more than any price. No matter what happens, you know you did your best, and if you go home it is because of them and not you."

Macie hugged Gladys and nearly started crying. "I better go check on the girls."

Macie started up the stairs, but when Gladys returned to the kitchen, Macie slowed her steps and watched until Gladys disappeared down the hall. When Macie was sure Gladys was gone, she tiptoed up the steps to make sure the girls' doors were still closed. It was. She hurried down the stairs to listen at the study door again. She didn't think Audrey would leave her room, anyway. She had been nearly asleep when she had finished her story.

"What does he know about breeding? He's nothing but a trainer." Mrs. Bailey hiccuped, and Macie wondered if she was crying.

"He's a vet. Your father paid for his schooling. Maybe it was part of his plan. That is why we house mares due to go into labor, so Daniel is on hand in case of an emergency." Mr. Baileys voice was faint. "He says he knows what to do. Just because his dad only trained doesn't mean he hasn't learned anything about breeding. You need to give him a chance."

Daniel was a vet? Why was he training horses? Macie focused on the conversation in the other room.

"Where do you suggest we get the money to do any of this?"

"Daniel told us we already have five horses your dad planned on breeding," Mr. Bailey said.

"How would Daniel know my father planned on adding breeding? I'm his daughter, and I've seen his will. He doesn't say anything about what he wanted for his business. He just left it all to me. If I sell, that bloke Callum gets it for chump change. If Callum wants it, he gets first dibs." Mrs. Bailey's voice grew shriller with every statement. "We could save money by selling those horses. Then we don't have to pay to feed them."

"If you don't want to sell the estate, then we have to try to make it work. Otherwise we will have to sell our London townhouse."

Mrs. Bailey gasped.

"The estate is several people's livelihood," Mr. Bailey went on. "We can't leave them out in the cold."

Mrs. Bailey's voice rang out clear. "I don't care a fig about the people who work for me. They can find other jobs. I just have to figure a way around the stipulation that Callum have the opportunity to buy first."

A chair scraped. Macie raced up the stairs and sat in the chair she used to watch the girls' doors. After her breathing slowed, Macie carefully opened Charlotte's door, then Audrey's. They were both sound asleep. Time out on the lawn must have sufficiently tired them out.

Macie had no sooner sat down when she heard her name called from the base of the stairs.

"Macie, come into the study, please."

Was it over already? Macie hurried down the stairs to avoid upsetting Mrs. Bailey further and curtsied when she reached the doorway as she had seen Daisy do. Though her curtsy probably looked more like she stumbled into it. And it probably was odd to curtsy in jeans.

"Have a seat." Mrs. Bailey gestured to the chair in front of the large oak desk where she sat. Shelves lined the wall up to the ceiling behind her. It was completely covered with books. Mrs. Bailey's eyes were bloodshot, and Macie didn't know if it was her place to ask Mrs. Bailey about her welfare. Macie finally decided it would be the only polite thing to do.

"Are you well, Ma'am?" Macie asked, mimicking Daisy's formal way of addressing her.

Mrs. Bailey waved a hand. "Oh, yes, just some troubling news, but it will be fixed soon enough."

She leveled Macie with a stare. Was she insinuating the troubling news had to do with her?

"You took Charlotte and Audrey into the stable earlier today while Evelyn was napping?" Mrs. Bailey pressed her fingers together in front of her lips.

Macie wondered briefly how she knew, but figured she could have spotted them from a number of rooms. The library faced the back of the house. Macie forced her face not to show her shock. "Yes, ma'am. I thought some exercise and fresh air would do them good."

"Fresh air in the stables?" Her accent made the incredulity in her voice even more pronounced.

"I thought they might want to see the baby horse. Then we played in the yard. We didn't stay in the barn for long."

"But you left Evelyn unattended." Mrs. Bailey arched a perfectly formed eyebrow.

"Gladys suggested it, so I thought it was okay. We were only gone for about an hour and a half, and Evelyn was asleep when we returned."

"It was irresponsible."

Macie tried not to let the panic rising in her throat show on her face. Irresponsible was what Macie had been called when Tommy hid from her when she was sixteen. Yes, they had been playing hide and seek, but she had given strict rules he hide in the house. He hadn't been found until after the parents returned, and they were understandably beside themselves. They thought Macie let him run away, and after an hour of searching for him, she had started to believe them. They told everyone in the neighborhood about Macie's blunder, and she was never asked to babysit again.

Tears stung Macie's eyes as she pushed the memory away. She focused on Mrs. Bailey, fighting to keep the tears from forming completely.

Mrs. Bailey took a deep breath. "If you take the girls on an outing, take all of them. But..." Mrs. Bailey took another deep breath. "Do not take them to the stables. I do not need their clothes soiled. They are very expensive."

"Could they have one set of clothes specifically for that purpose?" Macie hedged. She really wanted to get to know the horses. Nate would help her; she was sure of it.

Mrs. Bailey pursed her lips. Macie thought maybe she was thinking, but then Macie realized Mrs. Bailey was holding back a laugh. Macie wasn't sure what she had said that was funny.

"I am raising my girls to be ladies, not stable hands. They have no reason to be around the horses."

"Ladies can ride horses." At least Macie thought they could. She didn't know much about ladies these days, but she was pretty sure ladies in English past rode horses, even if it had been side-saddle. Macie wondered if the girls even owned pants. Was this woman so old-fashioned she didn't let her girls wear pants or was that the girls' preference?

"Do they have a pair of pants they could wear in the stables?"

Mrs. Bailey's hand flew to her mouth. "Pants?"

Macie studied her own jeans, wondering what was wrong with wearing them.

Mrs. Bailey laughed, but it was a relieved, short burst of sound echoing from Mrs. Bailey's mouth. "Oh, you mean trousers."

"Um, yeah." Macie didn't know the difference besides the name.

Mrs. Bailey's face lost all traces of humor, and her lips disappeared behind a thin line. "My girls will not ride horses."

"Yes, Ma'am." Macie turned to leave but stopped and took a deep breath. "Do you think I could learn?"

Mrs. Bailey laughed then, but it was a derisive sort of laugh. "When would you have time? Caring for children is a full-time job."

"Yes, Ma'am." *Though I'm not sure how you would know that since you don't spend a minute with them.* Macie bit back the remark, smiled, curtsied, and left.

Macie double-checked to see that Charlotte was asleep then made her way to her room. The baby monitor was set up in Evelyn's room, so Macie would hear her at night. Macie figured she would take it with her whenever Evelyn was sleeping until she went to bed. That way she could show Mrs. Bailey she was responsible. She just wished she had thought of it earlier.

After clipping the small portable monitor to her pants, she went to the kitchen to see if Gladys needed help. She needed someone to talk to. Gladys was washing dishes when Macie entered but turned to greet her. "I didn't expect to see you again tonight. You must be tired."

Macie sighed, grabbed a towel on the counter. She dried the dishes and put them in a pile. They were silent for a time before Macie started the conversation.

"So the Bailey's help mares give birth? I heard Daniel say it was someone else's colt."

"Daniel is a vet, so many people send their horses here when they are close to due. It is a bit cheaper than having the vet on call." Gladys gave the last dish to Macie and drained the sink.

Macie nodded. That bit of information she had learned from her evesdropping.

Gladys went on so. "Training horses is the main part of the business. Mrs. Bailey's father, Thomas Martin, was one of the greatest horse trainers this side of London, along with Daniel's father. They had this place thriving. I came on as cook when my Nate was a toddler. Mrs. Bailey moved home six months ago to take over the business when her father died, even though she didn't want to."

"Why did she?"

"I'm not sure. Mrs. Bailey's used to high-society London life. She doesn't get that here, even with the bigger house. But it isn't my business to know why people do what they do."

Macie ignored the burning in her cheeks knowing that she *was* making it her business. She couldn't help herself. Macie remembered what she had overheard. Something about someone named Callum. Macie decided to keep that to herself for now.

"Didn't she help around here growing up?" Macie asked, curious as to how someone raised with horses would hate them so much.

"She went off to a private school when she was young. After Daniel's father passed away, Thomas told some clients he couldn't train their next horses." Gladys was quiet for a moment. "Daniel is knowledgeable, but he has been running a one-man show here with a little help from my Nate. He can't keep up since Nate doesn't know much about training yet. Plus, Daniel tries to do some vet work on the side. I don't think Mrs. Bailey knows about his house calls, since that's his own little business Thomas helped him start."

Daniel's father died. Macie thought back to her interactions with him. Maybe that was why he was closed off.

"How long ago did Daniel's father die?"

Gladys sat on a stool. "Let's see... I think it was about three years ago. They had some extra help when Callum came on to help at busier times."

This was Macie's chance.

"Who's Callum?"

"Someone who went to school with Emma at the private school. He has an small estate not too far from here. I haven't seen him around here since Thomas's funeral but know he offered to buy the place."

Macie tried to stifle a yawn, but Gladys noticed.

"You better get to bed. You need to get your rest."

Macie smiled. "Thanks for talking with me." Macie wanted to talk more, but knew Gladys was right. She needed her rest.

Macie was asleep as soon as her head hit the pillow.

CHAPTER 10

DANIEL MUCKED THE STALLS with gusto to work out his frustrations. He reveled in the strain of his muscles as he scooped manure out of the stalls. Mrs. Bailey was impossible.

Daniel wanted to do what he needed to save Thomas Martin's estate, even if his daughter didn't seem interested in doing so. He owed it to the man he considered a second father. Even if he did want to leave, he couldn't leave his mother.

No matter how difficult Mrs. Bailey was, he would endure and find a way to keep the business afloat, even if Mrs. Bailey didn't care whether it failed or not. He felt he owed it to Thomas Martin to keep his estate alive. Thomas was the reason Daniel was now a certified veterinarian. He would check to see if Jack was still in the study. Then he needed to get home to check on his mother. Daniel was sure Jack would see reason.

He finished the stable and put the shovel away. Gladys would let him through the kitchen, and it would be better if he washed his hands first.

Daniel jogged to the kitchen door and lightly tapped on it, not wanting to wake Gladys if she was already asleep. The door opened almost immediately, and Daniel blinked at the sudden brightness.

Nate sat at the breakfast nook, eating a scone.

"Do you want some?" Gladys asked.

"I need to get home." He'd missed dinner, which meant his mother probably had as well. He needed to get home to feed her. He couldn't sit and eat and take the time to talk to Jack.

"Are you okay, Daniel?" Gladys asked.

Daniel's face heated as he remembered Gladys had also been right outside the room.

"How much did you hear?"

"I didn't hear anything."

Daniel grunted. He didn't believe her. Macie had been standing on the stairs and Gladys in the hall leading to the kitchen.

Gladys handed a paper bag filled with scones. "For your Mum. You keep fighting for what Thomas wanted. I don't know what Mrs. Bailey has against horses and such, but she isn't one for business. You have the know-how. You have to convince them you know best."

"We could find customers who need a stud without them knowing," Nate suggested.

Daniel chuckled. "They write the checks to the Bailey's, mate. They'd find out sooner or later."

"But with a check staring them in the face, why would they refuse?"

Nate had a point. If he became desperate, he might do just that. Daniel thanked Gladys for the scones and took the paper bag with the hot scones to the study, hoping Mrs. Bailey wouldn't be there... but Jack would.

The door was wide open, and the light was on. No one was inside. Maybe Jack would be back soon, but Daniel didn't want to wait too long.

He set the bag of scones on a side table next to the chairs and went to the desk, determined to leave a note for Jack to call him. If he said it was about something urgent, Jack was sure to call.

Daniel checked all the drawers in the desk. They were nearly empty. It didn't make sense. Where did the Baileys keep their receipts and such? Thomas had kept them in the drawer. He moved to the bookshelf. A sliver of gray behind the books caught his eyes. He removed a few books to find a small safe. Daniel was sure it had not been there long. Daniel had spent a lot of time in here with Thomas Martin. When would Thomas have put it in? More curious than ever, Daniel was tempted to figure out the combination but couldn't. Whatever was in that safe was none of his business.

He returned the books to the shelf and wondered if Mrs. Bailey even realized the safe was there. The books that covered the safe were large and held information about different types of horses. If the Bailey's weren't interested in breeding, they wouldn't feel the need to read those books.

He grabbed the bag of scones, grateful they were still warm, and hurried to the back door. He could talk to Jack later. A night to think about what he would say would probably be better anyway.

***

Callum strode to his neighbor's door. He had heard they had a horse that was almost ready to give birth. Vin said create an opportunity where everyone important was away from the Bailey Estate, so Vin could do something to help undermine it.

He knocked, and a woman with a young child clinging to her legs opened the door. "Cheers, Mrs. Jones. Is Joseph here?"

Mrs. Jones nodded. "He's out back. You can go around the house."

Callum nodded. He had worked hard to befriend this family, even though he preferred to stick to himself, but the prescription drugs to help him relax and forget his guilt about arranging Thomas Martin's death made meeting with people bearable.

Callum made his way around the large house and looked in the direction of his estate. The hilly landscape and copse of trees made it impossible to see his house, but he could see his barns. He relaxed at the assurance that his privacy was assured, at least from the neighbors.

Joseph was walking out of the barn. Callum raised his hand in greeting and jogged across the lawn. Joseph smiled and shook his hand.

"Callum. What brings you here today?"

"I heard you have a mare nearly ready to give birth. I know you're new here. Are you going to birth it yourself?"

Joseph shook his head. "I know there are rarely problems, but I was thinking of calling a vet when the time comes."

"I know an estate that houses mares when they are about to give birth. They have a certified vet onsite. It might be cheaper than hiring one to come to you."

"I don't know. I'd really like to be there for the birth." Joseph looked at his barn. Callum could understand his hesitancy. Joseph was trying to grow his stock, and the thought of letting his one mare out of his sight most likely felt risky.

"I'm sure if you asked, they would call when she first showed signs of labor. I personally know them. The vet does great work and even makes house calls, so if you need a vet later, he can check on the colt for you. He charges less than most vets around here."

Joseph rubbed a hand over his stubbly chin and looked hesitant. Maybe saying that gave him the idea Daniel was less capable.

Callum went on. "I can give you the number, and you can set up a time for them to talk with you. Have Mrs. Bailey come since she is the one who works the contracts. The vet and the hired stable hand can come too so you can get to know the people who would actually be taking care of your horse."

That was the best Callum could do. If Joseph didn't take the bait, he would have to find another way to get the estate empty for Vin.

After a long pause, Joseph nodded. "That would be great. Would you come over to make introductions?"

Callum nodded. Joseph was playing right into his hands. If Callum was there when they came, he would know exactly when to tell Vin they were gone. There would be no risk as long as the nanny and house staff stayed indoors, which Callum knew they normally did from watching the Bailey place since Thomas's death.

***

CHAPTER 11

"WILL YOU PLEASE EAT and stop telling me how someone else does it?" Macie snapped at Charlotte. "This is the way I serve lunch, and this is the way I will *always* serve lunch. So, get used to it."

Macie had been here almost a week, and Charlotte had questioned everything she did. She argued with her methods of teaching. She argued with how she served meals. She argued over how she played with them. Macie was doing her best not to let it wear her down, but something had to give. Somehow, she had to show Charlotte she was not someone she needed to fight, and Macie would be a cheerleader for her. The constant back-talking was starting to wear on her. She tried to console herself in the knowledge that Mrs. Bailey had decided she would give Macie another month. So far, she had proved her worth.

It had been a long morning. Charlotte had been sulky and yelled about everything Macie had told her to do as part of her schoolwork. She had even done the opposite of what Macie asked several times. Macie knew she was pushing her boundaries, but she was at her wit's end with the girl. She suspected it was a reaction to her mom's announcement at breakfast that Macie would be staying on at least a month. Macie was grateful Audrey and Evelyn were willing to do what she asked, but then again, they got to play during school time.

Gladys came into the kitchen and smiled at Macie but directed her comment to Charlotte. "Macie's right. There's no one way to feed someone lunch." Then she pulled Macie into a hug. "Don't let her get under your skin," she murmured.

Macie took a deep breath and huffed it out.

"Mrs. Bailey went with Nate and Daniel to talk to someone who might have them house a mare until she gives birth," Gladys said. "I'll finish feeding them. You take a break."

Macie nodded. "Thanks. I don't know how moms do it when they never get a break."

Gladys set her hand on Macie's shoulder. "All mums need to find a few minutes to themselves at some time, or they'll have a mental breakdown."

Macie flung her arms around Gladys's waist before she could stop herself. This woman was so kind and understanding. "Thank you."

Gladys patted her back. "You never have to be perfect."

The murmured words sent warmth flitting through Macie. But, even if Gladys was understanding, she knew Mrs. Bailey expected perfection. She would take a quick break while Gladys fed the girls and go back to trying even harder to be the perfect nanny.

Macie made her way out the kitchen door that led to the back yard. It was raining lightly, so she grabbed her jacket where she had stored it in the mudroom. She took a deep breath when she stepped outside. The bright pink and white blossoms in the orchard on the other side of the house beckoned to her, so she headed to the grove. She breathed in when she got to the edge of the orchard. She opted not to wander among the trees, since that would get her even wetter. The moisture in the air amplified the stillness around her. It was almost unnaturally quiet, and she shuddered slightly as a wave of nervous energy swept through her. She wandered around the edge of the grove, wanting to revel in the scent without walking among the dripping leaves.

She jumped as her phone vibrated in her pocket. She glanced around then remembered Mrs. Bailey was gone. It wasn't often she got texts here. She had texted her sister off and on throughout the previous week, needing to vent her frustrations to someone, but not wanting her parents to know how much she was struggling.

Katie: How's it going?

Macie: Okay. You're up early.

Katie: Sick kid. (frowny face emoji)

Macie: I'm sorry. Charlotte is giving me grief. I don't know how to convince her to like me.

Katie: You can't convince her. Just be your wonderful self, and she will eventually come around. She's had a lot of change in the last six months from what you tell me.

Macie: Yeah. It is so hard to remember that when she's sassing me.

Katie: I understand, believe me. (Smiley face)

Macie: I better get back to work. I'm not supposed to be on my phone while on duty. I'll call you in the morning—my morning.

Katie: Don't forget. (winky face)

Macie put her phone in her pocket and turned toward the house. A movement near the back of the barn caught her attention. Was there another hand she wasn't aware of? It could have been a horse. Her feet moved quickly to the barns even as dread filled her belly.

She cautiously walked toward the side door of the barn, keeping a sharp eye out. The feeling of dread spread from her stomach and seeped through her veins, as the cold drizzle of rain coated her clothes and hair, making her shiver. As Macie turned into the barn opening, she bumped into someone exiting the barn, and a horse reared up and kicked.

CHAPTER 12

MACIE FELL ON THE seat of her pants, landing in a shallow puddle. A man swore and pulled on the lead rope in his hands to keep the horse from running.

"Who are you?" Macie asked as she picked herself from the mud, then stared at her feet. Her cheeks blazed with embarrassment and shame.

"I should be asking you the same question," the stranger said as he continued to struggle to calm the spooked horse.

Macie noticed the muscles under his shirt tense as he pulled on the lead rope to keep the horse from bolting. Her eyes flicked to the horse, trying to decide if it was going to trample her. She picked herself up out of the puddle, the seat of her pants soaked through.

"I'm Macie, the nanny." Macie forced confidence in her voice she didn't really feel.

"Then what are you doing out here?" The man's short tone made Macie take a step back. Was she not supposed to do that? Her breathing hitched, but she forced her face to remain passive. She couldn't let the man know she was nervous. She had learned if she let her insecuries show too much, people easily took advantage of her nievete.

"Taking a short break." Macie was distracted by the odd tattoo partly revealed through his partially unbuttoned shirt. She pulled her gaze away from the tattoo and looked at his face, but his hat was pulled down low over his eyes, shadowing most of his face. Rainwater dripped off the front in a steady stream. A bandana was wrapped around his mouth, most likely to keep the dust out. Though there wouldn't be any dust today. Macie shivered, unease coursing down her spine.

"So, why are you here? I haven't seen you around. Do you work here, too?" Macie doubted he did. Sure, she had only been here a week, but she had spent some time outside with the girls every day and had never seen the man. The Baileys seemed to employ as few people as possible, and Macie was sure he would have been at the birth of the foal if he worked here, but she didn't know how else to get the man to give some hint as to who he was.

The man turned his head, as if looking over his shoulder, though Macie couldn't see his eyes to be sure. "No, I came to see how the training was going for my horse."

Macie didn't miss the fact that he avoided giving his name. Her heart flipped, and she searched for something to say. The sense that something was wrong was growing inside her. She glanced around to see if there was anyone around who might be a witness to what was going on. When would Daniel and Nate get back?

Macie swallowed. She wasn't sure whether to detain the man or run for help. Most likely, she was overreacting, but the way the man kept moving his head as if looking for anyone nearby and his short non-answers, Macie figured her caution was the best route to take. She had to get some sort of explanation out of the man since no one was here. Gladys had told her both Nate and Daniel were gone along with Mrs. Bailey. She had learned last Sunday at dinner that Mr. Bailey worked and lived in their townhouse in London during the week. He wouldn't be home until tomorrow. Maybe she would be rescued from this mess, and Daniel would show up.

Macie glanced toward the house, wishing she could see the driveway from here. Her eyes flitted to the man and were immediately drawn back to the tattoo. It appeared to be a dragon, but she was uncertain. She wouldn't know without seeing the entire thing. But a reptile-like face was visible in the opening of his shirt, its jaws gaping as if ready to swallow Macie whole. Shivering, she tore her eyes away from the fearsome creature and focused on the shadow where the man's eyes were hidden.

"Did Mrs. Bailey know you were coming? She isn't here right now, but I can deliver a message if you need."

"No," the man assured her, his head swiveling as if he were checking the area around them. "I'm satisfied the horse is coming along nicely."

"What's your horse's name?" she asked, trying to be polite and cover up her unease. Macie looked at the horse. It was beautiful, with a sleek black coat and matching mane.

"How long have you been here?" The man didn't know how to answer a question.

"A week," Macie admitted. "I don't think you should take the horse while everyone is gone. Could you come back when they are here?"

Macie realized she didn't know anything about how things were run at the stable. Would Daniel or someone be there to discuss the training before turning a horse over to its owner? Macie tried to think of a way to backpedal, to let the man know he could probably take the horse if that was what had been arranged, but the man spoke up before she said anything.

"I'm not taking the horse with me yet. It's clearly not ready." He turned and led the horse into the barn.

Macie's whole body relaxed. At least he wasn't going to push. The fact that the man had yet to offer his name didn't sit well with her. Something was off, but she would have to ask someone who knew how things were run to know for sure. She waited outside the barn until the man reemerged.

"I'll walk you to the front of the house." Macie took a few steps and then waited until he followed. Everything inside of her told her she needed to see the man to the front. She chalked the feeling up to being paranoid for most of her life. She figured she should follow the feeling and admit her error later if needed. She couldn't explain the compulsion she had to see him gone, but she figured it was the responsible thing to do. She wasn't about to be accused of being irresponsible again.

Macie led him past the orchard and around the house. He didn't say anything, and Macie gave up asking him questions. She kept his boots in sight as he walked a half a pace behind her. She tried to slow her steps so he would pass her, but he matched her stride. Macie stood by the front corner of the house as she watched him make his way down the long drive. His dark hair was visible under his cowboy hat. Where was his car or truck? Did he live close enough to walk? Macie had slept most of the drive here from the airport. She could see a roof about a quarter mile to her left past the apple orchards, but the area to her right was blocked by large trees that made it impossible to see past them.

Macie tried to shake the uneasy feeling that held her hostage. Something wasn't right, but she didn't know anything about the business of training horses.

Macie hurried to get the girls, knowing Gladys would be wondering what happened to her. She hoped Gladys wouldn't tell Mrs. Bailey she was negligent. Something was off about that man, but she determined to mull it over while she finished Charlotte's schoolwork. She didn't want to look like she was overreacting to a man checking on his horse.

"Oh, there you are," Gladys said as Macie hurried through the door. Gladys's eyebrows raised in question.

"Sorry." Macie didn't want to give an explanation in front of the girls. "Come on, girls. Let's finish up school, so we can do something fun while Evelyn naps."

"What fun can we have while it rains?" Audrey complained.

How had Macie forgotten about the rain? Drizzle that it was, it had still left her hair and coat soaked. "We'll come up with something."

Macie quickly hung up her jacket.

"I've done enough school today," Charlotte announced, folding her arms and stomping her foot.

"Sorry. The schedule Daisy gave me says we have to do reading."

"I'm usually done with school by lunch."

"Since I'm new, I probably went slower than you have before. Some extra time won't hurt you." Not to mention that Charlotte had fought her over everything she was asked to do, which no doubt slowed the process, but Macie didn't want to goad Charlotte into a fight. Macie walked with determination toward the school room, hoping her confident manner would get Charlotte to follow her without any more arguments.

"Then I want Daisy to teach me again."

Macie swung around. Evelyn clung to Macie's shirt to keep her balance. Audrey looked at Macie as if waiting to see how she would react. Macie considered for a brief moment, but Charlotte went on.

"Not that any of the nannies here have been as good as Celeste."

Again the first nanny that seemed to be able to walk on water in everyone's minds here. Macie didn't know how she would ever be able to measure up with someone so perfect.

"Come on," Macie said, choosing not to take the bait.

Charlotte slowly stepped forward, and Macie waited until Charlotte passed her before following her to the school room. But Macie was only able to get through one reading passage with Charlotte before her mind wandered to her encounter with the man with the tattoo. Images of the man with the horse kept flashing through her mind, and Macie wondered about his appearance. She was almost positive he had been hiding his identity. If she needed to tell Mrs. Bailey or Daniel, she wouldn't be able to describe him well except that he had dark hair and was wearing blue jeans and black boots and had a creepy tattoo on his chest. She also knew he was wearing a brown cowboy hat.

At dinner, Macie tried to bring up the topic, but Mrs. Bailey didn't give her a chance to speak, talking over Macie as she described the luncheon she would get to go to with some neighbors the next day. At least Mrs. Bailey was happy today.

Macie got the girls to bed and peeked into the study. The room was empty. She wandered the house, glancing into all of the main level rooms. She didn't want to disturb Mrs. Bailey if she was in her room, so after a fruitless search Macie made her way to the kitchen where she found Gladys making bread.

"Gladys," Macie started. She wasn't sure if Gladys was the one to tell but holding it inside was suffocating her. Gladys would know how urgent the matter was and tell her who she should report it to. "When I went outside today, a strange man took a horse out of the barn. He put it back, but something seemed off. I tried to tell Mrs. Bailey about it at dinner but couldn't get a word in."

Gladys gave Macie her full attention. "Customers usually make appointments to pick up their horses. That does sound a little strange. What did he look like?"

"Umm, tall. Black hair, brown cowboy hat. He had his face covered with a bandana, and he had a tattoo on his chest—some picture of a kind of reptile with gaping jaws and sharp teeth." Macie shivered at the memory and tried not to be embarrassed about her dismal list of descriptors. If only he hadn't had his face covered.

"Mrs. Bailey doesn't like to be bothered about problems with the horses. You should probably mention it to Daniel. He's in charge out there."

Macie cringed, and Gladys thumped her hand on Macie's back. "Don't judge him too harshly. He's had a hard time these past few years."

"Because of his father's death."

Gladys nodded. "That's part of it."

"Is Daniel here? He doesn't live here, does he?"

"He lives in the house west of here. He's probably at home." Gladys gave Macie Daniel's number.

After Macie retired to her room, not anxious to have anybody witness how she feared this conversation would go, she called the number. After several rings, it went to voicemail, and Daniel's voice came on the line. "This is Daniel. If you have questions about the Martin Estate training schedule, please leave your name and number, and I will call you back." Then the tone sounded.

"Daniel, this is Macie. Um... Gladys gave me your number, because, well... This afternoon when you were gone—"

"Macie!" Macie jumped at the sound of her name. She gritted her teeth, hoping Mrs. Bailey wouldn't wake Evelyn.

"Call me." Macie quickly hung up and ran out to find Mrs. Bailey in the sitting area that separated the kids wing from the adult wing.

"Are the girls all asleep already?" Mrs. Bailey's tone made Macie think she doubted it.

"Yes, Ma'am."

Mrs. Bailey arched her brows before she nodded. "I wanted to let you know I will be gone most of the day tomorrow. I have a luncheon in London, so I will be leaving early.

Macie nodded. It wouldn't be much different for her whether Mrs. Bailey was there or not, since in her week there Mrs. Bailey hadn't once dropped in to spend some time with her girls. Mrs. Bailey stood and made her way to her bedroom and Macie returned to her room, hoping Daniel would listen to her message and not dismiss it entirely. Leaving him the message would at least put someone on alert in case the man came back and wasn't who he said he was. She would just have to be patient and wait for his call.

CHAPTER 13

A LOUD KNOCKING ECHOED through Callum's house. That had to be Vin. Callum had been pacing the floor, wondering if he was able to take advantage of Callum getting the Mrs. Bailey, Nate and Daniel out of the house. He hadn't expected to have to wait until dark to hear from him.

He opened the door, and one look at Vin's face told him things hadn't gone well. His hair was mussed, and his dark eyes flashed. Callum took a step away from him, and Vin took that as an invitation into the house.

"I thought you said the estate would be empty," Vin seethed.

"I can't guarantee anything with the household staff and the girls, but I told my neighbor about the Baileys housing mares until they gave birth, and he wanted to meet them with me there. Emma, Daniel, and Nate were all at my neighbor's house. Jack was still in London; I was sure."

"So you're drumming up more business for them? How is that going to convince them to sell?"

"You wanted me to clear the estate. That was what I thought of." Callum strode into his study and grabbed a shot glass. He poured a glass for himself and his cousin, but Vin waved him off. Callum shrugged, trying to seem unconcerned and drank the fiery liquid in one gulp. It seemed he needed more and more to drown the guilt threatening to overwhelm him. Vin's threatening presence was not helping him tonight.

"Well, we have to figure out another way to get rid of the Bailey's and their trainer," Vin said. "The nanny caught me leading a horse Emma had marked for me out of the barn and she wouldn't leave without seeing I was gone. I was afraid she'd report me if I did anything more suspicious."

"I heard Emma say she was leaving for London early tomorrow. She had been chatting with my neighbor's wife as Joseph talked to Nate and Daniel. You don't have to worry about her, but you have to figure out how to get rid of Daniel."

"Fine," Vin growled. Then he paused and studied Callum. Before Callum could ask any more questions, Vin shook his head and left.

***

Daniel stared at his phone after listening to the voicemail a second time. Why had Macie called him? What had happened yesterday afternoon that she felt the need to tell him and not Mrs. Bailey?

He figured whatever she was calling about was important if Gladys gave Macie his number. Gladys never gave his number out without asking him first. He would find Macie sometime this morning, maybe after the morning chores.

He strode to the fence separating their property from the Martin Estate, intent on finishing the morning feedings quickly so he could find Macie. His phone rang as he walked toward the barn, and Mrs. Bailey pulled out of the driveway.

"This is Daniel," Daniel said into his phone.

"Daniel. This is George Morris. Clay says the colt I brought home from your place last week is sick. Could you come check him?"

Daniel's mind raced through different scenarios, but all the guessing in the world wouldn't let him relax unless he saw the animal in person.

"I'll be right over." Macie would have to wait. It hadn't sounded like what she had to tell him was an emergency.

"I won't be home," George said. "My daughter just had her baby, and my wife is anxious to get to the hospital, but Clay will stay here until you arrive. He has some errands to run when you get here."

"I'm on my way."

Daniel hung up and sent a text to Nate, telling him he had an emergency vet call and Nate would have to do the morning feedings. Daniel grabbed the keys for the estate truck off the hook inside the garage and pulled out.

Fifteen minutes later, he jumped from the truck and rapped on the front door of the Morris house to make sure they were already gone. No answer.

Daniel wandered to the back to find Clay. He checked the small barn, the sheds, and the corrals. He didn't see a sign of him.

Daniel went to the barn to check Mr. Morris's colt. He wished Mr. Morris had told him what was wrong, but figured he would conduct a thorough examination. Daniel rubbed his hand along the colt's legs to check for swelling and looked into his mouth. He finished the exam, but the colt seemed fine. A quick search of the other stalls in the barn didn't turn up any more colts, so Mr. Morris must have meant the one he checked. He decided to err on the side of caution and performed a quick examination of all the horses.

Daniel jumped in the truck after checking all the horses, anxious to get to the estate. He needed to find Macie. He had a feeling she would never call him unless absolutely necessary. She didn't have a high opinion of him, and he understood why. He hadn't yet proved to be friendly. He turned the key. The truck didn't start. Daniel groaned and opened the bonnet. The Baileys needed to buy a new truck.

He sent a text to Nate to let him know the truck was not starting, and he might be later than he thought.

He looked at the time. He had been here three hours. He ground his teeth in frustration. He shouldn't have taken the time to examine all the horses. Mr. Morris had said colt. He should have left after he looked him over. He threw his phone on the seat and opened the truck bonnet. He found the problem easily, but it took him a while to figure out how to fix it.

He checked his phone again as he got into the truck. Macie had called again. He missed it by ten minutes. He called her back, but she didn't answer. She probably had it on silent so it wouldn't distract her from the girls.

***

Macie paced the room as Charlotte continued to struggle with her math facts. She didn't have the mental bandwidth for this. She had to tell someone about the strange man. Macie asked Gladys to tell Nate to pass on the message that she needed to talk to Daniel as soon as possible. She stepped out of the room for a moment to sneak a phone call since Mrs. Bailey was gone. No answer. She almost wished she had told Katie about the strange man when she called her this morning, but hadn't wanted to worry her. Katie couldn't do anything about it, anyway. It was Daniel who needed to know about the man. She was sure of it.

She set the phone on a bookshelf and approached Audrey to help her form her letters. She had learned she shouldn't hover over Charlotte and had decided it was best if Charlotte had to ask her for help. It felt hotter than it had been all week, and her anxiety made the room feel stuffy. She threw the window open and breathed in the fresh air.

The schoolroom was at the back of the house, but a large bush right outside the window obscured her vision of the barn. She couldn't see Daniel from there. If she had, she would have yelled for him, but from this window all she could see was the area around the door leading to the kitchen and the garage.

"Macie?" Charlotte's voice was whiny.

"Yes?"

"Subtracting nines is so hard." Charlotte threw her pencil across the room. "I'm never going to get it."

Macie took a deep breath. "If you would like my help, you can ask nicely."

"I don't have to ask. You are *supposed* to help me. It's your *job*."

Macie willed herself to stay calm. "It may be my job, but you can still be polite. I will not help until you ask nicely."

Charlotte stared at Macie, then her eyes filled with tears.

Macie forced herself not to run to soothe her.

Audrey stood and put a hand on Charlotte's arm. She didn't pull away like usual. Audrey whispered, but Macie was close enough to hear her words. "She will help you if you are nice."

"It's not worth being nice if she's just going to leave us," Charlotte hissed.

Macie wanted to reassure her she was not going anywhere, but that could be an empty promise. If Charlotte's mom said she had to leave, she would have to leave.

"Charlotte." Macie's voice was soft. "I will not leave unless your mom makes me. I want to help you." Macie's heart hurt for Charlotte, and she couldn't help adding. "I know what it feels like to feel forgotten, Charlotte."

Charlotte met her eyes. All the anger faded out of her tear-streaked face and then it crumpled. "Will you help me, please?"

Macie ran to Charlotte's side, wrapped her arms around girl, and let her cry until the sobs subsided.

Macie leaned on her heels but kept a hand on Charlotte's back for comfort. "What do you need help with?"

"I can't subtract nines."

Macie smiled. "Well, my little brother had problems, too, and his teacher taught him a trick. Can I teach it to you?"

Charlotte nodded, but she didn't look convinced that any trick would help her.

"If it is a number between ten and nineteen you are subtracting nine from, a trick is to add the digits of the top number together. So if it's thirteen minus nine, you would add one and three. That equals four, so thirteen minus nine is four."

Charlotte stared at her doubtfully. Then did the next problem. She did the trick first then had Macie help her use her fingers to double-check her answer. Charlotte grinned. Macie's stomach did a little flip. It was the first time Charlotte had directed a smile at Macie since she had arrived.

Macie kept Evelyn occupied with the play tea set but couldn't stop glancing toward the door. Audrey and Charlotte worked on an art project nearby and, hopefully, didn't notice her nerves. She couldn't believe Gladys wouldn't have delivered her message to Nate. Surely Daniel would be at the estate by now.

By the time the girls finished their art project, Macie's insides were twisting. She couldn't take it anymore. She hoped Daisy would come soon to tell them lunch was ready. It was a little early, but she couldn't stand the tension in her body and didn't want to get in trouble by leaving the girls or dragging them around the estate, looking for Daniel.

"Daisy?" Macie called out of the room, hoping she was within earshot. Daisy came out of a room down the hall.

"Will you ask Gladys if lunch will be ready at noon? She mentioned yesterday she was going shopping."

"Yes, Miss."

Macie shook her head at the formal address, but Daisy insisted she would get fired, so Macie let it go.

Daisy came back a few minutes later. "I can't find her. She isn't in the kitchen, and the groceries are on the counter. She must be back from the convenience shop."

Macie's stomach tightened. She was probably being paranoid after waiting to talk to someone about the man yesterday, but she wanted to make sure. "Can you check around outside?"

Daisy's face paled. "I'm not supposed to go outside when I'm working."

Macie's hands trembled. She couldn't stand the stress in her body. "Okay, I'll go if you can watch the girls."

Daisy nodded, relief evident on her face.

Macie ran to the kitchen. The groceries were on the counter, as Daisy had said. She hurried out the kitchen door Gladys would have used to bring in the groceries.

"Gladys!" Macie called. She peeked around the corner of the house. Gladys's car was parked next to the garage, the trunk open. Macie checked the trunk and found more groceries waiting to be brought in. Macie's heart thumped, and her breath hitched.

Something was wrong.

A lump grew in Macie's stomach. She tried to swallow the nerves since she was prone to getting paranoid, especially since she lost Sammy. Macie shook her head. Nothing was wrong. Maybe Gladys went to the garden to see if any of the spring vegetables were ready. Were any vegetables ready in May? Macie wished she knew something about anything.

Macie made her way to the garden but stopped when something outside the barn caught her eye.

Macie squinted. As her eyes strained, Macie made out the shape of a body.

CHAPTER 14

MACIE FROZE, HER BREATH catching in her throat. The dark figure lay sprawled on the ground. Her heart pounded as she sprinted forward, dread tightening her chest.

Please don't be dead.

The distance between her and the figure seemed to go on forever. She propelled herself harder, faster. Dirt and grass kicked up around her as she gained even more speed. Glancing to the sky, she sent up a silent prayer.

The distance closed. Macie took in the familiar dress, and her heart stuttered again. She dropped to her knees. "Gladys!"

Gladys lay motionless. Blood seeped down the side of her face. Macie rolled Gladys over so her face wasn't in the dirt. Macie lifted Gladys' head to put it in her lap, and her hand touched something wet and sticky. Macie tried not to think about it as she gently brought her hand away, covered in Gladys' blood.

"Daisy!" Macie screamed as loud as she could, cursing herself for not grabbing her phone from the bookshelf where she had set it after she tried calling Daniel. Would Daisy be able to hear her? Macie had opened the schoolroom window. "Help!" Macie screamed in case anyone else was around. Where were Nate and Daniel? Macie continued to alternate between calling for Daisy and screaming for help.

Macie's pant leg stuck to her skin. She tried to forget that the wet sticky mess on her pants was blood. She needed to stay focused. She needed to put pressure on the wound. She had a tank top on under her button-up shirt. Her fingers fumbled with the buttons. She let out a small yell of frustration as her fingers slipped on the button a third time. She could feel her pant legs getting stickier. Unbuttoning the shirt was taking too long. She gripped her shirt with both hands and pulled as hard as she could. Buttons went flying. She ignored them and slipped the shirt off and then wadded it up. She lifted Gladys's head slightly to put her shirt on the wound.

Macie's voice was growing hoarse. Daisy couldn't be so worried about leaving the house that she wouldn't answer Macie's desperate calls for help, would she? Macie's hands trembled, but she refused to let Gladys down. She would not freak out.

Macie finally decided that it would be better for her to leave Gladys long enough to run for her phone when the back door next to the kitchen opened. Daisy rushed out.

"Call 911!" Macie yelled at her. Was it called 911 here? "Call an ambulance," Macie amended.

Daisy's hand went to her mouth. She ran back inside. Macie gritted her teeth. A few minutes later, Daisy looked like she was talking to someone just inside the kitchen

"Call an ambulance," Macie repeated.

"I've got to get my phone." Daisy sprinted to the house again.

"Bring me a towel or something. She's bleeding badly," Macie called after her, grateful Daisy's room was near the kitchen. It wouldn't take her long to get her phone, but Macie could feel the blood soaking through the thin shirt she held against Gladys's head.

Macie searched the area around the barn, hoping to see some sign of Daniel or Nate, though she knew they would already be here with the noise she was making.

Daisy exited the house a minute later with her phone to her ear and holding a dish towel. She stopped a few paces away from Macie and threw her the towel. Her face was pale, and her eyes were glued to Macie's hand covered in Gladys's blood. Macie carefully folded the towel and lifted Gladys's head enough to put the towel over the wadded-up, blood-soaked shirt. She prayed Gladys would be okay. Macie wouldn't be able to survive here without her gentle guidance.

"Do you know what happened?" Daisy asked, obviously repeating whoever she had on the line.

Macie shook her head. "I found her face down in the dirt with a head wound."

Macie zoned out as Daisy continued to talk into her phone.

The sound of a garage opening brought Macie out of a daze. She looked at Daisy.

"They say someone is on the way." Daisy ran toward the garage to intercept Mrs. Bailey.

Macie breathed a sigh a relief when Mr. Bailey came out of the garage in front of Mrs. Bailey. He must have come home at the same time. Mrs. Bailey's hand flew to her mouth. Mr. Bailey turned and shooed his wife inside.

Daisy tossed her phone to Mr. Bailey. He caught the phone and started talking immediately. Macie watched Gladys and held her breath until she could discern the slight rise and fall of her chest. Macie wanted to cry, but she wasn't done here yet.

"Where's Nate?" he asked.

"I haven't seen him." Macie frantically searched the grounds to see if she could see Nate lying somewhere behind her. She hadn't even thought he might also be hurt.

Mr. Bailey looked at the barn. He sprinted to the opening in the middle of the barn and stopped short. He sprinted out of sight. Dread seeped into Macie's veins and left her limbs feeling cold. "Please don't let him be dead," Macie mumbled out loud, hoping the God she learned about in her youth was listening.

Mr. Bailey didn't emerge and a heavy weight settled in Macie's chest, making it hard to breathe. The silence surrounded her, thick and heavy, as her only wish was to hear some sort of siren that meant help was near. Gladys's chest was still rising and falling, but Macie could feel the sticky wetness of blood through the towel she was holding to her head. She was losing a lot of blood.

The sounds of sirens filled the air, and Macie breathed a little easier.

Soon Macie could see the faint flashing lights on the grass in front of the house. The sirens turned off. Two men with stretchers sprinted toward the barn.

"Where's the boy?" one man asked, and Macie pointed to where Mr. Bailey had disappeared into the barn, figuring that was where Nate was.

Macie concentrated on answering the questions asked and helping them get Gladys situated on the stretcher. She was rushed off, so Macie went to the barn where Mr. Bailey was standing behind the paramedics as they worked on Nate. His dark skin was streaked with blood, and Macie was afraid to ask, but she had to.

"Is he—?" Macie couldn't even say the word.

"He'll live," a paramedic said.

A policeman came up to her.

"Mr. Bailey says you are the one who found the woman. Do you know what happened?"

Macie shook her head. "I found Gladys on the ground and didn't even know Nate was hurt."

The man turned to Mr. Bailey. "Do you know who would have done this? Is anything missing?"

Macie felt the blood drain from her face. The man with the black horse she saw yesterday. Could it be the same guy? If Gladys died because she hadn't tried hard enough to tell someone about the guy, Macie would never be able to forgive herself.

"I'm not sure where each horse is kept. I'll call Daniel," Mr. Bailey replied.

The policeman nodded. "The guy might have known Nate was here and didn't want him warning anyone, so dealt with him first."

Mr. Bailey absently handed Macie Daisy's phone as he walked by. "Go in and have Daisy help Emma."

Macie didn't need to be asked twice. Now that Gladys was on her way to the hospital, she wasn't needed out here. She found Daisy in the kitchen feeding the girls, trying to keep her voice calm as she attempted to placate them.

Macie laid a hand on Daisy's shoulder. "I'll take care of them. Why don't you go find Mrs. Bailey and let me know if she needs something?"

Daisy fled through the door.

Evelyn was crying but not screaming. Tears rolled down Audrey's face, and Charlotte's lips trembled. Macie looked at the clock. The girls were eating lunch almost an hour late. It was still a little early to put Evelyn down for a nap, but Macie figured that would be okay.

"I don't want Gladys to die," Audrey blurted, still focused on her plate of food.

"She's not going to die," Macie assured them.

"How do you know?" Charlotte asked.

Macie tried to hold her own tears back, but they splashed onto her cheeks. "I don't know, Charlotte. I'm just really hoping." Macie kneeled down and held her arms out, but the girls gaped at her and stumbled away.

Audrey gasped. "Macie. You have blood everywhere."

Macie glanced at her blood-soaked jeans and tank top. She jumped up to the kitchen sink and scrubbed her hands vigorously.

"Are you girls done with your lunch?"

Audrey nodded, wide-eyed. Macie had to get changed. She would put Evelyn down for a nap, then have Audrey and Charlotte wait while she found clean clothes.

"Charlotte, can you and Audrey help Evelyn up the stairs?"

Each girl took their little sister by the hand, and they slowly made their way up the stairs.

"Sorry, Evelyn. No rock-a-bye right now."

Evelyn started crying.

"I can rock her," Charlotte's voice was timid, and Macie nodded, smiling at her.

"Thank you."

Macie tried to sneak away to change, but a slight noise of protest from Evelyn stopped her. Macie sighed. She could wait another minute.

Daisy rushed toward Macie as soon as she shut the door. "Mr. and Mrs. Bailey need you in the study." She gestured to the girls. "Mrs. Bailey asked me to take them to the playroom while you talk."

"Can I change first?" Macie indicated her clothes.

Daisy took a step back, disgust evident at Macie's appearance, but she shook her head. "The detective is here."

Macie cringed but nodded. She would just have to be filthy a little longer. She couldn't keep the detective waiting.

CHAPTER 15

THE DOOR TO THE study was wide open, so Macie walked in. Mrs. Bailey was reclining on a chair in the corner next to the open window. She was fanning herself with a piece of paper. She stared at the wall opposite her with a vacant expression on her face, and it scared Macie even more. Mr. Bailey sat behind the desk, and the police officer who had been at the barn sat in a chair near the desk, opposite Mrs. Bailey. He stood when Macie entered. He was tall, and his blue eyes were so penetrating she was sure he never missed anything when dealing with crimes.

"You wanted to speak to me." Macie tried to sound calm and confident, but her voice trembled. She clasped her hands together and looked down, but the sight of her blood-soaked clothes made her stomach turn, so she forced herself to make eye contact with the police officer.

The man stepped forward and offered his hand. "Detective Inspector Clark. I want to hear your side of the story."

Macie shook his hand, grateful she had at least cleaned those, and tried to clear her thoughts enough so she could tell him what happened. It was starting to blur in her mind, and she hadn't been knocked in the head.

"Well, it was getting close to lunchtime. I sent Daisy to ask Gladys if lunch would be ready soon. I knew she went shopping, so I wasn't sure if lunch would be a little late because of it."

Detective Clark made a rotating motion with his hand as if to speed up her story.

"Uh, said she couldn't find her."

Detective Clark's hand shot up with his palm facing Macie. "Who couldn't find who?"

"Oh, Daisy came back saying she couldn't find Gladys. I suggested Daisy go look for Gladys near her car in case she was still bringing in groceries. Daisy said they were on the counter."

"The groceries were on the counter?" Detective Clark repeated.

"Yes, sir. Daisy seemed scared to go outside, so I offered to search for Gladys. I left Daisy—"

Mrs. Bailey gasped. "You left my girls alone when a murderer was on the loose?"

"I didn't know someone was here who wasn't supposed to be, Ma'am. The girls were with Daisy. They weren't alone." When the detective cleared his throat, Macie rushed to continue. "I went outside to check Gladys's car. She wasn't there, so—"

"What's wrong, sir?" Daniel burst through the study doors. His frantic eyes searched Mr. Bailey as if he could find the answer to his question on his face.

Macie fell silent.

The detective flashed his badge. "Detective Inspector Clark. I'm afraid there has been an incident."

"You picked a perfect day to be absent from your duties." Mrs. Bailey's steely voice made Macie flinch.

Mr. Bailey waved his hand. "Never mind that. I need you to check the barns to see if any horses or tack are missing. Nate was found in the barn with a head wound."

Daniel's eyes widened, and he ran out of the room.

Macie had a sinking feeling he would find something gone. Everything inside Macie told her this, whatever it was, was related to the man she had seen the day before.

"Do you want me to continue?" Macie asked the detective, anxious to finish this part of her story, so she could tell him about the man with the horse.

The detective waved his hand at her while he watched the door. Macie clasped her hands together and fought the urge to pace. It was obvious he wanted to wait to see what Daniel found.

Daniel's face was red as he re-entered the study and leaned over to catch his breath. "Shadow... is... gone."

Mr. Bailey slapped his hand on the desk. "One of *our* horses is gone?"

Macie felt her body sway, and Daniel reached out and steadied her. His reassuring touch contrasted with the stony look on his face. Macie shook herself and pulled her arm out of his grasp, not wanting to seem weak. A horse was gone. Shadow? It was the perfect name for a black horse. Fear and anger formed a knot so tight in Macie's stomach she thought she might vomit. She suddenly needed to sit down, but remembered she had blood covering her clothes. If only she'd been able to tell Daniel about the man and the horse. Maybe they could have avoided this whole thing, and Gladys would be safe in the kitchen. The room felt too hot, and her legs turned wobbly.

Daniel focused on Macie. "Is she a suspect?"

Macie barely registered the words before her legs gave way, and blackness engulfed her.

***

Daniel caught Macie as her body went limp. That was when he noticed the blood. He had been so angry to find Shadow gone he had jumped to conclusions. Had she been hurt as well?

He laid her gently on the floor and made eye contact with Detective Clark.

"She was the first on the scene with the woman. She probably saved her life."

Daniel thought about his accusation. It was idiotic. Macie wouldn't know how to put a halter on the horse. She admitted to wanting to learn to ride, but Daniel had the impression she hadn't been around horses much.

Daniel glanced around, realizing he hadn't seen Nate out in the barns. "Where's Nate? Did he go to the hospital with his mum?"

"He went to the hospital," Detective Clark said. "But he went in his own rig. He was gravely wounded as well."

Daniel's shoulders slumped under the weight of the situation.

Macie's eyes fluttered open. They clouded for a moment, then cleared. She blinked several times and moved to sit up. Daniel studied her, worried.

Detective Clark reached around Daniel and gently pushed Macie down. "Just lie still for a moment." He looked at Mr. Bailey. "Can we get her something to drink?"

Mr. Bailey nodded and left, returning a minute later with a glass of juice. Daniel helped Macie sit, and Detective Clark handed her the drink.

"Do you feel up to finishing your story?" Detective Clark asked.

Macie tried to stand. Daniel put his hand on her shoulder to keep her sitting.

"Help her sit in this chair." Detective Clark pulled a wooden chair away from the wall.

Macie's eyes flicked down at her clothes and shook her head.

"It will be okay, Macie," Mr. Bailey assured her.

Macie's gaze flicked to Mrs. Bailey, but before Mrs. Bailey could refute the idea, Daniel pulled her up enough to set her on the chair.

Macie met Daniel's gaze for a moment. The hurt that flashed in her eyes cut him to the core and told him she had heard his accusation before she passed out.

"Macie?" Mr. Bailey prompted.

Macie shook her head slowly. Then looked at Detective Clark.

"Oh. Well... Um, where was I?" Macie asked.

"You didn't find Gladys at her car," Detective Clark supplied.

Daniel listened in horror as Macie finished her story. He couldn't help but be impressed with her levelheadedness in helping Gladys.

"Where was Nate?" Daniel asked.

"He was unconscious in the barn," Mr. Bailey put in. "I found him when we got home."

"Which horse was Shadow? Did it have a dark coat and matching dark mane?" Macie asked.

"Yes." Daniel studied Macie for a moment. How could she know that?

Macie's mouth dropped open. She looked at Mr. Bailey, stammering for a second. "Yesterday, when Mrs. Bailey, Nate, and Daniel were all gone, Gladys was feeding the girls. I was a little restless..." Her eyes flicked toward Mrs. Bailey, but Mrs. Bailey was staring at her hands, clearly not listening. "Gladys told me to go outside for a minute. I wandered through the orchard. I decided to head to the house when I noticed movement near the barn. Everyone was gone, so I went to investigate."

Daniel folded his arms and kept his eyes on Macie.

After a small pause, Macie went on with her story. "I ran into a man leading a dark horse with a dark mane out of the barn."

"Did you get the guy's name?" Detective Clark asked.

Macie's eyes darted from Daniel to Detective Clark. Daniel tried to make his face more open.

"Well, the guy refused to give me his name, even though I asked for information several times."

"What did he look like?"

"Umm," Macie started, then her face flushed. "He had blue pants and brown boots. He was wearing a brown cowboy hat."

"Like an American cowboy hat?" Daniel interrupted. Detective Inspector Clark shot him a look but nodded at Macie to answer.

Macie's gaze flitted to Daniel's hat in his hand. "Like yours."

Daniel nodded, understanding that it did look a little like a traditional cowboy hat in America. "This is smaller than those. It's a trilby."

Detective Inspector Clark cleared his throat. "We understand the type of hat. Let's move on."

Daniel's cheeks heated slightly, but he shook off his embarrassment. The goal was to find who had taken Shadow.

"And he had a strange tattoo on his chest that I could only see a part of since his top two buttons were undone. It was some kind of reptile with his mouth open as if it could jump off his chest and bite me." She shivered, and Daniel understood why it was the thing she could describe the best. It had definitely made an impression on her.

"What color were his eyes?" Detective Clark asked.

"I couldn't see his face. His hat was pulled down, and he was wearing a bandana over his mouth and nose." Macie shrugged. "I don't know how he could even see where he was going."

Daniel shoved his hand through his hair in frustration. Why didn't she mention this earlier?

"He had a tattoo," she repeated, as though she knew that was the only identifying thing she noticed.

"Did you mention this to anyone?" Detective Clark asked Macie.

She nodded. "I told Gladys. She said to tell Daniel, but he didn't answer when I called." She blushed, her whole face reddening. That was why she'd called him? Why didn't she leave this in a message? Then Daniel remembered hearing Mrs. Bailey's voice faintly calling for Macie at the end of the message.

She had called to tell him all this. He had let the emergency at the Morris farm keep him from seeking her out immediately. And that had ended up not being an emergency. If he would have talked to her first, then maybe they could have avoided all of this. But, Daniel also knew himself. He would have promised to look into it later but still rushed to the Morris farm, and they would be in this situation, anyway.

"You may leave," Detective Clark told Macie. "Go clean up."

Macie glanced at her clothes again and paled. "Thank you."

Daniel watched as she made her way to the office door, keeping her eyes lowered.

"Daniel. I have a hard time believing you were away the whole time this was happening," Mrs. Bailey said, bringing his attention back from where Macie had gone.

"I had a vet call. I texted Nate—"

"Just last week, you mentioned wanting to breed horses," Mrs. Bailey said. "Now one of our best horses is gone. That's highly suspicious."

Daniel didn't know how she knew Shadow was one of their best horses. She never went near the barn.

"Now, Emma," Mr. Bailey said. "It will not do to start accusing everyone in the house. Why would it do him any good to steal the horse? He wants to use our barns. He doesn't have his own."

"My lawyer warned me about this," she hissed. Mr. Bailey put up his hand and shook his head.

"We can talk about that later. I think the most likely suspect is the person Macie saw." Mr. Bailey placed a hand over his wife's.

Mrs. Bailey scoffed. It was clear she didn't think much of Macie's description. "The only thing that can identify the man is a tattoo on his chest." She paused and thought for a moment. "I don't know anyone with a tattoo like that."

"How many men's chests have you studied lately?" Mr. Bailey asked.

Daniel coughed to cover up a laugh. Detective Clark covered his mouth and turned away momentarily before speaking to Daniel. "Let me get your contact information in case I have more questions."

CHAPTER 16

DANIEL STOOD OUTSIDE THE office for a moment after the detective left. The office door was ajar.

"I'm sure it was Daniel. There's no reason to bother the police further," Mrs. Bailey said, her tone almost hysterical. Daniel paused to listen further.

"He wasn't even here when the horse was taken."

"He could be working with someone else."

"Who would he be working for?" Mr. Bailey pressed.

"How should I know? Any number of people could be jealous. Even his mom. She was always rubbing it in that her son was following in his father's footsteps. She probably wants him to start his own business, but they can't afford to buy a colt to get started. My lawyer said he might try to take over the business, then wouldn't share the profits, and we would be left destitute. I would have sold if my father hadn't stipulated that Callum got first choice of buying the estate."

Confusion cleared the anger Daniel had been feeling. Why would Thomas give Callum first choice on buying the estate? Callum had only worked here a handful of times during the six months before Thomas's death. Doubt niggled at him. Something wasn't right, but he couldn't put his finger on what.

After training hard and giving himself time to think and sort some of his anger out, Daniel thought back to the conversation. Mrs. Bailey was acting out of fear. She never wanted the estate and would have sold it if not for the stipulation that Callum should get the chance to buy it first. What did Mrs. Bailey have against Callum? Daniel was doing his best to keep his father and Thomas Martin's legacy alive by keeping this estate running. If Mrs. Bailey didn't want to sell to Callum, why was she not doing anything to save the estate? Thomas had been a second father to Daniel. Mrs. Bailey hadn't set foot on the estate since she was old enough to go to a private school in London. A sense of betrayal filled Daniel. Why had Thomas not put *him* as the person to have the first choice to buy the estate? Not that he had the money to do so, but the betrayal hurt.

Now that he was a prime suspect in Mrs. Bailey's mind, he knew how unfair it had been to accuse Macie. All because of the call from the Morris's. And they hadn't even been there.

Nate? His young friend's face flitted through his mind. If he had been here, maybe Nate wouldn't be in the hospital. Daniel slumped to the ground, folded his arms over his knees, and rested his head against his arms. Tears fell unheeded. It would be his fault if Nate died. Daniel hadn't been able to save his father, either. No matter how he tried, Daniel couldn't seem to keep the people he loved safe.

His thoughts went to his mother. She needed him. It was his responsibility to care for her. He couldn't do that if he were in jail under false charges. He leaned his head against the wall behind him when another thought struck him.

Mr. Morris had said Clay would be there to meet him. Daniel knew it wasn't Mr. Morris' fault Clay wasn't there. Could Clay be the thief? Daniel had never met the man.

The only person who had seen the thief was Macie. That meant he had to work with her.

Daniel rested his head in the palms of his hands. Shadow was gone. It felt like a part of him had been ripped away. He knew the horses better than anyone else on this estate and had cared for a lot of them since becoming a vet. He would get Shadow back and bring Nate and Gladys's attacker to justice. But would Macie help him after he accused her of being the thief? If it meant getting some answers, he would swallow his pride and beg her to help.

He thought of what Mrs. Bailey said about her lawyer. Why would Mrs. Bailey's lawyer warn her about Daniel taking over the business? That didn't make sense with the news that Thomas had given Callum the opportunity to buy the estate first. Had Thomas's will said something about Daniel? How would the lawyer know his name otherwise? Mrs. Bailey insinuated that Daniel would take over the business. Why would she think he would have any right to do that? It didn't make sense.

The more he thought about it, the more he was sure the lawyer wouldn't have known Daniel's name if his name wasn't somewhere in the will. Or had Mrs. Bailey mentioned him? Maybe this had nothing to do with the will and everything to do with Mrs. Bailey's hatred of the estate. He wouldn't know for sure unless he saw a copy of the will.

The urge to run into the house to see if Thomas had a copy of it somewhere propelled Daniel to his feet. His feet stayed planted, though. He had no reason to go into the house and would be questioned. He thought about the small safe hidden in the bookshelves. That would have to be where it was, but he couldn't go into the house while Mrs. Bailey was there unless she summoned him. That would only make her more suspicious.

***

"Did you have to make such a scene that people were sent to the hospital?" Callum asked Vin as soon as his cousin opened his front door. He had heard about the investigation going on at the Bailey Estate and hurried over immediately.

"I didn't have a choice with the boy. I assumed he would go with the trainer to check the colt. The woman must have seen me. I heard her calling for the boy, so I had to keep her from identifying me."

"Now there is a full-blown investigation going on."

"It will be okay. We'll be done with our business before they figure anything out."

"They won't ignore the fact that two people were attacked on the estate."

Vin shrugged. Somehow Vin made the gesture threatening. "Our timeline has moved up. You need to convince Jack Bailey to convince his wife to let you buy the estate."

Callum sighed and nodded. The sooner this was over, the better he would feel.

***

Macie wasn't sure she should call her sister, but knew if she didn't check in, Katie would text. Better to call her when she had a few moments. Macie had woken early with nightmares. It was only six in the morning, but she didn't dare go back to sleep for fear the dreams would return. Her sister answered on the first ring.

"Macie. How are you?"

Macie considered lying, but figured she needed someone to talk to. "We had an incident at the estate. My friend, the cook, was beaten as well as her son. They are at the hospital."

"I'm so sorry. Are you safe? Was it someone they knew?"

"It was a theft, and they were at the wrong place at the wrong time." Macie didn't want Katie thinking she was living with someone who would do such a thing.

"Have they caught the person?" Katie's voice was tight. Macie would have to make sure she didn't report to Mom and Dad.

"Not yet. But I am perfectly safe. Don't tell Mom or Dad."

Katie was silent for a moment before she answered. "Okay... if you think you are safe."

"I am, and Mom and Dad would only worry. I want to last at this job."

"Macie, you have nothing to prove."

"I know," Macie said, but she didn't know. Her sister had been out of the house by the time the babysitting fiasco happened. She had heard about it, but hadn't been in the house to see Macie fail again and again in almost everything.

Evelyn cried. It was early for her, too. Maybe she was also having nightmares.

"The baby is awake. I better go."

"Okay. Take care of yourself, Macie."

"I will," Macie reassured her. She could hear the worry in Katie's voice. Maybe she shouldn't have told her, but Macie knew she would keep her promise and not tell her mom and dad about the theft and attack.

Macie turned her phone to vibrate and stuck it in her pocket after she dressed and hurried to get Evelyn. It was going to be a long day if Evelyn was already crying.

***

Mrs. Bailey informed Daisy she was not well and would take her meals in her room. She also gave strict orders to keep the girls quiet. Macie hoped the stress from the weekend before wouldn't make Mrs. Bailey ill for too long. Macie didn't blame her. Her stomach tightened and nausea surfaced when she thought of Gladys on the ground.

When that thought entered her mind, she forced herself to replay the instant she had entered the playroom after changing her clothes and dumping them in the garbage. Charlotte had flung herself into Macie's arms.

"I don't want you to go. I'm sorry I've been so horrible, but you've been the best nanny yet."

Macie was shocked, but she took what she could. At least she was winning over Charlotte, even if she wasn't with Mrs. Bailey.

Mr. Bailey also told Macie at breakfast that morning before he left for London that both Gladys and Nate were in stable condition. Unfortunately, neither had regained consciousness for more than a few minutes at a time. It had been a long weekend, keeping the girls entertained while the police finished investigations of the barn. That morning, Detective Clark had come in and said they were clear to go outside again. They were done collecting evidence and taking pictures. Macie didn't know how Daniel had taken care of the horses during their search for clues.

In order to keep the girls away from Mrs. Bailey's room, Macie forewent school even though it was a Monday. She took them on a walk through the orchard, and Evelyn's delight with the many blossoms that were starting to turn to fruit almost had Macie believing it was a normal day. Evelyn seemed to have forgotten the events of the weekend before. Macie wished she could forget as easily.

"Macie!"

Macie jumped at the shrill sound of her name. She looked around to find the source of the sound.

Charlotte pointed to the house, and Macie saw Mrs. Bailey's face in one of the second-story windows.

"What are you doing outside with the girls? It's still morning. They should be doing school."

"Yes, Ma'am," Macie called. Then she grabbed Audrey's hand while holding onto Evelyn. "Come on. We'd better do some schoolwork until lunch."

"You said we could take a break for another day." Charlotte's voice trembled slightly.

"Yes, but we'd better listen to your mom. We'll do a picnic out here on the lawn for lunch." Macie hoped that would be enough of a concession. She couldn't go against Mrs. Bailey's wishes.

After school hours, she made their lunch and packed it in a picnic basket. They walked to the edge fence that bordered the lawn and one of the pastures and watched the horses. One made its way to the fence. Audrey glanced at Macie for permission to pet the horse. Macie nodded her approval. Audrey got up, slowly walked to the fence, and put her hand up. The horse nuzzled her hand. Audrey giggled and smiled back at Macie.

"Do you think she misses her friend?" Daniel's voice behind them made Macie jump.

Audrey turned to him, tears already forming. "She lost her friend?"

Daniel nodded. "But we'll find him, Lass."

Macie wasn't sure if Daniel really believed that or if he was saying it to placate Audrey. His eyes met hers. Her heart stuttered. His green eyes radiated a compassion she hadn't seen in him before. Macie reminded herself he had accused her of stealing Shadow. Was he faking to trick her into a confession?

"Can we talk for a minute, Macie?"

Macie nodded numbly. Daniel hadn't sought her out the entire time she had been here. "You girls stay here on the blanket. I'll be right over there." Macie pointed to a nearby oak that shaded part of the yard.

Daniel put out his hand in front of him, indicating Macie should lead. Macie made her way to the tree and stood in a way that gave her a full view of what the girls were doing. Then she looked at Daniel. He was tall. She was surprised she hadn't noticed how much taller her was than her. He stared at her curiously, and Macie resisted fidgeting under his scrutiny. His green eyes were inquisitive. Macie couldn't figure out why he was suddenly being amiable toward her.

As the seconds went by without Daniel saying anything, Macie couldn't stand the silence any longer. "Well?"

He asked her to talk, which meant he had something to say. She didn't want to wait all day to hear it, even if his strong jaw and shaggy blond hair made her breath catch. Macie didn't want to let him know he was having any sort of effect on her, so she folded her arms and stared at him, waiting for him to speak.

"Mrs. Bailey thinks I stole Shadow."

"Because you suggested they start breeding?" Macie spoke before she remembered she'd overheard that conversation. Before she could feel ashamed, Macie raised her chin to meet his gaze and acted like that was common knowledge among the staff at the Bailey Estate.

He cocked his head slightly, then one corner of his mouth twitched up before returning to rest in a grim line. "Yes."

"So, is Shadow a good horse to have on hand to breed?" Macie knew nothing about breeding.

"Yes, he's a thoroughbred."

"If Mrs. Bailey doesn't want to breed horses, how did the Baileys end up with Shadow?"

"Thomas bought him a year before he died."

Macie shook herself. She was asking the wrong questions. "Why did you need to talk to me?"

"The only clue we have is the guy you saw with Shadow the other day. I think you were lucky he didn't knock you to the ground—"

"Or let the horse trample me," Macie muttered.

"What?"

Macie waved a hand of dismissal. "When I turned into the barn, I startled the horse, and he reared up. The guy had a hard time calming him down."

Daniel nodded. "If we can figure out who this guy is, maybe we can convince Mrs. Bailey to keep looking. She doesn't think the police need to look for anyone else. Not that the police are going to go off of her suspicions, but having some evidence will help me keep my job."

"We?" Macie shoved down the feeling that he might actually think she could help him. "You no longer think I'm guilty?"

"No, and I'm sorry I accused you. I jumped to conclusions." He removed his hat and ran a hand through his blond hair before replacing it. "I was hoping you'd help me out."

Macie tried to think rationally, but so many emotions flooded into her chest she could barely breathe. There was anger that he had accused her, even though he had apologized. There was fear that if she let herself get involved and helped Daniel, Mrs. Bailey would fire her. And swirling around it all was the hope that maybe he really thought she was capable.

She took a deep breath, trying to focus.

"Why don't you ask the owners whose horse you went to check out and tell the police what time you were there? You don't need my help to do that."

"They weren't home. Their daughter had a baby, so they left for the hospital. Their hired hand was supposed to be there, but he wasn't. I checked out the colt anyway, so I could reassure them it was fine without having to return. I took the time to check the other horses in case Mr. Morris had misheard Clay." Daniel's neck reddened. Macie wondered why he was embarrassed, then she took in his stance and clenched fists and realized he was angry.

He breathed deeply. "Please, Macie. Think of Gladys and Nate. You could help catch the person who hurt them."

Macie stared at him. He was begging her. She felt bad for him. He cared about Nate and Gladys, and he cared about the animals. He wouldn't have taken the time to check all of the horses if that wasn't true. He was doing his best, and now he could lose his job and go to prison because of someone else's actions. Right now, the only argument that stuck with her was that she could help find the person who hurt Gladys. Macie's mind raced, and she caught onto an idea of where to start looking.

"Well, you are either guilty as charged or the people at the farm you went to are also in on the whole horse heist."

Daniel actually smirked. "Horse heist?"

Macie grinned. The phrase sounded even better with his accent. "It has a nice ring to it, don't you think?"

"So, you don't think I'm guilty?"

"I never did. The guy I saw with Shadow the other day was clearly not you, unless you are hiding a chest tattoo and like to wear dark wigs in your spare time. When I caught him leading the horse out of the barn, he would not identify himself. That was just one day before the horse was actually stolen. If you would have called me back, you would have known."

Daniel's shoulders slumped. "I realize I should have found you before I went to the Morris farm, but your message didn't exactly make it sound like an emergency."

His actions didn't match his words, and Macie wondered if he was beating himself up for the fact that he had not found out what she wanted first. But he did have a point. It hadn't sounded like an emergency in the message.

"I didn't realize it was an emergency. I thought it was odd, and the guy gave me the creeps, but I..." Macie trailed off. It wasn't either of their faults. They couldn't see the future. That was what her mom had told her when she had suffered through so much guilt for losing Sammy. Macie had suspected her parents were disappointed in her and the rumors that came after the incident. Some even said that her parents were to blame for her irresponsibility, but her parents had cared about Macie's feelings. Her mother's advice certainly applied in this case.

"It doesn't matter. We can't change the past."

"You're right." Daniel rubbed the back of his neck. "The guy probably would've taken Shadow that day if you hadn't shown up. Both Nate and I were gone. It would have been much easier."

Warmth filled her veins. What he said rang true, but she tried to tamp it down. She always messed things up. A slough of her past mistakes ran through her mind: trying to help her mom with laundry, but using bleach instead of laundry detergent; helping her brother sew up a hole in her pants only to sew the leg shut. Her life seemed to be one misstep after another.

Daniel seemed to be praising the fact she had stopped the horse thief, but she had only stalled him. She thought back to when she held Gladys's bleeding head in her lap. She saved Gladys. At least that was what Detective Clark had suggested. Maybe she could help Daniel catch the guy who sent Gladys to the hospital.

"So, do you think Mrs. Bailey will find evidence to prove it is you?"

Daniel's eyes darkened. "Who knows."

Macie faltered. "I'm not sure it is a good idea for me to help too much. I'm needed with the girls."

Daniel nodded, looking crestfallen and resigned.

Guilt threatened to smother her, but she was sure she wouldn't be much help, anyway. She hoped Daniel would find out who had hurt Gladys and Nate and help the police bring them to justice.

A shout echoed from behind her. Macie spun around.

Daisy was waving from the kitchen door. "The hospital called. Gladys is awake. Mrs. Bailey said we can visit her if we want."

Charlotte gave a shout and ran to the house.

Macie followed Charlotte, grabbing Evelyn.

"Wait for me!" Audrey called.

Daniel picked Audrey up and swung her around so she was riding piggyback. She squealed with delight.

Daniel smiled, and Macie realized it was the first time she had ever seen him smile. She shook her head. She had been wrong about him. He may have been a little dismissive the first day, but he must carry a big burden to take care of the horses, train them, and keep his job while dealing with Mrs. Bailey. For more than a week, she had let herself believe he was arrogant, but she had never let herself see any situation from his point of view. For the past several years, she hadn't tried to see anything from anyone's point of view. In order to stay invisible, she couldn't think about others And she had chosen invisibility over vulnerability.

CHAPTER 17

DANIEL HELPED GET THE girls into the car.

"Do you want to drive?" Daniel asked Macie.

Macie blanched and shook her head. "I've never driven on the left side of the road."

"I can drive," he reassured her. He hoped Mrs. Bailey wouldn't mind. He wondered if she had meant Macie and the girls could go to the hospital but hadn't meant that he could. But, he reasoned, Macie didn't want to drive. Daisy didn't offer to drive either, so he figured he could use that as his excuse. He wanted to go see Gladys and Nate as much as Macie seemed to.

When they got to the hospital, Macie hurried to the desk to ask where they could find Gladys and followed the directions she was given. Daniel followed behind her through the halls, the smells of the hospital threatening to remind him of the last time he was here—with his dad. Macie turned suddenly and rushed to Gladys's side.

"Oh, Gladys. I'm so glad you're okay." Macie wiped at her eyes, and Daniel tried to avoid looking at Gladys. He loved Gladys and was so grateful she was awake, but he didn't want to see her like this, either.

Gladys patted Macie's hand. "The detective told me you were the one to call for help and that you helped them find my Nate as well. He would have died without you." Gladys teared up.

"I'm so glad you're okay!" Audrey cried and clasped Gladys's arm.

Evelyn babbled something unintelligible, and Charlotte also stepped up but seemed reluctant to touch Gladys.

Daniel shifted his focus, but looking at Gladys didn't help his emotions.

Memories reared up, bringing the past forward with startling clarity. He was in the hospital after his father had been thrown from a horse and hit his head on a fence post. He was with his mum, trying to be brave, and told his father he would be okay even though his father hadn't been awake the hear him. His mum fell to the ground as the doctor delivered the news that his father hadn't made it through the surgery. His own grief surged wider in his chest as he watched his mum, wracked with such emotional pain. Daniel left the hospital bitter and upset, with a promise he would do all he could to help Thomas Martin. He felt the weight of that promise. His mother had become a shell of herself and couldn't, or wouldn't, come back to him. He was alone in his world, but he was afraid to let anyone else in. The loss of his father convinced him that loving someone only led to intense pain.

Anger surged. He had to find who did this to Nate and Gladys. They had survived, and he had to protect them.

Macie turned to Gladys and laid her head on the bed. Gladys gently rubbed Macie's head for a few minutes until her breathing deepened and slowed. Daniel paused, taking in the scene.

He backed to the threshold of the room. The memories swirling around him were too much, and he didn't want to show his emotions in front of anyone. He waited in the hall, breathing deeply to rid his mind of all the memories.

Macie emerged with the girls a few minutes later.

"Are you ready to find Nate?" Daniel asked, hoping that was what they wanted as well. Daisy came up behind Macie.

"I'll stay with Gladys for a moment. Come back after you visit with Nate."

The poor girl looked exhausted, and she probably wanted to stay with Gladys for a chance to rest for a minute.

They found Nate's room, and Daniel walked to the bedside as Nate tried to smile up at him.

"Alright, Mate?" he asked, repeating what they always asked each other if they were bucked off a horse.

"They'll never keep me down for long," Nate repeated the usual response, though his voice was slurred.

Daniel gripped his hand as he would if he were going to help him up. "I'm so sorry I wasn't there."

Nate moved his head slightly, but then winced. "Not to worry, mate. Just don't hire someone else to replace me yet." He gave a weak smile.

"Never, mate."

Macie stepped forward slowly. Daniel stepped back, not wanting her to think she was interrupting or unwelcome at the bedside.

"I'm so glad you're okay. I was so worried." Her voice cracked, and a tear streaked down the side of her face. Daniel almost reached for her to comfort her, but she stepped away before he could move.

"I'm going to sit with Gladys for a moment." She smiled at Nate then turned a shy smile up at him. "You guys chat for a while."

***

When Macie got back to Gladys's room, Daisy was in a chair, fast asleep, and Gladys was watching her with a concerned expression. Poor Daisy was being overrun. She had done the cooking in Gladys's absence over the weekend.

Gladys gestured to the T.V. "You girls can watch a show if you turn it down."

Charlotte and Audrey nodded and turned on the T.V. They sat at the foot of Gladys's bed, so Macie set Evelyn between them.

Then, she pulled up another chair to sit next to Gladys.

Gladys beckoned Macie to lean closer. "The detective asked if it was Daniel. Said that was who Mrs. Bailey accused."

Macie nodded.

Gladys scoffed. "Sorry, Macie, but where would she get such an idea?"

"Daniel asked me to help him figure out who the guy was since I saw him."

Gladys raised her eyebrows slightly.

"Remember the man I told you I saw earlier last week?" Macie prodded.

Gladys shook her head.

Macie closed her eyes until the sting of tears went away. Just because Gladys couldn't remember didn't mean she had permanent brain damage.

"I saw a man leading Shadow from the barn, but he wanted me to believe it was his horse he was having trained. You gave me Daniel's number. I tried calling him, but he didn't answer. Daniel and I think it is the same person who hurt you. I didn't get a good look at his face, but I'm hoping I can recognize him if I see him again."

"It's good that Daniel has you on his side. He needs someone rooting for him."

Her words tightened Macie's throat. She hadn't exactly agreed.

She changed the subject, promising herself to tell Daniel she would help. It was time to let go of her grudge. She immediately felt her chest lighten.

Macie chatted with Gladys while they waited for Daniel. She asked Gladys about her childhood, how she got on with Thomas Martin and such. She laughed at Gladys's stories, but she noticed that she kept talking about memories that included Daniel as a young boy. Gladys's eyes closed, and her sentence trailed off.

Macie patted her hand.

"Turn the T.V. off. Gladys is tired."

The girls complied, and Macie glanced at the door, wondering how much longer Daniel would be. But Daniel was standing in the doorway, watching her with an expression Macie couldn't read. He nodded toward Daisy.

"I guess we have to wake her. She must be knackered."

Macie smiled at the English phrase that was becoming more familiar. She picked up Evelyn before she fell off the bed. She put a hand on Daisy's shoulder.

"Daisy?"

Daisy's eyes flew open.

Macie smiled at her. "It's time to go."

Daisy stood quickly, apologizing profusely for falling asleep, while Macie reassured her.

They rode to the house in silence, each lost in his or her own thoughts. Even the girls were subdued and eventually fell asleep.

Daisy rushed into the house as soon as they pulled into the garage, so Daniel helped Macie get the girls out. Both Charlotte and Audrey woke when they were unbuckled, but Evelyn stayed asleep, even as Macie carried her up to her room and laid her in her crib. She ran to her room and grabbed the baby monitor, not sure if the change in position would wake her. The girls followed.

Macie hurried them downstairs before their mother caught them with shoes in the house and hoped Daisy wouldn't have extra work because of it.

She had to talk to Daniel right away, so she ushered the girls out the back door and saw Daniel leading a horse toward the corrals.

"Daniel!" she called.

Macie turned to Charlotte and Audrey. "You can play in the yard. I'll be right back." Since Daniel was in her sight, she would be able to keep an eye on the girls.

Macie launched into speech as soon as she was close enough for him to hear her easily. "Sorry to bother you, but I remembered I never gave you an answer before we went to the hospital."

He cocked his head slightly. Maybe he'd forgotten what he had asked. Or maybe he had assumed she had been telling him no.

Macie pressed forward. "Umm. I'll help you find who took Shadow." She paused. "If you still want me to, that is."

"You'll help me? Even after..." He trailed off. Macie hoped an apology was at the end of that sentence, but he never finished. She reminded herself he had already apologized. How many times did she expect an apology, especially an apology for something that was probably more in her head than reality? Plus, she had already decided to let go of her silly grudge.

"Of course. I want to do all I can to bring the person who sent Gladys and Nate to the hospital to justice."

***

Another week went by, and Daniel hadn't come to her or told her something she could do to help. Macie was now sure he had thought better of it and realized she wouldn't be helpful after all. She tried to focus on the girls as they played in the nursery. There was no school since it was Sunday, and Macie was never sure how to handle Sundays. It was nice not to have to do school, but she also didn't know how to keep the girls entertained. At home, her family went to church, but Mr. and Mrs. Bailey hadn't dragged her to any church since she got here. At home, Sunday was also a day they lounged around. The girls weren't okay with that, so Macie found herself wishing the Baileys went to church just to break up the monotony of the day. Daisy was dragging when she came into the nursery to let her know dinner was ready. While the girls cleaned up—something Macie insisted on since it was not for the maid to clean up after them—she sidled up to Daisy.

"Are you okay?"

Daisy nodded. "I'm just knackered."

"Mrs. Bailey hasn't hired a temporary cook?"

Daisy shook her head, her eyes going moist before she blinked. "I asked about it, and she said I was doing a fine job. There was no reason to pay for a temporary cook."

"Why are you doing so much? Mrs. Bailey can't be paying you that much more."

Daisy shrugged. "I need all the money I can get. Beggars can't be choosers."

Daisy didn't seem like a beggar to Macie. She seemed like an overworked woman who should be taking a night off to go out. But Daisy always went into her room after the girls had their evening teatime. She wanted to say something, but didn't know what. They walked to the kitchen. Macie had insisted they eat there as long as Mrs. Bailey wasn't eating with them. Once they were all served, Macie turned to the girls.

"Girls, tell Daisy thank you for making dinner."

Charlotte raised her eyebrows at Macie, but said thank you with her sisters. Macie still hadn't seen Mrs. Bailey, and it had been more than a week since the horse theft. She had ordered Daisy to bring her meals to her room. Anger at the woman surged through Macie. The nerve of the woman to take advantage of Daisy.

Mr. Bailey walked in as the girls said thank you. He smiled at Macie. Daisy nearly dropped the bowl of soup she was filling.

"Oh, Mr. Bailey. I'm coming."

Mr. Bailey raised a hand to keep her from sprinting through the room with the tray laden with food.

"I'll take it to her tonight. You go rest. You deserve a break."

Tears welled up in Daisy's eyes, and she curtsied and hurried away.

Mr. Bailey put a hand on Macie's shoulder. "Thank you for keeping the girls on a schedule. I know it has probably helped this past week. I'm sorry I'm not around to help."

He looked as exhausted as Daisy, but Macie wondered if it was more mental fatigue with all the worries about the estate and his wife.

Mr. Bailey then kneeled down next to Charlotte and Audrey. "You girls are doing great. I hope you are helping Macie as much as possible. We all have to do our part while Gladys heals."

"Yes, Papa," Audrey said.

"Is Mum sick?" Charlotte asked.

Mr. Bailey considered Charlotte for a moment. "Yes, she is, but it isn't anything you can catch. You just concentrate on your schoolwork. I'll worry about Mum."

Charlotte nodded but didn't seem to believe her father. Her blue eyes held that defiant glint Macie had become familiar with since her arrival. The trauma of Gladys' attack seemed to have bonded the girls to Macie. Macie was glad she could be there for them, since their mother couldn't for whatever reason.

"I have good news, though." Mr. Bailey waited until he had all of their attention. "Gladys and Nate have been cleared to come home. I'll be bringing them home tonight. You will still have to help, but at least they will be home."

The girls all smiled at this news, and Mr. Bailey took the tray of food for Mrs. Bailey out of the room.

A few days later, Macie got the girls to bed and made her way to the kitchen to clean the dishes so Daisy wouldn't have to.

She walked into the kitchen to see Gladys leaning over the sink, obviously exhausted.

"Gladys! What on earth are you doing?"

Gladys harrumphed. "Well, I was trying to do my job."

"Sit. I'll do the dishes. You can keep me company if you insist, but you really should be in bed. You have only been home from the hospital a few days."

"If I had more energy, I'd fight you on that, but I suppose I'm not as well as I hoped. I feel so bad you and Daisy are having to work so hard while I recoup."

"You don't need to push yourself. Otherwise, you'll put yourself back into the hospital." Macie led Gladys to a chair and started washing the dishes.

Gladys sighed as she leaned back. "I'm so glad to have someone in the house to talk to. Daisy only talks as necessary because she is afraid it would put her job in jeopardy." She paused and studied Macie. "Not that I blame her."

"How long has she been here?"

"Mrs. Bailey hired her when she moved in after Mr. Martin died six months ago. Mr. Martin hired house cleaning once a week but didn't have a live-in maid." Gladys grimaced and shifted her position.

A comfortable silence settled around them as Macie washed dishes. She wanted to insist Gladys go to bed but knew she couldn't boss her around.

"I wish I could remember something from that day. It's all a blur."

Macie glanced at Gladys and was dismayed to see tears rolling down her cheeks.

"It's okay, Gladys. I'm sure we'll figure it out."

"I hope so. Mrs. Bailey came into my room right before dinner demanding to know if it was Daniel." Gladys sat up slightly before giving in to her pain and slumping against the chair's backrest.

Macie stared at Gladys. Mrs. Bailey had come out of her room? Macie hadn't seen her at all since the theft.

As if their conversation had summoned her, Mrs. Bailey appeared in the doorway to the kitchen. Her dark hair hung down her back, and it contrasted sharply with her white skin. Her eyes seemed hollow, even if there was a spark in them, which she directed at Macie.

"Why were the girls in those dreadful play clothes? It is irresponsible to keep them in those dirty clothes all the time. My girls will always be well-dressed."

Without waiting for a reply, she turned and left the room. Heat flooded Macie's face. When had she seen the girls? Maybe Mrs. Bailey did spend time outside her room, but not with anyone.

Gladys stood and put a hand on Macie's shoulder. "Don't you worry about her."

Gladys's arms wrapped around Macie, even though Macie could feel she had to support Gladys physically as Gladys gave her emotional support. Macie took a deep breath, trying not to feel like a failure.

Gladys muttered something under her breath. After a few moments, Macie backed away and looked out the window, not wanting Gladys to see the sheen of tears in her eyes. She saw Daniel shutting the gate to the barn. She took a deep breath and decided she needed to talk to him.

She helped Gladys into her bed and hurried out the door with the baby monitor on her hip, hoping she wasn't too late.

She caught sight of Daniel as soon as her eyes adjusted to the fading light. He was leaning against the front wall of the barn, looking exhausted.

He made eye contact as her shoes crunched against the gravel surrounding the barn.

"Have you thought of any way we can figure out who the thief is?" Macie asked.

Daniel shook his head. "I've been too busy to even think about it."

"Why don't we let the police take care of it?" Macie asked. "I'm sure Detective Clark is doing all he can."

Daniel grunted. "I overheard Mrs. Bailey speaking to Mr. Bailey. She told the police not to worry about finding the horse. They will still investigate the attacks, but right now they have no leads. He came by yesterday and asked me more questions."

Daniel slammed his fist against the side of the barn. Macie jumped, and Daniel looked at her, regret in his eyes.

"Sorry. Mrs. Bailey said it was probably a personal attack since the two people hurt are related. She insists the attacks weren't even connected to the horse theft."

Macie tentatively reached out and touched his arm. He flinched, and she immediately pulled her hand back.

"I'll help any way I can, but I'm not sure how. You'll let me know if you need me?" Macie was sure her insecurities were written all over that statement, and she tried to keep her voice from showing it.

Daniel nodded. "Thanks."

Macie backed away, the myriad of emotions coursing through her, confusing her. She was suddenly hoping Daniel really would find a use for her. Daniel was someone she wanted to figure out, but she couldn't understand why.

CHAPTER 18

THE NEXT DAY, DANIEL burst into the playroom where Macie was playing with Evelyn while Charlotte did math and Audrey practiced her letters. Macie figured she had one more week of homeschooling until they could stop for the summer. Evelyn jumped.

"George Morris wants me to come and look at that colt."

Macie stared, trying to figure out what he was talking about. Who was George Morris?

"The Morris farm where I went on the day Shadow was taken."

Macie still didn't know why she would be involved.

"You can come and meet them and his help." Daniel waited, obviously expecting her to figure out some hidden meaning.

Macie cocked her head. "The same colt? But it's been two weeks."

"He just got home from visiting his family. Apparently, his wife insisted they stay at their daughter's house to help her. He said he figured it was all taken care of. When he asked Clay about it this morning, he claimed I never came. And Clay *insists* the colt is still sick." Daniel shrugged. "It could be now, since it has been two weeks, so I will check anyway, just in case."

"But why didn't Mr. Morris call Clay earlier to ask?"

"I'm not sure, but I figure this is my chance to get out there and bring you." He gave Macie a significant look.

Understanding dawned on Macie. Macie would help to either identify or clear both Mr. Morris and Clay as the horse thief.

He turned to the girls. "Do you girls want to help me check on a colt?"

"Brilliant!" Charlotte and Audrey said at the same time.

Macie wondered if Mrs. Bailey would approve. She didn't like them near the horses, but they could stand outside of the barns while Daniel did whatever he needed to do. Mrs. Bailey might not even find out. She was still staying in her upper wing of the house.

They were almost done with their schoolwork, so it shouldn't be a big deal for them to go anywhere.

"Let's pack a picnic," Macie suggested, raising her eyebrows at Daniel, hoping he would go for it. Macie knew Mrs. Bailey would allow a picnic.

He smiled. "Sounds like a good idea to me."

The girls cheered, and Macie shushed them before Daisy came in to say they were being too loud, even though Macie doubted Mrs. Bailey could hear them where she stayed.

Half an hour later, they were all piled in a truck with the Martin Estates logo emblazoned on the side. Luckily, it could seat five, so they wrestled Evelyn's car seat into the truck and were on their way. An uncomfortable pit settled in Macie's stomach.

Despite the worry Mrs. Bailey wouldn't approve, Macie was grateful to get out of the house. It was a shame she couldn't see more of the country while she was here.

She knew there were lots of plants in England, but she was surprised at the constant row of hedges lining the road. The road was a lot narrower than she thought and was sure Daniel was taking some backroad to the Morris farm. She was used to wide open spaces in Idaho. The inability to see past the road on either side was making her a bit claustrophobic.

After riding in silence for fifteen minutes, Macie dared a peek at Daniel out of the corner of her eye. Charlotte and Audrey were chatting happily, and Evelyn would occasionally add a word or two. Macie smiled at their happy chatter. She didn't know if this would end with Charlotte purposefully or accidentally tattling to her mother about their adventure because she enjoyed it. Either of those scenarios could result in Macie getting fired.

Macie pushed the thought from her mind. "How far away is the Morris's farm?"

"We'll be there in about five more minutes." He didn't look away from the road in front of them.

Macie was still getting used to being in a car driving on what she considered the wrong side of the road, but then again, the steering wheel was on the wrong side of the car.

"I wish the Baileys would jump into breeding," he said quietly. "It could save their estate."

Macie turned in her seat, curious to see if Charlotte had heard, but she was pointing out a bird flying in the distance to Evelyn. Macie didn't want Charlotte to know about her family's financial affairs. Macie was sure *she* wasn't even supposed to know about their financial troubles. If what Gladys said was true, she was only supposed to stay long enough to take advantage of room and board along with her low pay.

"So... " Macie started, wanting to understand this guy who suddenly decided she was an okay person to team up with. "Are you hoping I can identify the guy, so its worth putting up with my presence?"

He raised his eyebrows at her but didn't answer. Macie hoped he wanted her around because he thought she was smart. It was probably stupid, but a part of her wanted him to tell her he believed she could help as more than just a face identifier. Macie gritted her teeth and looked out the window. It didn't matter what Daniel thought. She would never let Daniel know she craved his approval for some reason even she couldn't fathom.

She squared her shoulders, determination filling her. Yes, she would help solve the mystery of the stolen horse, but more so to help bring Gladys and Nate's attacker to justice. She didn't need Daniel to think she was smart and capable of handling anything thrown at her. Her actions the day of the attack showed she was capable. She would continue to be helpful and capable. She would be good at something. But those were all words she didn't really believe, as much as she wanted to.

Macie focused on the road when she felt the truck vibrate slightly as Daniel slowed down. "Why is it doing that?" she asked.

"The vibration?" Daniel asked.

Macie nodded.

"Something is wrong with the axle, but Mrs. Bailey won't let Mr. Bailey spend the money to fix it."

Macie's eyes widened. "Is it safe for us to be driving?"

"We'll be fine. I drive slowly."

Macie wasn't convinced. A quick glance at the girls told her they didn't notice anything out of the ordinary, but she didn't know how often they even got in a car. Since Macie had arrived, the only time they got in a car was when they went to the hospital. Macie shifted her gaze to Daniel. Maybe they should find somewhere to have a picnic off the main road. Macie didn't want to go back on the picnic idea since the girls were so excited about it, but the bouncing truck scared her. Finally, Daniel pulled into a break in the hedge, and she got her first glimpse of a much smaller house than the mansion the Baileys owned.

Daniel jumped out of the truck to meet a guy who definitely was not the tattoo man. This guy had fully gray hair and was maybe an inch taller than Macie. He was also almost as round as he was tall. Macie helped the girls out of the truck.

The man squinted at Macie when she approached with the three girls. "Who is this?"

"This is Macie, the new nanny, and these are the Bailey's daughters." Daniel turned to Macie and the girls. "This is Mr. Morris."

"Nice to meet you." Macie put out her hand, and Mr. Morris shook it.

Mr. Morris clapped Daniel on the back. "I thought you might be hiding a wife and kids from me."

Macie blushed. She was only twenty, and Charlotte was eight. Though, Mr. Morris wouldn't know that. Red crept up the back of Daniel's neck as well.

"No, sir."

Mr. Morris eyed Daniel. "Since when do you bring the nanny and the girls with you on calls?"

Daniel lifted a shoulder. "The girls are interested in knowing more about horses."

"Seems to me that Mr. Bailey mentioned Mrs. Bailey doesn't want them to have anything to do with horses. Which is preposterous, since they should be hoping one of them takes over the family business." Then he mumbled, "Either that, or they secretly want Callum to take it."

Macie looked at the girls to see if they had heard or recognized the name.

"Callum Davies?" Charlotte asked.

Daniel's gaze flicked to Charlotte.

Mr. Morris shook his head. "Sorry. I was thinking aloud."

Macie followed Daniel around to the back of the house. Daniel and Mr. Morris led them to a barn much smaller than the Bailey's.

"I'm sorry we weren't home when you were supposed to come. I figured all was well until Clay said you hadn't come," Mr. Morris said.

Daniel glanced at Macie and seemed to be trying to communicate something with her, but she had no idea what. Her mind-readings skills were definitely not what Daniel thought they were.

Macie stared at the young horse, still in the pen with its mother. "Is that the horse that was born my first day?"

Daniel met Macie's gaze and grinned. Macie's heart fluttered.

"Yeah. How could you tell?"

Macie pointed to the white spot on his head. "I mean, I don't know if horse's spots are similar, but I remember thinking that spot looked like the head of a unicorn." Macie blushed and distracted herself by adjusting Evelyn on her hip.

"I thought the same thing."

Macie glanced to the spot where Mr. Morris had been standing, but he was no longer in the barn. Daniel said that? She looked behind her to be sure someone else wasn't speaking behind her. Daniel chuckled.

"Yes, Macie, I agreed with you." Daniel's voice, full of humor, brought her attention fully to him. "It was either that or a frying pan, and it resembles a horse's head too much to be a frying pan. Do you think that makes him lucky?"

Macie let the corners of her mouth turn up slightly, sure he was making fun of her. "I guess it could be, but I think that luck will go to Mr. Morris."

"Maybe if I rub it, I will get some of the luck. I need all I can get right now."

Macie stared at him, sure now he was teasing her, though his eyes held a glint of determination that suggested he was serious about needing some luck right now. "I guess." Macie kept her answer short.

Daniel studied Macie for a minute with his head cocked to his side. His eyes brightened like he thought he had figured something out. She was sure he was wrong, no matter what conclusion he came to. What would he know about her?

"I'm not making fun of you, Macie. If that's what you think."

It wasn't exactly what she was thinking, but close enough. Macie didn't believe him. She folded her arms around Evelyn and raised her eyebrows at him. Macie was sure the toddler in her arms ruined the desired effect, but she had to work with what she had.

"So, is the horse still healthy?" Macie asked.

Daniel stepped into the stall and started rubbing the horse and looking into its mouth. He studied the mother horse before returning to his inspection. When he was done, he leaned against the gate.

Daniel turned his attention to the girls. "Do you want to pet him again?"

They all, even Charlotte, nodded eagerly. Macie carried Evelyn into the stall, so she could also pet the horse.

Daniel leaned over and whispered in her ear, making goosebumps appear on her arms.

"We need to see if we can find the hired hand here," he murmured. "I'm guessing Mr. Morris wasn't the one taking Shadow."

Macie's breathing became more shallow at his closeness, but she shook her head. Warmth spread through her, and she was turning hot. She had to focus on the task at hand, but Daniel's closeness was clouding her mind.

Daniel backed away, and Macie breathed a sigh of relief. Having him so close was messing with her mind. She barely knew him, and this was the first time since she had arrived they had spent more than five minutes together. Macie adjusted Evelyn's weight on her hip. *Focus, Macie. We need to find information that Mr. Morris or his help is involved with Shadow's disappearance.*

"Should we see if Mr. Morris will let us see the rest of his horses? I'm going to check the mom, so you guys better wait outside the stall." Daniel jutted his chin toward the gate. Macie turned around to see Mr. Morris had returned, followed by a woman even shorter than Mr. Morris.

"This is Mrs. Morris," Mr. Morris said. "Did I hear you say something about wanting to see the other horses?"

"Yes, sir," Audrey said. "Can we, please?"

Mr. Morris smiled, and it reminded Macie of her grandfather. Her heart squeezed at the reminder. Her grandfather and grandmother were the only ones who never let Macie disappear. They took the time to see her and wanted to know what she thought, even if it was trivial. Her grandfather's face came to mind. He didn't look like Mr. Morris at all, but the kind eyes and ever-present twinkle that let Macie know he loved her was visible in Mr. Morris's eyes as well. She could tell he cared about the people around him. Macie couldn't believe Mr. Morris would be involved in the horse-napping scheme.

"I don't see why not. Should we wait for Daniel?" he asked.

Audrey nodded. "He likes horses too. He might be sad if we saw the other horses without him."

Macie heard a snort behind her, and she saw Daniel duck behind the horse as he ran his hands around the back legs. Was that Daniel's snort? It could just as easily have come from the horse.

After a few minutes, Daniel exited the stall. "Everything checks out with both the baby and the mother. He seems to have gained weight, so I assume he is eating okay?"

Mr. Morris nodded. "Yes, I watched him feed this morning, and everything seems great."

"Maybe if we find Clay, he can help enlighten us."

Audrey grabbed Daniel's hand. "Let's go see the horses."

Macie smiled as Audrey dragged him to the next stall. Then she remembered her promise to herself to stay out of the barns. Macie sighed. It was too late now. Hopefully, Mrs. Bailey wouldn't find out about this.

CHAPTER 19

THE HIRED HAND WAS in a tack room at the end of the barn.

"Ah, Clay," Mr. Morris said. "Daniel came to check on the colt, and everything is fine. You never did say what you noticed wrong with him."

Macie glanced at Daniel, and he met her gaze with a raised eyebrow. So this man was the one who insisted the horse be checked.

Daniel put his hand on Macie's back to propel her toward Clay while putting his other hand out to shake. "How are you, Clay?" Daniel asked. "This is Macie, the Bailey's nanny."

Clay smiled, looking smug. "Nanny is the perfect fit for a pretty girl like you."

His accent was a little heavier, making her need to focus on his words. Her face heated at his compliment, though she felt she should be offended.

Macie forced herself to meet his eyes. His voice was different from the man Macie had run into, but she studied him to make sure. She examined his chest. His shirt wasn't unbuttoned enough to see any tattoo, but thick hair stuck out from his collar. Macie didn't think she would have noticed a tattoo without noticing hair. She determined he couldn't possibly be the same guy.

Clay winked. "Do you like what you see?"

Macie's eyes widened in horror, and her face flushed hot. He thought she was checking him out. "No!" she blurted. "I mean, yes... I mean..." Could her cheeks get any hotter? She didn't like what she saw, but didn't want to offend him, either.

A call from Charlotte tore her attention immediately to the girls. Charlotte was on the fence. "We can't reach him, Daniel."

"He probably doesn't want to be pet right now. You better not bother him." Macie ran over and helped them from the fence. "I'll be just a few more minutes."

Macie returned to Daniel's side, swinging Evelyn to her other hip. Daniel was staring while Clay smirked in return. Clay stepped forward as Macie joined them and put his hand on her shoulder. Macie stepped back enough that it fell back to his side. Her heart ramped up, and she felt the urge to flee. She looked to Daniel for support, but his steely gaze was on Clay.

"When's your next day off?" Clay asked. "I could show you a good time. Show you a bit of England. What are you, Canadian?"

"I don't have a day off."

He didn't need to know where she was from.

His mouth dropped open. "How can you not have a day off? Isn't that against some labor law?" His eyes moved from smiling at Macie to glaring at Daniel like it was his fault.

Was it? Macie had been so intent on pleasing Mrs. Bailey that she hadn't even fought her on it. Gladys hadn't said anything. Macie shook her thoughts away. It didn't matter right now. Mostly, she needed to get away from this guy.

Daniel's fists tightened. Would he punch Clay? There was no way he was feeling protective or jealous. Daniel didn't even want to be her friend. He only wanted her help clearing his name.

"You work on getting a day off and let me know when it is. I'd love to get to know you better."

Macie took a step back. "Thank you." That felt like the wrong thing to say. She'd never had a guy come on to her. "But I'd rather spend my days off by myself." That part was true.

Clay smirked. "What fun would that be?"

Macie shrugged, unsure of what else she could say that would dissuade him.

"I am perfectly capable of showing her around England, if that is what she wants to do," Daniel said through clenched teeth.

Macie didn't know what shocked her more; that he offered to show her around England or that he was so angry at Clay's advances. Macie wouldn't want to spend time alone with Clay. She suspected he had something to do with Shadow's disappearance. She only needed to find some proof. Which seemed almost impossible. But...

"Maybe you could show me around the stables now? My own private tour." Macie tried to smile coyly, though she never considered herself good at flirting.

Daniel grasped her elbow. "Can I talk to you a minute?" He glared at Clay. "Alone."

Clay grinned at Daniel. "I'll be right here, waiting to take you on that tour. I'm sure Daniel has things to discuss with Mr. Morris."

"Charlotte, Audrey, can you stay with Mrs. Morris for a second while I talk to Daniel outside?" Macie asked.

They both nodded. Macie tried to hand Evelyn to Mrs. Morris, but Evelyn clung to her neck tightly, so she gave up and took Evelyn with her.

Once they were out of sight, Daniel turned on Macie. "What are you doing?"

"Getting information." Macie raised her eyebrows, hoping he would get her meaning without having to spell it out.

"I don't trust him." He glanced around the corner into the barn.

"I don't either, but I have a feeling he is somehow involved with Shadow's disappearance. Maybe if I get him alone, he might let something slip."

Daniel gripped Macie's elbow. It wasn't threatening. In fact, it felt reassuring, even though the grip was tight. "I don't feel good about it. What if he tries to hurt you?"

"I'll scream."

Daniel studied Macie for a long time. He let his hand drop, and Macie felt the difference immediately. It felt vulnerable.

Macie shifted Evelyn, so she could look her in the eye. "Can you stay with Daniel for a few minutes?"

Evelyn shook her head.

Macie sighed. It was flattering that Evelyn preferred and trusted her, but Macie needed to be alone with Clay. "Please?"

"After Macie is done, we can go have the picnic at my mum's house," Daniel put in. He held his arms out to Evelyn. "Aunt Jessie?"

Evelyn flung herself at Daniel. So Daniel's mom was the Aunt Jessie they wished they could visit.

"Aunt?" Macie asked, unable to keep all of her curiosity to herself.

"She asked them to call her that. There's no family relation."

Macie shrugged and then peeked around the door. "I'm ready for my tour." She turned to Charlotte and Audrey. "Stay with Daniel. I'll be right back."

They both nodded. Clay held out his arm. Macie tentatively put her hand in the crook of his elbow. She kept her eyes lowered as they made their way to the pastures, determined to hide the fear that flared up in her chest.

Macie met Daniel's gaze once more. He and the girls had followed Macie and Clay out of the barn. His hard eyes were on Clay. Macie smiled, hoping he wouldn't think she wanted to go back to Daniel or something.

Clay winked at Macie. "Forget him. He can't do anything for you."

"And what can *you* do for me?" Macie asked.

"Whatever you want." Macie raised her eyebrows but kept any thoughts to herself. She couldn't very well tell him she wanted to know if he was guilty of being an accomplice in the horse heist. Her hand tightened on his arm. He patted it.

"No reason to be nervous. I have my ways of getting ladies to relax around me."

"And how many ladies have you helped in such a way?" Macie looked around the pastures, distracted.

His arm jerked slightly, and Macie almost took her hand away, but his grip became firmer. Great. She probably offended him. Macie guessed his conquests with the ladies was not something he wanted to quantify to his current target.

Macie cleared her throat. "Umm, well. What is first on the tour?" She pulled him slightly toward the pastures straight ahead so they would still be in view of Daniel. Macie didn't know why she trusted Daniel, but she knew he would try to keep Clay from hurting her.

Clay clutched her hand to keep it firmly planted on his arm and turned abruptly toward some sheds. "I thought you might want to explore something a little more secluded," he said in a low voice.

Not really, Macie thought. Maybe this wasn't a good idea after all.

"Since I don't know you very well, I would prefer to get to know you while looking at the horses in the pasture here." Macie nodded toward the fence and forced her hand from his arm.

Clay stepped up beside Macie and put an arm around her shoulder. "You want to take things slow. I get it."

Macie ducked away. "Not really. I don't know you, so I don't know if your intentions match mine."

Macie leaned against the fence, folding her arms on the top rail and resting her chin on them.

He leaned forward, forcing her to meet his eyes. "So what are your intentions?"

"To get to know you and what you're like and maybe to know a little more about how things are run here."

He nodded, but seemed thoroughly uninterested in getting to know each other.

"How long have you worked for Mr. Morris?"

"A couple of years."

"Do you like it here?"

He shrugged. "It's a job."

This was getting nowhere. "Why did you think the colt needed checking on?"

"He wasn't eating very well." Clay's gaze went out over the pasture. But Macie wasn't sure if he was looking away from her because he was lying or not.

"So why weren't you here?"

Clay turned his head sharply. "It isn't my job to be on site when a vet comes to check on the horse."

Macie tried to remember the details of Daniel's visit. "So did you tell Daniel when to come?"

Clay growled. "I came out here to show you the best places on the estate, not to answer all these questions about Daniel's animal checking schedule." He kept his eyes on the shed in front of them. "Let's go back to talking about me."

Macie smiled. She had him riled. "I'm not sure I'm ready to see the best places on the estate. I'm really curious about how you run things. Do you make most of the decisions for the horses?"

He leaned toward her. Macie focused on not backing away, even as everything inside of her warned her to step cautiously. Was he trying to make business talk romantic? This guy was giving her the willies.

Macie forced herself to keep talking. "Daniel hasn't told me anything about how things are run with the horses."

"He's willingly giving up the opportunity to spend more time with you? He's a fool."

"Well, he doesn't really like me." Macie clamped her mouth shut. Clay's eyebrows rose toward his short-cropped hairline.

"Do you want him to?"

"I prefer not to be around people who hate me." Not that she saw much of Daniel, but she had to give this guy something.

Clay dramatically wiped his brow. "Whew! I was afraid I would have some competition. Not that Daniel is much competition. I mean, what does he have? A dead father and a dependent mother? Not much to offer a pretty young thing like you."

Macie tried to keep her face neutral, though her teeth clenched. "If he *were* competition," she said evenly, "putting him down to set yourself on some kind of pedestal wouldn't be very impressive." Macie smiled, reminding herself she was here to get information, not defend Daniel. "Why not tell me what's so great about you?"

"Well, for starters, I know how to run a breeding business. Training only is not profitable anymore. Daniel hasn't seen the trends."

Macie almost said that Daniel wanted to do just that, but she had to keep some information back if she was going to maintain the upper hand. "And how do you run a good breeding business?"

He leaned over and whispered. "You get the best horses."

Macie narrowed her eyes. Why was he whispering?

"And where do you find the best horses?" Macie asked, sounding too innocent. "It must take a long time to raise them. You could always steal them?"

Clay's eyes flashed, and he clenched his fists. Then he turned toward the horses in the pasture. Macie watched him breathing rapidly. She had hit a nerve, and now she was going to push him more. A voice in her head told her to tread cautiously, but caution wouldn't get them the information they needed.

"Do you only work for Mr. Morris?" Macie tried to make her voice as light as possible.

His eyes darkened. "Why would you think I work for anyone else? Most people around here work for one employer. It's enough to keep one person busy."

Macie stepped closer and put a hand on his arm. His gaze darted to her hand. The urge to get her alone no longer sharpened his stormy eyes. He reminded her of a caged animal. She pushed further.

"But wouldn't it be lucrative if you worked for more than one person? I mean..." Macie raised her eyebrows, hoping he would get that it was an example. "If you took the connections from Mr. Morris and then used them to help another employer, that would end with you on the upper hand and able to stick with whoever paid you more."

His arm yanked out from under her touch, then his hand connected with the side of Macie's face. Macie staggered backward, her vision temporarily blurring.

Clay's eyes narrowed. "I would watch your mouth, if I were you."

CHAPTER 20

"MACIE!" DANIEL WRAPPED HIS arm around Macie and pulled her away from Clay. Clay looked stunned, as if he had forgotten they had an audience.

"Clay!" Mr. Morris's voice was loud and firm. "You're fired! Get off my property."

Daniel stepped between Macie and Clay, his protective instinct going into overdrive.

Clay raised his hands. "Sorry, sir. I lost my temper."

Lost his temper? He'd hit Macie. Daniel should have intervened when he saw Clay getting agitated. But he didn't think Macie would say something to make him lose control and hit her.

Daniel took a step forward, "He said to get off his property."

Clay stepped away, fury written all over his face. Daniel immediately turned to Macie, wanting to reassure himself she was okay.

Macie's brown eyes were luminescent with unshed tears, so he pulled her in close. His anger burned even hotter. Daniel held her tightly for a moment. He shouldn't have let her talk him into attempting to get information out of Clay by herself. He wanted her help but didn't want her to get hurt because of it.

"Of all the stupid things to do," Mr. Morris muttered. "To act like that in my presence. He's out of his mind."

Daniel ignored Mr. Morris and took Macie's hand. He led her to Charlotte, Audrey and Evelyn. Charlotte and Audrey stared at Macie with wide eyes, and Evelyn cried and reached for Macie. Macie pulled her hand free of his as the girls flung themselves at her. The feeling of loss when she let go of his hand surprised him. He shook himself. He was obviously too worked up after seeing Clay hit her. He felt bad for practically throwing Evelyn to Mrs. Morris when Clay hit Macie. But his only thought had been to get to Macie.

"I'm such an idiot," Macie whispered, though Daniel didn't think she meant for him to hear.

"Did you satisfy your curiosity?" Daniel bit his lip. This was not the time to lecture her. He tried to tamp down his own anger. She didn't deserve to get the brunt of his emotions since the real cause was stalking past the house. Macie's contemplative look gave him pause. Had Clay given her a clue?

Macie soothed Evelyn. When she settled Evelyn on her hip, her free hand rubbed her slightly red cheek, and his blood boiled all over again.

"What happened?" Mr. Morris asked, making his way over.

Daniel shook his head. Only Macie could answer that question, but she averted her eyes. Daniel spoke up to fill the uncomfortably long silence. "I'm not sure why he had you call me in the first place. There was nothing wrong with the colt."

Mr. Morris glowered, but Daniel knew it wasn't at him.

Mr. Morris turned to Macie. "I'm sorry about that, Miss."

Macie blinked rapidly as if she were fighting off tears. Daniel had to find something to distract himself from what happened or he might track Clay down and let him know what he really thought about him hitting Macie.

Daniel debated on confiding in Mr. Morris about what happened at the Martin Estate. Mrs. Bailey would go ballistic if she found out Daniel was talking about it to the neighbors. Even though Mr. Morris likely saw the story on the news, but he couldn't be sure, especially since Mr. Morris hadn't mentioned it. No, he would wait to hear what Macie had to say. They needed more evidence before he could ask others to help him.

Daniel shook the man's hand. "Thank you, sir. Let me know if you have any more problems."

***

Macie shifted Evelyn when they got back to the truck. Mr. Morris had called the police and reported Clay. They each gave statements, but Macie left most of the details of her and Clay's conversation out of her statement. She wasn't sure she understood them herself. She pushed too far, she knew that, but she wasn't sure why he had reacted so violently.

Mr. Morris took her hand and covered it. "I'm deeply sorry. You won't have to worry about him anymore."

Macie didn't know if that was true. With Clay out of a job, he would be free to find her at the Bailey Estate, but that could just be her paranoia speaking. Clay had no reason to come after her based on their exchange. "Thank you, sir."

Daniel offered his hands for Charlotte and Audrey to hold. They both gripped his hands with both of theirs. Macie felt bad they'd witnessed Clay hitting her, but the sight of them looking to Daniel for support sent warm shivers up her spine.

Macie fought back tears as they buckled the girls in the truck.

Right before they turned onto the road, Macie turned around and saw a glimpse of Mr. Morris standing in the driveway, watching them. "He's a good man."

Daniel glanced at Macie, then in the rearview mirror. "He is."

Macie faced the front. "Why did you become a vet?"

Daniel shrugged. "Thomas helped pay for my schooling. He figured it would be good to have a vet on hand, especially with the plans to breed. It was always my plan to stay on the Martin Estate. I would help breed, train, and do house calls as needed. Once we started breeding, the plan was to stop offering to let owners keep their pregnant mares at the barn so I would be on hand. Thomas Martin even talked about leaving me the business, but I guess he didn't get his will changed in time." He trailed off, and Macie gave him a moment of silence.

"So, why did you rush to see the colt? Did Mr. Morris think it was an emergency?"

"He wasn't sure, but he sounded panicked, so I figured it was better to be safe than sorry."

"But you still went back to check on the colt today?"

"It's been almost two weeks. Something could easily have come up."

Macie looked at the girls. They were all staring at her with frightened expressions, their eyes wide. Tears were still wet on Evelyn's face.

"Aunt Jessie's?" Evelyn asked.

"Yes, Evelyn. We'll go to Aunt Jessie's for our picnic," Daniel said.

That brought up other questions. Clay said Daniel's mother was dependent. What did that mean? Macie guessed she would find out soon enough.

Daniel pulled into a driveway not far from the Bailey's estate. The drive was as long as the Bailey's, but it led to a small cottage in comparison. It was a two-story brick house with large windows. Macie thought it might be larger than the house she grew up in but couldn't be sure. The roses around the house flourished, and the dark green of the shrubs in front of the house brought out the red in the bricks.

"Oh, it's lovely," she breathed.

Daniel gave Macie an incredulous look. "It's a lot smaller than the Martin Estate house."

"I love it."

Daniel studied her for a minute as he turned off the truck. Then he shook his head and climbed out. "Let's get this picnic started."

The girls cheered, but it lacked the excitement from earlier. Macie felt bad that going alone to talk to the Clay creep had ruined the girls' mood and marred their excitement.

Macie carried Evelyn, staying a pace behind Daniel, while Charlotte and Audrey rushed forward to knock on the door.

"I don't know if she'll be able to come to the door today, girls. She's not feeling well." Daniel patted Charlotte's shoulder then reached over her to open the door, being careful not to hit either girl with the picnic basket.

"If she isn't feeling well, should we be bothering her?" Macie asked, standing at the bottom of the steps. Trepidation coursed through her. She had heard nothing about this woman. She knew the girls missed being babysat by her, and she had lost her husband, but what if she hated surprise visitors? Macie's mom hated when someone showed up without her having at least a day's notice.

Charlotte and Audrey scampered under Daniel's arms into the house, shouting, "Aunt Jessie!"

"Do I hear my favorite girls?" The reply was faint, but still clear.

Evelyn was wriggling in Macie's arms, so she set her down. Evelyn climbed up the stairs and toddled into the house.

Daniel set the basket down inside the door and came down the steps to Macie. "It's okay, Macie." He tugged lightly on her elbow. "My mom hasn't felt well for a couple of years. Some days are better than others, but she hasn't been the same since my father died."

Macie stood frozen to the ground, unable to make her legs move. Her grandmother, who had been young enough, deteriorated rapidly after her grandfather passed. A vision of walking in her house to visit, her grandmother a shell of what she used to be, tumbled into Macie's consciousness. Is that what she would see? It nearly undid her to see the strong woman who had been her one main support besides her grandfather, unable to recognize her, unable to give her the encouragement she needed after Katie moved out and got married. She'd felt so alone in a house full of siblings—siblings who could all do something better than Macie could. Grandma always said Macie had something special, but it was buried deep, and it would take time to dig it up so it could shine and others would see it.

Grandma passed a short month after that visit.

"Macie?" Daniel's voice brought her back to the present. "What's wrong?"

Macie shook her head. "Bad memories," was all the explanation she could force out.

A strange understanding passed through his green eyes, and for the first time, Macie felt that Daniel saw her. It unnerved her. It felt too vulnerable since she had barely decided to forgive him.

Daniel took Macie's hand. She hardly noticed it. Her eyes were focused on the door, but she wasn't seeing the beautiful white double doors. In Macie's mind's eyes, the door was a plain wooden one in the small, two-bedroom house. It was going to open, and Macie wouldn't see her grandmother because it was the day after her funeral. Macie's mom said she needed her help going through Grandma's things. Mom wanted to get rid of everything. Macie wanted to keep everything. Her breathing hitched slightly. That was almost four years ago, so why was it all coming back now?

CHAPTER 21

"MACIE?" DANIEL'S VOICE INTERRUPTED the daydream.

Macie forced her lips up into a smile, but she could see from his concerned expression that it looked as stiff as it felt, like she was trying to bend a stick, but if it bent too far, it would crack.

Daniel led Macie through the door and into the parlor, where a tall woman was sitting on a loveseat reading a book with the girls. She smiled at Daniel, then her eyes flitted to Macie.

"Mum. This is the new nanny, Macie."

Audrey smiled up at Aunt Jessie. "She's my favorite."

Macie wanted to know if that included the great Celeste, but refrained.

"Well then, I think she must be my favorite, too." Aunt Jessie patted Audrey's hair.

"Macie. This is my mum, Jessie."

Macie stepped forward to shake Jessie's hand. "It's good to meet you Mrs..." Macie stopped. She didn't even know Daniel's last name.

"Oh, call me Jessie. I prefer it to the stiff Mrs. Evans."

"Nice to meet you, Jessie."

"Mum, the girls are ready for a picnic. Where do you want us to set up?"

"Oh, it's such a nice day. Let's do it out back." Jessie started to move the girls to get up.

"We can take care of it," Macie hurried to assure her. "The girls would love it if you could finish reading to them."

Jessie settled herself back onto the loveseat and pulled the girls closer.

Daniel grabbed a blanket from a cupboard in the hall, and Macie followed him out the back door. Macie paused right outside the door. Flowers bloomed on both sides of the path that led to a grassy meadow shaded by a large willow tree. Not far beyond that was a small pond. Daniel set the blanket up at the edge of the flower garden.

Macie moved slowly over the stone path to join him, inhaling the mixed scents of the flowers, grounding herself in the here and now, forcing the memories that had plagued her away.

"How far back does your property go?"

"See those trees behind the pond?"

Macie looked across the pond. Long grass blew in the wind before giving way to the trees Macie was sure bordered the Bailey's property. She looked around, wondering if her sense of direction was correct. Sure enough, to her left, she saw a white picket fence and the flowering orchard beyond. The Bailey mansion rose above the tops of the trees.

"It has kind of been neglected the past few years, but my mum finds joy in caring for the flowers, at least."

Daniel didn't elaborate, but Macie wondered if it coincided with his father's death.

Daniel touched her shoulders, making her jump. He leaned over so he could look into her eyes. "What happened back there?"

Macie wasn't sure if he meant the incident with Clay or not, but that was the only thing she felt comfortable talking about at the moment. "I just talked to him. I did try to rile him up to get him to drop some useful information."

"No, Macie, just now as we were coming to the house."

Macie swallowed. "Nothing."

Daniel looked half disappointed and half concerned.

"I was just thinking. When you said your mom wasn't well enough to come to the door, I thought maybe I would walk in and find a shell of a person, and it made me think of my grandma."

Daniel turned and looked at his house and heaved a heavy sigh. "She is a shell of what she used to be, but the girls wake her up a bit. She loves them so much. Mrs. Bailey had her babysit for a while when there was a lag between the Bailey's arriving and getting a nanny. But when the next nanny left, she didn't ask her to babysit. My mom said it was probably too much of a hassle to bring them here when Mrs. Bailey was so busy, but my mom was willing to watch them for free. It gave her something to look forward to. I never understood why Mrs. Bailey would pay Daisy extra to watch them on top of doing all her regular work, but also have them sit in the study while Daisy cleaned."

Macie raised her eyebrows. He knew a lot more about what happened in the house than she would have thought.

He grinned. "Gladys knows everything, and thus Nate usually hears it and tells me."

Daniel stepped back, and she shivered slightly, then pushed the feeling away. She was overwrought from everything that had happened. It had nothing to do with him. She saw he could be a good friend and hoped that working together on this mystery would help deepen that friendship.

"Am I going to be in trouble when Mrs. Bailey finds out I brought them?"

Daniel shrugged. "Maybe, but after today, I think you can handle anything."

Tears unexpectedly pricked at Macie's eyes, and she blinked them away. Why did his words have to mean so much to her? Macie pivoted to hide her emotions.

Daniel moved so his face was in front of hers again. "I owe you an apology. I brought you into this deeper than you already were. We are dealing with a violent person." He took a deep breath. "If you want to step away from helping me find the person responsible, I'll understand. I should have never asked you to put yourself at risk."

Macie met his gaze fully, surprised at the admission. "You thought I would be in danger?"

Daniel shook his head. "No, but I see now this is more dangerous than I expected. Clay hit you." He shoved his hand through his shaggy blond hair, and Macie watched his jaw muscle work.

"I wanted to help," Macie said. "I hope I didn't make things worse."

Daniel moved as if he was going to grab her arms or something, but then he stopped and his hands dropped to his side. "You didn't. And you have surprised me in more ways than one. I believe you're a lot stronger than you let on."

Macie looked at her shoes, wanting to believe him, but her brain wanted to reject the compliment. Her grandma and grandpa had seen something in her, but she had never been able to see it in herself.

She found Daniel's probing eyes. "Daniel. I'm almost certain Clay is involved somehow with Shadow's disappearance, but he wasn't the one who actually did the taking."

Daniel inclined his head away from the girls as they raced out across the lawn to where they had set up the blanket and walked to a spot where they could talk without being overheard.

He turned and studied her. "Are you okay? From getting hit, I mean." He moved his hand and cupped her face, moving it from side to side."

Warmth flowed from his hands, and a new kind of heat shot up her neck at his attention. She had tried to ignore the pain in her head. When Daniel had hugged her briefly after the incident she had all but forgotten the pain completely, but her face was starting to sting.

"I'm a little tender." Macie put a hand over the spot. Daniel pulled his hand away so slowly that his fingers brushed against her cheek, sending tingles down her spine.

"I'm so sorry."

Macie tried to shrug his concern off. "It was the only way to find out something."

His eyebrows rose. "I don't think it was the *only* way."

"It was the quickest way," Macie pointed out.

"So, what did you learn?"

Macie sighed and looked out across the pond behind Daniel's house. The water reflecting the sun's light caused her to squint. She thought this might be the sunniest day she had experienced in England.

"He got really mad when I asked if he was working for two people and suggested I knew too much. I also mentioned stealing horses." Macie grimaced and raised her head to meet Daniel's eyes. His eyes were dark as he considered her words. She went on before he could chastise her for being so blatant in her questions. "I think he was more than just offended."

"So, Clay is working for the horse thief?" Daniel raked his hand through his hair. "You said he wasn't the one who did the taking?"

Macie grimaced. "It's definitely not him. Remember the tattoo?"

Daniel dipped his head once.

"Clay has too much chest hair. It's like a shag carpet."

Daniel snorted and then put his hand to his mouth.

"And he thought I was checking him out," Macie mumbled under her breath as her face warmed.

Daniel laughed out loud for a split second before he coughed. He cleared his throat. "I'll believe you on that count."

Macie's face burned even hotter and got the conversation back on track. "You said Clay was supposed to be at the Morris' farm when you arrived."

"Which should have suggested he was the horse thief." Daniel pointed out.

"But it wasn't the person I saw leading Shadow out of the barn. What about that day?"

"What about it?"

"I'm sure he was planning on taking the horse when I stopped him, but I just happened to show up. How did he know you were going to be gone? Where were you?"

"Callum told his neighbor about our services to house his mare until she gave birth. So, Nate, Mrs. Bailey, and I all went to see him and the horse. The man was insistent on meeting all of us. He even had Callum there to vouch for us."

So the two incidents didn't seem to have any connection. Macie was sure Daniel would have mentioned Clay being there if he had been. The silence stretched on, and Macie had decided she'd better join the girls for lunch. No answers had been found in the course of this conversation, only more questions.

Daniel studied her, his green eyes holding a depth she hadn't seen before, and Macie lost track of everything else she had been thinking. His lips twitched slightly. He wasn't laughing at her. It was like he actually saw her, and this time it didn't scare her. She turned abruptly and walked to where the picnic was set up and sat down on the blanket, not sure whether she felt shock or awe. It had been years since someone had actually seen her.

Daniel was the last person she expected to look at her like that. What was she supposed to do with that information?

Macie sat up straight. It didn't mean anything. He wasn't avoiding her, and that was great. She was helping him save his job. He was grateful for her help. That was all.

The girls' laughter brought her attention fully back to them. Macie pushed the odd feelings away. She would never stop trying to prove that she was valuable. Even if she felt like a failure.

Audrey and Charlotte nearly bowled her over as they wrapped their arms around her. "Is it time to eat?" they yelled.

Well, she thought, *the girl's affections are probably real.*

Macie dished out bread, cheese, and sliced meat along with grapes and carrots. The girls chatted animatedly with Jessie, though Macie held back from joining the conversation. She felt uneasy around this woman. She didn't know what to say and didn't want to say something that would either offend her or make her shut down as Daniel had described. The logical part of her knew she probably wouldn't say something that could immediately shut her down, but Macie stayed quiet and only spoke when spoken to, just to be sure she didn't mess up this happy moment in their day.

Macie watched Jessie's countenance improve with every interaction with the girls. It was like someone lit a fire, and it was slowly coming to life. Did this happen every time the girls came? They should visit more if that were the case, even if Macie would have to fight the unease lingering in her body.

Macie kept from feeling completely awkward by thinking over her conversation with Clay and what Daniel had said about his call the day Shadow was taken. It didn't add up, but she wasn't sure if her suspicions were enough to show that Clay was part of the horse theft.

***

Daniel couldn't help but stare at Macie throughout the picnic. He couldn't figure her out. He had misjudged her. She seemed so timid that first day. He was sure she would leave after one day with Charlotte. Gladys had mentioned that Charlotte tried to make the nannies' lives miserable, even though his mother had never experienced that side of her. But Macie was something special. She had won over the girls and helped everyone around her, even when it wasn't part of her job description.

He remembered watching Macie with Gladys in the hospital before she knew he was there. She had been so relaxed, but he could see how much she cared about everything Gladys said. He hadn't wanted to interrupt the moment. Macie laughed at something Gladys said, and Daniel realized he didn't really know Macie. He had been so intent on his own problems that he hadn't even tried to get to know her. Every time he caught a glimpse of her, she always had an edge of nervousness he couldn't explain. But in the hospital with Gladys was the first time Daniel had seen her look relaxed and at ease. A sudden desire to have her be that relaxed with him flared inside of him.

Daniel's smile faded as he thought of Gladys hurt and unable to do her work. Nate was also still laid up in bed. Macie had been there for her, making sure Gladys was taken care of.

She acted more at ease with the girls. Nate had told him Mrs. Bailey had given her until the end of the month to continue to prove she was worth keeping. At least that was the way Nate worded it. Mrs. Bailey was direct, but would *she* word it that way? No wonder Macie was on edge. As he watched her with his mother though, he realized she seemed even more uneasy around his mom, who was usually able to make almost anybody feel at ease.

Was it just his mum or was something else making Macie uncomfortable? Daniel's mind jumped back to Clay and the slap. Anger bubbled up inside of him again, but he tamped it down.

Daniel checked his watch. "The lunch hour is over. Do you want to take the shortcut with me?"

The girls all glanced at Macie.

"Do we have to leave already?" Audrey asked.

Macie studied his mum and frowned. He took in his mother's appearance. She did seem tired, despite the genuine smile that brightened her face—the smile Daniel rarely got to see. He was almost sorry to end this time, wanting to keep that smile shining, but he could see his mother didn't have the stamina.

"We'd better get back. Your mother might wonder where we are," Macie said.

"She won't leave her room," Charlotte said.

Macie's eyebrows rose in a strangely attractive way.

Charlotte shrugged.

Daniel reached out to help Macie stand. Warmth spread up his arm, and Macie's cheeks reddened. His heart thumped hard once. He smiled at Macie, trying to hide the effect she had on him.

He helped clean up the picnic and walked with Macie and the girls back to the Martin Estate. The thought of it being the Bailey Estate didn't sit well with him, even after six months of being in the employ of Emma Bailey. He missed Thomas.

As they walked, Macie took one more look over her shoulder.

Daniel's gaze immediately followed, but his mother had already gone inside. "What is it?" He couldn't help the panic that rose in him. Had Macie sensed something he should be aware of?

"Sorry. Clay made your mother seem like an invalid."

Daniel's fists clenched at Clay's name. "She's not really invalid, but she doesn't function well. She gets lost in her memories and forgets to take care of herself."

"Or you?" Macie's soft voice sent a shiver through him.

"It's my job to take care of her. That's what I promised my dad." Even though his dad couldn't have heard him, Daniel didn't resent his mother. He could take care of them both and be the man of the house, but he often wished she would talk to him more often instead of staring out the window as if waiting for his father to come home from some holiday. Daniel knew how she felt; he just wished she would continue living her life and make the most of the time she had with her son.

Macie rested her hand on his arm. Her eyes seemed hesitant yet full of compassion. With a jolt, he realized maybe Macie could understand how he felt. Part of him wanted to sit and tell her how hard life had been since his father died and how the pain had been amplified by Thomas's death, but he couldn't burden her with all of that.

He boosted Charlotte and Audrey over the fence before taking Evelyn from Macie. Macie's foot slipped as she climbed. He automatically reached out to steady her, his hand resting on the small of her back. She really was beautiful and a lot stronger than he had given her credit for on that first day. He hoped she would stay. Hoped Mrs. Bailey would keep her for longer than a month. He wanted to really get to know her.

CHAPTER 22

DAISY RAN UP TO Macie the moment she and the girls walked in the door. Daniel headed directly to check on the horses.

"Mrs. Bailey wishes to see you. She wanted to see the girls, and I told her you took them on an outing." Daisy was wringing her hands.

"Does she want to see the girls now, too?"

"No. She got mad when I told her you were on an outing and said the moment you came back, I was to take the girls to the playroom so she could speak with you alone.

Macie groaned.

"She's in her room." Daisy took Evelyn and hurried the girls down the hall to the playroom.

I will not cower. I will not be weak. Macie thought of a million other things she should not be, but her body ignored the nots. She'd messed up again. Mrs. Bailey would be disappointed and see Macie's failings. It was the same as everything else she tried.

"Come in," Mrs. Bailey called after Macie knocked lightly.

Macie stepped into the dim room. Mrs. Bailey had been holed up in her room for days now. When was she going to move forward and do something? Macie's irritation with Mrs. Bailey surprised even her. Mrs. Bailey wasn't even trying to save her estate.

Maybe she was resigned to the fact that she was going to lose everything and was already mourning her loss.

Macie's irritation grew, and she straightened her back. Maybe Mrs. Bailey was ready to give up, but Macie wasn't. Even if Mrs. Bailey didn't want Macie to solve this crime and save her estate, Macie would do it. Not for her boss's sake. Macie hadn't seen anything in her boss that made her want to fight for her sake, but for the girls and for Daniel. He needed to be close to home.

Macie pulled herself away from her tumbling thoughts and took in Mrs. Bailey's appearance. She was facing the large window with the drapes tightly shut, her back to

Macie. Maybe she had migraines brought on by the stress. Macie could sympathize more easily if that were the case, so she let herself believe Mrs. Bailey had migraines.

Macie cleared her throat since Mrs. Bailey hadn't yet moved. "You asked to see me?"

She remained still. "Yes. Come to the other side of the bed."

Macie obediently walked across the small sitting area that separated the door from the bed and walked so she was standing in front of the covered window. Macie desperately wanted to fling the curtains open and let in the light. She could feel her own mood dropping the longer she stood in the darkness.

"Daisy said you took the girls on an outing."

"Yes, Ma'am."

"You didn't inform me of your plans."

"I knew you were not feeling well and didn't want to bother you. I was not aware you wanted to know our daily plans. I will let you know in the future." Macie hurried through the apology, hoping that would help cut this meeting short.

"And you went with Daniel?"

"Well, yes. I don't have a car and—"

"Next time, use mine," she interrupted. Her voice was still soft, but the sharpness in her tone made Macie jump.

"Yes, Ma'am."

"You didn't visit his mother, did you?"

Macie hesitated. Maybe she should lie. Macie huffed out a breath. She couldn't lie. The girls were bound to mention it. "Daniel suggested it, and the girls were so excited I couldn't refuse. They love her."

"I know." The bitterness in Mrs. Bailey's voice was apparent. "They love her more than they love me."

"That might be because she spends time with them," Macie suggested.

It was the wrong thing to say. Even in the dim light, Macie saw Mrs. Bailey's eyes darken. "I have an estate to run. I don't have time to play all day with my girls. Do you think I don't want to?"

"No Ma'am. I believe you love them." *But*, Macie added in her head. *You aren't currently running an estate holed up in your room.*

The irritation was returning. Macie had to leave before she said something else that would offend her boss and get her sent home immediately. She couldn't go home now. Charlotte, Audrey, and Evelyn needed someone to show them love.

"If that is all, Ma'am. I need to put Evelyn down for her nap."

Mrs. Bailey waved her hand dismissively. Macie hurried out of the room, closing the door on the darkness behind her. She leaned against the door for a second and took a deep breath before making her way to the playroom to collect Evelyn for her nap. She was an hour late as it was.

Macie picked up Evelyn and was about to walk back upstairs, when Daisy caught her arm. "Daniel asked me to give this to you."

She handed Macie a slip of paper.

Macie's heart rate increased slightly at the mention of his name.

Macie slipped the paper into her pocket, gestured to Charlotte and Audrey to come with her, and left so Daisy could do her work.

They were about to turn toward the girls' rooms at the top of the stairs when Macie stopped, marched with the girls to Mrs. Bailey's room, and knocked. Daisy had said Mrs. Bailey wanted to see her girls, so Macie would let her see her girls.

"Come in," came Mrs. Bailey's voice.

Macie opened the door. Charlotte and Audrey peeked into the dark room, seemingly hesitant to enter.

Macie spoke from the door. "Daisy mentioned you wanted to see the girls, so I figured I would bring them by before I put Evelyn down for a nap."

Mrs. Bailey waved her away. "I don't have the energy. I mostly wanted to see if they were happy." She turned her attention to the girls. "Are you happy?"

Charlotte and Audrey both nodded.

"Oh yes, Mum." Audrey said. "Macie is so great. She took us to see Aunt Jessie."

"I told you not to call her that," Mrs. Bailey hissed.

Audrey took a small step backward. "Sorry, Mum."

"That is all." Mrs. Bailey shooed them out with her hand. She hadn't even called them over.

Macie held back a sigh, and Charlotte straightened her spine.

Macie took Evelyn to her room with Charlotte and Audrey trailing behind her. She heard a sniffle and noticed Audrey wiping away a tear. Charlotte's brown eyes showed all of the hurt she was feeling.

Macie sang two songs, laid Evelyn down, and then took the girls to the playroom.

After she got the girls started on a game, she discreetly opened the note. *Meet me at 9:00 at the fence by the orchard. D.*

An inexplicable urge to run out to the stables to talk to Daniel right away came over Macie, but he specifically asked to see her tonight, and she couldn't upset Mrs. Bailey any more than she had already. She could be patient. Would she get in trouble for taking a little walk after the girls were asleep?

***

After an hour, Macie couldn't stand being in the playroom anymore.

"Can we play hide-and-seek?" Audrey asked.

Macie's chest tightened, and her vision went black for a second. Hide-and-seek led her to losing Sammy. The parents were terrified and thought he had been kidnapped. Their fear leaked into Macie, making her doubt everything up until that moment, even though everyone eventually knew Sammy was only hiding.

"It's almost time for dinner." Macie hoped they would completely forget the idea. "Let's go see if Daisy needs some help. Gladys still isn't feeling well. We should make sure she isn't up and overworking herself." Macie hoped the woman was in bed since Daisy was still in charge of cooking. She had only been home a week, and it had only been two weeks since the incident.

Charlotte smiled.

"Okay." Audrey's enthusiastic response brought a smile to Macie's lips.

Macie was surprised to find Gladys in the kitchen. She was chopping vegetables.

"Gladys!" Macie hurried over and gave her a light hug. "What are you doing? Why are you up? I thought Daisy was cooking dinner."

"Macie. I'm going to go plum crazy if I have to lie in that bed a minute longer. I told Daisy she didn't need to cook and to get her own work done so she could have the night off. Nate went out to the stables today, and he's doing fine after being hurt even worse than I was."

Macie highly doubted Daniel let him do anything too strenuous. Right now, she was worried about Gladys overdoing it.

Gladys set the girls to polishing the silver. Macie made Gladys sit on a stool near the sink as she followed her directions to prepare dinner, letting Gladys feel like she was doing something.

"Gladys," Macie said in a low whisper. She checked to see if the girls were listening, but they were happily chatting about their visit to Jessie's and weren't paying attention. "Can you remember anything?"

Gladys sighed. "I brought some groceries in and went back out to get the rest and shut the trunk in my car when I noticed a movement around the stables. The person wasn't Nate. I knew Daniel had gone earlier. I tried to rationalize that Daniel could be back, but I couldn't shake the feeling that something was wrong, so I went to the stables to investigate."

She looked at the girls. "You girls getting that silver polished?"

"Yes, Gladys." They pointed to all the silver already polished.

"Good girls. You are a great help."

The girls grinned and went back to polishing. The memory was probably painful, but she needed to know what Gladys remembered.

"Then what happened?"

Gladys shook her head. "I'm not sure. I remember seeing someone step from behind the barn, but I didn't really get a good look before everything went black."

Macie cringed, almost wishing she hadn't asked. The fear she had felt for Gladys that day came roaring back. She would not stop her investigation until she found out who had done such an awful thing to her friend.

Macie heard Evelyn on the baby monitor. Macie told the girls to stay in the kitchen, then ran up and grabbed Evelyn.

When Macie opened the door, Evelyn stood and reached for her. Macie changed her diaper before she placed her on her hip for the walk downstairs.

Evelyn wrapped her little arms around Macie's neck. "Luv you, May May."

Macie choked back tears. She couldn't remember the last time someone had said they loved her. In her family, it was assumed. Macie squeezed her back. "I love you, too, Evelyn." Macie swung Evelyn, so she was sitting on her other hip. "Should we go help cook dinner?"

"Mummy eating?" she asked.

Macie's chest tightened. This little girl already missed seeing her mother at dinner. It had been the only time the girls had gotten to interact with their mother since Macie arrived. Since Mrs. Bailey now took dinner in her room, they never saw her. Macie was suddenly glad she had taken them to see her before her nap. Heat burned in Macie's belly, and she had to control her face so Evelyn wouldn't know she was angry. Macie took a deep breath. "I don't know, sweetie. I hope so." *For your sake.*

CHAPTER 23

MACIE AND THE GIRLS ate in the dining room. She would have insisted they eat in the kitchen again, but Daisy had said Mrs. Bailey might be at dinner, but that changed at the last minute.

Charlotte ate in stony silence. Audrey chatted about the day. Macie listened attentively even though she was there for the visit to the Morris estate and to Aunt Jessie's. Even if Mrs. Bailey didn't approve of their choice of outing, Audrey deserved to have a parent listen and care about what she enjoyed. Evelyn slapped her hands on the high chair tray if Macie took too many bites of her own food before giving Evelyn another bite.

The door opened, and all three girls looked expectantly in that direction. Macie stood when Mr. Bailey entered.

"Mr. Bailey. You're home." Macie quickly sat down again, embarrassed at her reaction.

He chuckled. I left work early today to check on Emma. He turned his attention to the girls.

"How are my girls?"

"Why are you ignoring us?" Charlotte asked.

Macie's eyes shot to Mr. Bailey, worried about his reaction. Charlotte was always willing to speak her mind.

Mr. Bailey rushed to her side and kneeled next to her. "I'm not trying to ignore you. I have been in London for most of the week. There's a lot going on right now, and your mum isn't doing well. We may have to move."

"Why would we need to move?" Audrey asked. "I don't want to move." Her blue eyes pled silently with her father.

"Neither do I." Mr. Bailey stroked her hair. "But your mum hates it here, and things are not going well."

He gave her a pat on the back as he stood. Macie could read between the lines pretty well. Things not going well most likely meant financially.

Macie's eyes misted. What if they moved before they figured out who had hurt Gladys and Nate? Would they take Macie with them, or would she be sent home? Macie didn't know.

Mr. Bailey squeezed Charlotte and Audrey's shoulders before making his way out of the room. The door closed with an ominous click. In the silence that followed, Evelyn startled Macie with a shrill noise and opened her mouth for more food. She gave Evelyn another bite, then studied Audrey and Charlotte. Something passed between them unspoken, then Audrey turned to meet Macie's gaze.

"If we move, will you come with us?"

Macie wasn't sure she would be invited, but she wanted to reassure the girls. "I will if your mother wants me to."

"She'll want you," Charlotte said confidently. She shrugged when Macie raised her eyebrows. "She would have to find another nanny otherwise."

Macie didn't bother mentioning that she had been on probation from the day she arrived. She changed the subject, asking the girls about Jessie and the times she had babysat them.

Both of their faces lit up, and they told story after story. She could tell they loved Jessie and Macie determined they would visit more often. They didn't need a car to visit Jessie. And Mrs. Bailey hadn't explicitly said they couldn't.

As diverting as their stories were, Macie's thoughts kept drifting to Daniel, the stolen horse, and what they could do to solve the mystery. A sudden thought sent Macie's heart into overdrive. Was it a one-time event? Or was the horse thief after more horses?

***

Callum paced the length of his bedroom as he talked to Vin on the phone.

"I'll talk to Emma tonight." Callum wished his cousin would relax a bit, but Callum knew he couldn't. That detective was still asking questions about the day the boy and his mother were attacked at the estate. They hadn't connected Callum to the crime, but he heard talk of neighbors getting asked if they had seen anything unusual. Apparently, one neighbor had seen a truck turn off onto the small road behind the Martin Estate, but couldn't remember details, except it was black: like Vin's. In hindsight, they were sure it was the person responsible for attacking Gladys and Nate, even though the small road went behind three or four different properties.

Despite Mrs. Bailey's insistence that they not worry about the stolen horse, the detective was still looking for the animal. Vin had even been stupid enough not to get on the horse right away. Tracks showed a set of boot prints along with horse prints leading to a gate at the back of the pastures. Tracks that were easily visible, thanks to the rain the day before the theft.

"Turn on that charm of yours, Callum." Vin's voice startled Callum. He had almost forgotten he was talking to him.

Callum rolled his eyes. "I'll do my best."

"You haven't heard any talk about them finding Thomas's real will anywhere, have you?" Vin asked.

"No."

Later that night, Callum approached the Martin Estate with a sense of foreboding. He wished he could get out of this mess, but knew his cousin would blackmail him if he backed out. Since Callum was the one who arranged Thomas's accident, and his cousin had proof, Callum would be in jail before he could attempt to point any fingers. Callum had no proof his cousin was in on the scheme. Unless he could get his hands on the original will... but that could wait until he was desperate.

Callum looked at his watch as he parked his car in the circular driveway. It was 8:00... almost too late to be considered polite, but he knew the girls would be in bed and wanted to talk to her without fear one of the girls would get away from the nanny and run in on them or something.

Jack answered the door.

"Jack!" Callum's words caught in his throat as he tried to think of a reason he might be there to see Jack. Jack should have been in London.

Did he know something? Callum's unease heightened when Jack showed him into the study. Callum had almost expected Jack to refuse to see him, since it was no secret why he would be there. It was the only reason Callum had spoken to either Jack or Emma since Thomas's death. Jack sat behind the desk, dark circles under his eyes. He was obviously exhausted. Maybe talking to Jack would be better. Maybe Jack could be convinced to sell the estate to him.

Callum spoke while he had the chance. "Maybe it's time to sell." Callum tried to keep his tone sympathetic.

"You'd like that," Jack said sarcastically. "You've been on Emma to sell from the day Thomas passed. You didn't even mourn Thomas."

"I didn't know him well, so I am able to stay objective. Maybe you need to convince her. It's obvious things aren't going well."

Jack sat back in his chair. "You are the last person Emma would sell to. I don't know your history with her, but she hates you. Since Thomas's will states explicitly you get first chance to buy the estate at a specified discounted price, she refuses to give it up. Why did Thomas even put you in his will if you didn't know him well?"

Callum forced himself not to show how hard his heart was pumping. Beads of sweat formed at the back of his neck. Had Jack figured it out?

Callum worked to keep his face neutral. Jack didn't know Vin had changed the will completely. How Vin did it without anyone knowing was beyond Callum. Would Jack start digging to find the will? Jack had a conscience; Emma didn't. Emma thought only of herself. She always had. And she had always let Callum know how much better she was, which is part of why Callum had been agreeable to the plan. It was a way to get back at all the horrible things she had said to him at the stiff private school. He had to distract Jack from more questions about the will.

"Think of what is best for your family." Callum knew that wasn't the way to go about things as soon as the words left his mouth. Jack's face darkened, and Callum felt like withering under his cold stare, but Callum would not back down. Vin could send Callum to jail with the knowledge he had and wouldn't hesitate to turn him in if he failed to do his part.

***

"Can we play hide-and-seek tomorrow?" Audrey asked as Macie tucked her in for the night.

Although Macie hoped she would forget, she hated to disappoint Audrey. Macie closed her eyes and forced her brain not to freak out. They would be inside the house. The horse thief wouldn't come into the house with so many people around. Macie would make sure Mr. Bailey would be around before they started. It would be fine.

"We'll see."

Macie shut Audrey's light off and went to the sitting area. She pulled out her phone while she waited for the girls to fall asleep and sent a text to her sister. It would be the middle of the night there, but she wanted to let her know things were going well. Katie had said, "I told you so," when Macie had told her Charlotte had decided to like her, like it was common sense that everyone liked Macie. But Katie was her sister and was supposed to say things to make her feel better, right? She pushed send when she heard the voices from the study.

"What is it going to take to get you to sell, Jack?" a deep voice rang out. "You're floundering. Everyone knows it."

"As I said, I believe you only started helping Thomas to get in his good graces with the hope he would leave you something. Since you have the first option to buy, Emma isn't going to sell, even if she hates it here. She hates you more."

A slam echoed in the hall, and Macie jumped and caught her breath. "Which is why you *should* sell. She doesn't appreciate this land and the horses like I do."

"I'd rather sell it to Daniel than to you," Mr. Bailey said. "I think we're done here."

Macie's breath hitched. It was almost 8:30. She jumped up and peeked in on each of the girls to find them asleep. To avoid being seen from the open door of the study, she made her way to the servant's entrance. Someone who got first option to buy the land was here, but it was someone Mrs. Bailey did not like, and that was the only reason she was still here. Mr. Bailey wanted to sell it to Daniel. None of what she heard made sense.

Would Daniel know who was in the study? She quickened her pace to get to the fence through the orchard. The last light was fading from the sky, but it was still light enough to make her way to the fence separating the Bailey property from Daniel's.

A screech filled the air, and she switched directions to the barn. Maybe Daniel was there. A light flickered in the opening in the middle of the barn. It looked more like a flashlight or lantern. Why didn't Daniel have the barn lights on?

"Daniel?" Macie called.

As she came to stand in front of the opening at the center of the barn, a bright beam of a flashlight blinded her as it was aimed at her face. A deep voice swore, and Macie froze. That wasn't Daniel's voice.

CHAPTER 24

DANIEL SAT ON THE fence to meet Macie. He had come back to work for a bit after getting dinner and wanted some time to think, so he had decided to sit here while he waited. Daniel wondered how all the things he had learned came together to make some sense. The will Mrs. Bailey mentioned. The horse being stolen. Clay not being there that day. He couldn't seem to make any logical sense of it. The squeal of a hinge broke the night air and into Daniel's thoughts. Daniel jumped over the fence. It wasn't loud, but it was noticeable, and it was coming from the barn. No one should be opening a stall at this hour.

Daniel sprinted through the corrals to the side of the barn to catch whoever was there in the act. Horse hooves sounded, echoing through the dark night. He peeked through the gap the door made. The movement of a torch beam lit up a man bridling a horse. Daniel pressed his face harder against the wood, hoping to see who it was. The horse was coming from one of the stalls they kept the horses they were training in. No. Not another one.

"Daniel?" Macie's voice echoed from the front of the barn.

The horse danced sideways, and the man swore and swung himself onto the horse's back.

Daniel sprinted around the barn, his heart thumping wildly. If the guy was determined, he could force the horse to run over Macie.

The horse whinnied, and the stomping of hooves drove Daniel's stomach to the ground.

"Ha!" The yell wasn't loud, but it cut into Daniel's heart. Daniel saw Macie just inside the alcove in front of the barn. Her form was silhouetted by the light of the torch, but her facial features were clear as day. Macie stood frozen, staring into the barn, her eyes wide with horror. Hoofbeats reverberated in the barn. Daniel didn't stop to consider if the horse would sidestep Macie. He took two big steps and flung himself into Macie, knocking her to the ground. The horse leaped over his legs and galloped toward the main road.

Macie lay on the ground, gasping.

Daniel swore softly as he watched the thief take another horse. He couldn't make out a single detail about the man.

"Daniel?" Macie's voice was strained.

Daniel didn't move as the ramifications hit him in the gut. Another horse gone. And this one someone else owned. He was sure of it.

"Oof. Get off me," Macie wheezed.

"Sorry." Daniel backed off, felt for her arm, and helped her up. "Are you okay?"

Gripping her hand tightly, he pulled her to the barn and flipped on the light. He did a quick scan, but Macie didn't seem hurt—scared but not injured.

"I'm fine," Macie said, though her voice shook. "Was that his horse, or did he steal one?"

Daniel searched the stalls. One was gone. One he was almost done training was gone. He hit the gate of the empty stall, making several horses startle. "He stole one."

"How did you know I needed help?" Macie's voice reminded him he was still holding her hand. He had been dragging her with him. He relaxed his fingers to let go, but with her hand gripping his tightly, he found he didn't want to.

"I heard the sound of the gate and saw the guy getting on the horse. Then I heard you call for me." His hand gripped Macie's tighter. "I was afraid he would trample you."

His voice caught, and he cursed the fact that his fear had slipped out. He walked swiftly toward the back kitchen door, clinging to Macie's hand. He took long, determined strides. Mr. Bailey would know about this right away. Daniel was glad he had come home. He slowed when Macie stumbled as she tried to keep up with him.

He opened the door into the kitchen, but realized the house was quiet. They made their way to the entryway. He had to report this to Mr. Bailey but didn't want to go to his room himself.

Macie must have sensed his unease.

"I'll knock on their door. Wait here."

Daniel felt like a coward. He could dive to save Macie from getting trampled by a horse, but he couldn't bring himself to knock on Mrs. Bailey's bedroom door.

The soft knock echoed through the silent house. There was a murmur of voices, then Macie appeared at the top of the staircase. She waited for Mr. Bailey to join her. Mr. Bailey strode to the study and flipped on the light.

Daniel followed him in, but Macie stopped just outside the door.

Daniel wasted no time. "Another horse was stolen. One we are training."

"One we are training?" Jack must have realized he was shouting because he almost whispered, "When?"

"Just now. Luckily we witnessed it; otherwise, we wouldn't have known until morning."

Mr. Bailey eyed Macie. "What are you doing out so late?"

She took a couple of steps inside the room, glancing first at Daniel, then meeting Mr. Bailey's gaze. Daniel wanted to reassure her. Mr. Bailey was on their side. Of that he was sure. "I needed some fresh air. It was a long day. I helped Gladys today to give Daisy a little break."

Mr. Bailey's steely eyes locked on Daniel. "What are you doing here this late? The mare we brought isn't due for another week. She didn't go into labor, did she?"

"No, sir, but I came back after dinner to finish up a few things. I had stopped at the fence to have some quiet time to think when I heard the stall in the barn creak, so I went back to investigate."

That much was true.

"I didn't hear anything." Mr. Bailey glanced at Macie.

"I doubt you would have heard it in here. It wasn't that loud." Macie met Jack's gaze. "I heard noise in the barn, so I went to investigate. Daniel made sure I didn't get trampled, and the man rode away."

"I'm guessing you didn't get a good look at him." Jack said.

Macie shook her head, her face reddening. "It's too dark. But..." She stopped.

"But?" Mr. Bailey prodded.

"When did the guy you were talking to earlier leave?"

Mr. Bailey's eyes narrowed. "How did you know he was here?"

Macie blushed again, and Daniel couldn't help but admire her courage to even bring that meeting up if she was eavesdropping. "I heard voices in the study after I put the girls to bed. You were talking pretty loud."

"He wouldn't steal the horses, if that's what you're thinking. He's not a criminal. A pain in my side, yes, but not a criminal." Jack's voice trailed off a bit at the end of the sentence, and Daniel had the distinct impression that Jack was second-guessing his own assertion.

"Sir, we have to be open to any possibility if we are going to solve this thing," Daniel said. "Who was here?"

"It was Callum. Trying to get me to sell the estate."

"Callum Davies?" Macie asked.

"Do you know him?" Mr. Bailey asked.

"No, sir." Macie folded her arms as if suddenly cold.

Daniel thought to his conversation with Macie earlier that day. There had been no connection between the two days, but Callum was a common denominator between the day the guy tried to steal the horse and tonight.

Mr. Bailey started fiddling with a pen.

"Who is Callum Davies?" Macie asked.

Daniel answered. "A second cousin who helped Thomas Martin a few times during the last few months of his life."

Macie's head swiveled to meet his gaze. "Do you know him?"

Daniel nodded. "I've been around this estate all my life. Callum worked a couple of horses when Thomas and I couldn't keep up with the demand."

"Is he tall?" Macie asked.

"I guess he is, but I think you think everyone is tall," Daniel teased, even with the weight of another theft on his mind.

"I'm not that short," Macie retorted.

"He doesn't have a tattoo," Mr. Bailey cut in.

"You looked?" Macie asked.

"Not tonight, but I have never noticed one before. You make it seem like the tattoo would be obvious."

Macie nodded.

Jack took a deep breath and walked to the phone. It was obvious from his side of the conversation that he was talking to the police. After he hung up, he turned to Daniel. "The detective is on his way. You can both sit. I'll be right back."

Daniel sat as Jack hurried out of the room. Macie took the seat next to him.

Macie shivered, so Daniel reached over and took her hand. "Are you okay?"

She nodded, but her eyes were still wide with fright. She wasn't okay, but Daniel didn't feel it was his place to call her out. Instead, he squeezed her hand "We'll figure this out."

Jack came back in and they sat in silence. Macie's head bobbed as though she were fighting to stay awake. Finally, her chin settled on her chest. It was an awkward position, but Daniel figured she needed to get some sleep. She was probably overwrought from her encounter with the horse. A loud knock moments later startled her awake, and she sat up straight, glancing around, confusion reflecting in her brown eyes until they rested on him. Daniel could see the moment the reason she was in the study hit her, since she slumped back in her chair and took a deep breath.

Jack answered the door and showed Detective Clark in.

"Another horse was stolen?" the detective asked. "Was anyone hurt this time?"

Mr. Bailey shook his head. "But these two witnessed the theft."

"Can you identify the thief?"

Daniel shook his head, his hands clenching as his frustration grew.

Detective Clark turned to Macie. "Will you wait in the hall with Mr. Bailey while I ask Daniel for his side of the story?"

Macie nodded and followed Jack out of the room.

Detective Clark waited until they had left and then sat in the chair Macie had vacated.

"So, can you tell me what happened?"

Daniel relayed the events of the night. He thought about lying about the reason he was waiting by the fence but didn't want that to come back and bite him. Having the detective know he was meeting Macie at night wouldn't hurt him unless he told Jack. But even then, he didn't think Jack would fire him over it. Having to pay off the owner of the horse would be the tipping point to him losing his job, not meeting with Macie.

"Why were you going to meet Macie?"

Daniel shifted in his seat. "We're trying to find some sort of lead."

Detective Clark regarded him for a moment. "But she didn't show?"

Daniel shook his head. "I heard the creaking of the gate, and then I heard her voice. She must have been on her way to meet me when she heard the sound as well."

Detective Clark wrote something in his notebook. "Then what happened?"

Daniel detailed the events of the night the best he could then added, "You are still searching for Shadow, aren't you?"

Detective Clark looked surprised. "Of course. Our priority is the person who attacked the boy and his mother, but if we find him, we will likely find the horse." He paused. "Horses, now. At this point, I have to assume it is the same person who made off with one of the horses tonight."

Daniel relaxed marginally. Gladys had said she overheard Mrs. Bailey say she told Detective Clark not to search for the horse. It was good to see he wasn't following her orders.

"We also figure if we find the horses, we will find the person responsible for the attacks," Detective Clark said as if reading his mind. "It goes both ways."

Detective Clark wrote a few more things in his notebook, and Daniel fought the urge to read what he was writing.

"Will you tell Macie to come in, please?" Detective Clark asked without looking up from his notepad.

Daniel exited the room and nearly ran into Macie as she paced back and forth. Jack sat on the bottom step with his head in his hands, his fingers gripping his blond hair.

"He's asking for you, Macie."

Macie paled, so Daniel reached up and gave her arm a reassuring squeeze. Daniel studied her for a minute, capturing her eyes with his. Her eyes were wide, and she was trembling. He wanted to give her a hug but didn't know how she would react. He might be crossing boundaries as it was. How had she gotten under his skin so quickly? They'd been working together on this mystery for two days and already he couldn't get her out of his head. Her vulnerability tugged at him, and he wanted to do all he could to protect her.

Her face flushed slightly, making her olive skin appear even darker. She hurried into the room, shutting the door behind her.

Daniel thought the detective might want to ask some follow-up questions, so he leaned against the wall to wait. His mind raced through all the possibilities. The horse thief had tried to take Shadow the day Callum's neighbor had suggested a meeting with the Baileys. Then Clay was supposed to meet him at the Morris farm the day Nate and Gladys were attacked and Shadow was taken. Daniel was sure Clay was somehow connected to the theft. He trusted Mr. Morris. Then today, Callum was talking to Mr. Bailey when a second horse was stolen.

Daniel straightened. Callum was connected to two of the times strange things happened. Daniel didn't know how long it had taken for Macie to hear Callum in the study to when she had gone outside, but he figured it wasn't enough for time for Callum to leave, then backtrack and take the horse, which meant Callum was acting as a distraction for someone else to take the horse, but who?

He didn't know but figured he'd better share his theory with the detective in case it would help.

"You are free to go, Macie," the detective said. "I'll have Daniel show me the barn where the horse was taken and talk to Mr. Bailey."

Finally, Macie emerged with the detective.

Macie bobbed her head. "Thank you, sir."

Daniel watched her until she had disappeared at the top of the stairs. A strange stirring started in his chest and worked its way down to his toes, taking him by surprise. When had she become more than the new nanny and his partner in figuring out what was happening here on the estate?

Just now, he'd reached out and done his best to comfort her before she gave her statement. He cared about her, and it scared him. He didn't want to care for someone else. Everyone he cared for got hurt or died. First his father, and with his father, his mother's decline. Then Thomas had died and, recently, Gladys and Nate had been attacked. He was the common denominator. What if something happened to Macie? His breath hitched at the thought.

"Daniel?"

Detective Clark's voice ripped through his thoughts.

"Sorry," Daniel said.

Detective Clark swept his hand in front of him as if gesturing for Daniel to go first. "Lead the way."

With a start, he realized the detective had been waiting for him to take him to the scene of the crime.

"Right." Daniel started down the hall toward the kitchen door. Jack didn't follow but returned to the study.

"I'll be back to ask you some questions." Detective Clark waited until Jack nodded, then followed Daniel. Daniel had a feeling he might not be going to work after all the next day. He would have to be up early in the morning to drive into London.

While they walked, Daniel got right down to business with his suspicions about Callum. "Sir, I think Callum Davies is somehow connected to the crimes." He outlined what he knew about the three times a stranger had been on the estate.

"It is definitely worth looking into," Detective Clark said.

Daniel waited near the barns as Detective Clark took some pictures, asked a few more questions, and had Daniel point out the stall stolen horse had been housed in.

"What is this?" Detective Clark pointed to the side of the stall next to the one the horse had been in. It was the same small mark Daniel had washed off another stall earlier last week.

"I don't know," Daniel said. "I found another marking like that on another stall but washed it off."

"Let's have a quick look at all the stalls."

Daniel was surprised he hadn't noticed them before, but three more the Bailey's owned had the same symbol.

"It looks like someone with access to the barns knows which ones the Baileys own and has marked them for the thief."

"Callum," Daniel growled.

"I got pictures of all the marks. You can go ahead and wash them off. That will at least slow the thief down until we can catch him. Be extra vigilant. Don't ever leave the stables unattended. I'll set up a watch, but it may take a day to get the manpower I need."

"I'll stay her overnight." Daniel sagged against the barn as the detective left and wondered how he was going to have the stamina to do all of this.

Daniel immediately gathered a rag and some water, despite the late hour. He wasn't going to give the thief any hints if he came back.

CHAPTER 25

"Are you okay, Macie?" Audrey's voice brought Macie out of a sort of daze. Audrey: the one that was always astute about what people were feeling.

Macie nodded. "I'm just tired."

A complete understatement. She was exhausted. Even after she finally went to bed around midnight, it took her another hour to fall asleep. Her thoughts jumped from the horse barreling toward her, to Daniel checking to make sure she was okay, to his light reassurance as he squeezed her arm before she went in to talk to the detective. As she made her way up the stairs the night before, she could have sworn Daniel was watching her, but the thought was so ridiculous she hadn't turned to check. She was invisible, no one watched her.

"Luckily we don't have school, anymore." Charlotte's tone made Macie chuckle.

"Lucky for me, right?"

Charlotte nodded, her face serious, but Macie wasn't fooled. Charlotte was proving herself to be very adept at hiding her emotions if she wanted to.

Macie sighed. "All right. Let's go outside as soon as you are done."

"Brilliant!" Charlotte said and finished her breakfast.

Macie resisted the urge to smile at the British phrase. Some of them still caught her by surprise, even after being in the country for a month.

Macie didn't allow herself to sit while playing in the grass with the girls, afraid that if she sat, she would fall asleep.

"I think Daniel wants to talk to you," Audrey said.

Macie spun around. Daniel was standing not far from their game of freeze tag.

She turned to Audrey. "How do you know he wants to talk to me?"

Charlotte rolled her eyes. "He's been standing there for a while, and he has no need to talk to one of us."

There must be news about the horse theft. She shrugged. "Keep playing. I'll be right back."

Charlotte and Audrey both grinned at each other and sat on the grass next to Evelyn to entertain her. She had been content enough as they ran around her, but Macie figured the extra attention couldn't hurt.

"I kind of wish the horse stolen was one of ours, not one we were training. This is a nightmare," Daniel said, running his hand through his hair.

Macie cocked her head, confused at the start of the conversation. "You wish the second theft was another horse Bailey's owned?"

He grinned at her. "You're always ready to put me in my place, aren't you?"

"Just clarifying what you're saying. Though I do understand it, since you are responsible for the theft now." She paused. "Well, not you, but the Baileys. Will they have to pay the owner right away?"

"Luckily they like me and are will give the detectives a little time to recover the horse before pressing charges. If the Baileys have to pay out on this one horse, they could go bankrupt. Especially if others decide we can't be trusted with the horses." He removed his hat and ran his hand through his blond hair. His blue eyes seemed dull and his face a bit pale.

Macie reached out but froze just short of touching him. "Are you okay?"

"Yeah. Just tired." He studied Macie for a moment. "What about you?"

"Same." She winced. "And a little sore."

Daniel grimaced. "Sorry."

"I don't blame you. So, have you figured out anything new?"

"Well, I suggested to the detective that Callum might be involved, since he was part of the original plan to get us off the property, and he was here last night."

"What did Mr. Bailey say to that?" Macie wasn't sure what Mr. Bailey's feelings were about Callum.

Daniel shrugged. "He wasn't with us when I mentioned it."

Macie thought about what Daniel had said. If they didn't recover the horses, the estate would go bankrupt. Where would that leave her? "We have to figure out what is going on. If the estate goes bankrupt, Mrs. Bailey will have no need to keep me around. I can't go home yet."

Macie pursed her lips to keep from spilling any of her deep, dark secrets. Daniel didn't know what she had come to prove.

Daniel cocked his head to the side. "I'm not sure you'll go home. Mrs. Bailey doesn't want to be a mother and being bankrupt will make it so she can't afford to fly or drive a new nanny here very soon." The grim line his lips were forming softened slightly. "You're the best thing that has happened to those girls in a long time."

Macie's eyes stung, and she averted her gaze so Daniel wouldn't see the emotions lurking there. He thought she was useful, great for the girls. She cleared her throat and changed the subject. "Do you think your mother would mind if I took the girls over to visit her tomorrow?"

"Why do you want to do that?"

"The girls love her company," Macie hedged. She didn't want to tell him she could tell it did his mother good as well.

He studied her for another full minute. Macie wanted to look away. She felt like he was reading her mind. Macie wanted to continue to defend her decision to take the girls to visit Jessie, but she resisted and met his eyes with her arms folded. Macie even raised her eyebrow for emphasis.

One side of his lips twitched, and he nodded. "She'd probably like that."

"Great!" She took off to tell the girls the good news.

"Macie?" Daniel called before she got very far.

Macie stopped and turned to Daniel, afraid he'd changed his mind.

"Thank you." He smiled. Macie's legs went wobbly, and her stomach warmed.

Macie stopped herself short before she reached the girls. They were taking turns rolling on the grass and being rewarded with gales of laughter from Evelyn. Maybe she would tell them they were going on a walk when they left. Macie figured they would like the surprise.

Macie glanced at Daniel one last time. His arms were folded, and he was watching her. He raised a hand. Macie resisted the urge to check behind her to see if he was waving at one of the girls. Instead, she waved back. Macie was invisible at home. No one waved at her.

Macie's heart lightened, and she had the sensation that she was floating, except she could feel the pressure of her feet against the ground. She took a deep breath and took the few steps necessary to get to the girls.

CHAPTER 26

THE NEXT MORNING, MACIE called her sister before the girls woke up. The conversation was going well until she mentioned Daniel.

"Who's Daniel? I don't think you've mentioned him before."

Macie had purposefully not mentioned Daniel in their conversations. She was confused at the way he looked at her as if he could read her mind. She didn't know what to do with the feelings he invoked in her. They were just friends, she had to remind herself.

"He is the guy who really runs the business with training."

"So he's old? The way you said his name sounded like you kind of liked him. Please tell me you don't have a crush on a forty-year old."

Macie rolled her eyes. "No. He's not much older than I am."

"Oooh. That is a lot more interesting. Tell me everything."

"There's nothing to tell," Macie said, even as her cheeks warmed at the thought of him.

"Come on. I'm home all day with two small kids. I need some gossip to liven things up."

Macie laughed. "Sorry, but there really is nothing. We're friends."

"And..." Katie prompted.

"And nothing."

"It's not nothing. I can tell that something is going on."

"He makes me feel important somehow. I'm not even sure what it is about him. He doesn't say things just to make me feel good, but he's genuine." Macie realized how ridiculous this sounded. She barely knew Daniel and was sure he only thought of her as a friend and someone to help him find a horse thief.

Macie heard Katie clap her hands. "So you do like him."

"I guess so, but I'm sure he sees me as a friend, so don't get your hopes up or anything."

"You never know." Katie's voice carried an excitement that even made Macie's stomach flip. She quickly tamped it down. There was no way she was going to get her hopes up. No guy had ever been interested in her. There was no reason Daniel would be any different.

Macie rushed through breakfast after collecting the girls. She wanted time to go visit Jesse, and they couldn't go while Evelyn was napping.

"Do you girls want to go on a walk?" Macie asked. The girls cheered.

"I like you." Audrey informed Macie.

Macie smiled. "As good as Celeste?"

Audrey nodded enthusiastically, but Charlotte paused as if taking the question seriously. Finally, she smiled. "I think so," she announced.

"Where are we walking?" Audrey asked as they headed down the long driveway.

"Down the road a little." Macie didn't want to say too much. Mrs. Bailey knew everything that happened on the estate. The country road wasn't busy by any means, but she held Audrey's hand and commanded Charlotte to hold her other hand while Macie held Evelyn. There wasn't a lot of space between the road and the hedges that lined it.

"Turn here," Macie said when they reached Jessie's driveway.

Charlotte and Audrey both smiled brightly up at Macie. "We're visiting Aunt Jessie?"

Macie nodded, and the girls sprinted up the driveway.

"Aunt Jessie!" Evelyn cried, clapping her hands.

Macie was almost to the sidewalk that led to the front door when Charlotte and Audrey barged into the house.

"Charlotte, you should knock first," Macie called out, even though it was obviously too late.

Macie entered the house and shut the door behind her. She heard voices in the parlor. She wondered if Jessie sat in there every day. It would be a nice place to sit. She had a beautiful view outside the parlor window.

"Sorry they barged in," Macie said when she entered the parlor. "I hope you don't mind surprise visitors."

Macie hadn't thought about calling ahead or anything. Now that they were standing in Jessie's house, Macie realized how rude that was.

"I *love* visitors. Especially these darlings." Jesse met Macie's eyes. "Daniel didn't put you up to this, did he?"

Macie heard the wariness in her voice and wondered why Daniel would feel the need. "No, ma'am."

She waved a hand at Macie. "Call me Jessie."

"Yes, ma'am—I mean, Jessie. I asked Daniel if you would mind some visitors, but it was my idea. The girls loved it over here and have wanted to come again."

"Then I dare say you are better than him."

Macie's jaw dropped. Evelyn wiggled in her arms, providing the perfect distraction.

Jessie smiled at Macie. She hugged the girls. "Now what should we do?"

"A story," Charlotte said at the same time Audrey yelled, "A song."

Jessie laughed. "I think we can probably do both."

Jessie reached for a book. While she read, Macie studied her. Daniel had told her she got distracted and that he took care of her, but she seemed capable. In fact, as Macie watched her now, she seemed strong. She made a careful inspection, searching for anything that would suggest Jessie was in pain.

Her face was drawn and pale, but her eyes sparkled. Maybe they were dim when the girls weren't around. She could put on a little weight, but she wasn't so thin that Macie was worried about her health. It wasn't until after Jesse sang a song and read the book that she glanced briefly out the window and her eyes darkened, and for a second she was not with them anymore.

"Can we go outside and play here?" Charlotte asked.

Macie checked the time. "Yes. We have to get back in time to help make lunch in about an hour."

Audrey grabbed Jessie's hand, bringing the woman's attention to the people in the room. "Will you come out with us?"

Jessie smiled, but it didn't reach her eyes this time. "Yes."

She struggled to stand, so Macie stepped to her chair and held her arm. Jessie shook.

"Were you able to eat breakfast before we came?" Macie asked, knowing her mother got shaky if she didn't eat. "I'm sorry if we intruded and messed up your morning routine."

Confusion clouded Jessie's face. "I'm not sure. Daniel usually makes sure I eat, but he left before I was up. Maybe he left something in the kitchen?"

Since they had to go through the kitchen to get to the back door to the yard, Macie led her to a chair at the bar. Some beans and toast lay cold on the counter. She almost gagged thinking about eating either cold. Macie could make Jessie more food. "We can let you eat something before we play."

"Oh, no. I'll be fine. I can eat later."

Macie took in Jessie's trembling hands, then she thought of Daniel, doing all he could to help his mother but dealing with the thefts and Mrs. Bailey's accusations. No, Macie would help him by giving him one less thing to worry about for the morning.

"Please. Let me get you something to eat." Macie turned to the girls who were waiting by the door. "Girls, can you help me find some breakfast for Jessie? We came before she ate."

Charlotte's eyebrows shot up. "Why didn't you say you were hungry, Aunt Jessie?"

Jessie patted Charlotte's head as the girl wrapped her arms around her waist. "It is all right. I didn't feel hungry when you came, but I think I could eat a little."

Macie silently thanked Charlotte. Jessie may fight Macie, but it was apparent she would not disappoint the girls if she could help it.

The girls helped Macie gather the bread and preserves. She let Charlotte run the toaster and buttered the bread, and then Audrey put the preserves on top. Evelyn toddled between Macie's legs. Macie smothered a giggle as she watched Jessie carefully scrape off half of the preserves Audrey had put on her toast while Macie reheated the beans on the stove with a little water.

After Jessie surrendered and declared she couldn't eat another bite, the girls grabbed her hands and dragged her out the door. Macie followed them to where they helped Jessie sit on a bench at the edge of the garden. The bench had a great view of the entire yard and the pond beyond a large willow tree.

Macie sat next to Jessie as the girls ran to the big swing hanging from the willow.

"So, does Daniel come home for lunch?" Macie didn't think he ate at the house.

"Yes. He'll make sure I eat then."

Macie's face flamed. Jessie saw right through her, but her shakes had Macie worried, and she desperately wanted to help Daniel in some way.

Jessie patted Macie's leg. "I appreciate you caring so much. I've struggled a lot since my husband died." She took a deep breath. "Daniel does his best to hide his worries, but I know something is going on. He is worried about his job. I know he thinks he has to take care of me, and feels that keeping this job is the best to keep him close to home."

She sighed and watched the girls. Macie waited patiently, hoping Jessie would continue to share her thoughts.

"And he is right. I do need him." She nodded toward the girls. "Those girls bring so much life back to me. The rest of the time, I go through the motions. It's been at least two months since I saw them before you brought them the other day. And before that was three months."

"Did they visit a lot before then?"

"Not a lot, but Emma would have me babysit regularly until they could get the first nanny. And even after the first nanny left before the second one came. I guess she doesn't really need me much with you in town." Jessie's voice broke, and she cleared her throat.

Macie knew what it felt like to not feel needed. "Well, you must have made a good impression on the girls. They love you."

Jessie sighed. "That last time she came to pick them up, the girls complained about having to leave. I think Emma took offense."

"Jessie." Macie put her hand on Jessie's shoulder, wanting to give her a hug, but didn't want to invade her personal space too much. "I don't think she can blame you for that. Mrs. Bailey hasn't spent any time with the girls since I came." Macie felt judgmental for talking about Mrs. Bailey like that, even if it was true. "I understand moms can't always give undivided attention..." Macie's voice cracked.

Macie's thoughts went back to her own home, where she felt her mom gave attention to the older kids and her younger siblings, but she was usually brushed aside. Macie's mom's words echoed through Macie's brain. *"I'm glad you know how to stay quiet and are not so needy."* She always wanted to become more needy so her mom would pay attention to her, but Macie's need to please overrode everything else.

Jessie's thumb against Macie's cheek startled her. Macie's cheeks were wet. When had she started crying?

Macie brushed her tears away. "I'm sorry."

Jessie nodded toward the girls. "I think you're the best nanny these girls could have. You know how it feels to feel forgotten."

Macie choked on a sob but couldn't contain it as her shoulders shook.

"I don't know your life, but I can promise your parents love you, and they have not forgotten you."

Jessie blurred in Macie's vision as more tears formed. She didn't want to argue with this sweet woman. "I just want to be noticed for something that is me."

"You don't think they notice your strengths?"

Macie grunted. "They know I am independent, but I have only brought embarrassment to them with my mistakes. They know not one person in our neighborhood would ask me to babysit their kids because I lost track of a kid and couldn't find him until his parents came home. My parents were embarrassed by the gossip." Macie leaned forward on her knees. "I'm sure they wish I were like my siblings."

Macie studied the grass in front of her feet, realizing she was baring her soul to someone who was almost a complete stranger. Her own parents didn't even know these deepest thoughts.

CHAPTER 27

DANIEL WATCHED THE SCENE before him, his throat tightening. The girls played under the tree, their backs to him. Macie sat next to his mother on the garden bench. They were chatting as if they were lifelong friends. He didn't want to interrupt, but he also needed to make sure his mother had eaten. He knew she would not tell Macie if she was hungry.

"Macie?" Daniel took a few long strides toward her but stopped as she glanced up at him then looked quickly to her knees. Her face was streaked with tears. His breath caught. Why was she crying? A million explanations tumbled through his mind, but none of them caught.

Macie looked at her watch. She was probably wondering why he was here. It wasn't lunchtime.

"Nate had things under control, and I thought I should come home to make sure Mom had eaten breakfast," Daniel rushed to explain.

"I ate." Jessie laid her hand on Macie's shoulder. Macie kept her gaze on the ground in front of her. "Macie and the girls made sure of it."

Macie's cheeks reddened. Why was she embarrassed that she had taken care of his mother? It was the most endearing thing to Daniel. Macie was special, and this tightened the hold she was forming on his heart.

"We've been having a nice chat while the girls played."

Macie glanced at his mother. She winked at Macie, and Daniel's heart stuttered. His mother hadn't winked in almost three years, not since his father died. Macie's willingness to tell his mother whatever it was that made her cry made his mother feel needed. He could see it in the soft compassion that reflected in his mother's eyes as she studied Macie.

Macie stood, obviously avoiding meeting his scrutiny. "We should head back home. Is it okay if we cut through your property?" Macie asked his mother.

"Of course. You're welcome to come in through the back door next time." His mother stood and grabbed Macie's arm above her elbow. "Come see me again. I enjoy the company." She met Daniel's eyes and raised her eyebrows in question. He wasn't sure what she was asking. He was sure she knew better what was bothering Macie than he did.

Macie threw her arms around his mother, and a sob escaped her lips. "Thank you so much."

His mother's shock at the gesture was apparent, but she quickly recovered and wrapped her arms around Macie. Her face positively glowed as she pulled back. "No, thank you." Then his mother smiled the first genuine smile he remembered in years. He felt a quick stab of jealousy that Macie was able to pull her out of her depressed daze but quickly squelched it. At least someone had succeeded. He felt as though a huge burden had suddenly been lifted from his shoulders.

"I'll help you get the girls over the fence," Daniel offered.

"I'm sure I can manage." Macie tried to hurry past him to call to the girls, but Daniel stopped her with a hand on her shoulder. He knew she was embarrassed he had caught her crying, but he didn't want her to think he was put off by it.

"Macie?" He paused, waiting for her to make eye contact. Hoping she wouldn't pull away. He needed her to know he appreciated what she'd done for his mother.

Macie raised her eyes but didn't meet his gaze. Daniel moved his hand from her shoulder to lift her chin with his finger. Her eyes met his. Macie's breath hitched, and Daniel hoped that meant he had the same effect on her that she did on him. He wanted to tell her he wanted to be for her what his mother had obviously been. He wanted to be the one to comfort her in times of need, but he couldn't say it. What if she didn't want to confide in him? He was afraid to confide in her. He shouldn't expect her to open up to him if he wasn't willing to open up to her.

"Let me help you," he whispered.

Macie's eyes widened for a fraction of a second, then she shrugged. "If you insist."

"I do." He smiled. Macie's lips formed a small *o*. Macie's hand shook slightly as she raised it to push a hair out of her face. If his smile had this effect on her, he'd have to make sure he did it more often.

Charlotte, Audrey, and Evelyn were searching for something under the tree. The break in eye contact as Macie turned to them dissipated the blush creeping up her neck, and Daniel was almost sorry to see it go.

"Come on, girls. Say goodbye and thank you to Jessie. It's time to head home and help make lunch."

"Bye, Jessie. Thank you," Charlotte and Audrey shouted as they ran up and hugged the older woman. Evelyn toddled behind them. Jessie took a few steps to her and wrapped her in a hug, picking her up in the process and carrying her to Macie. It was the most life his mother had shown in a long time.

Evelyn dove into Macie's arms, and she held her close. Macie blinked rapidly, and Daniel knew she was still holding back emotions. He wished she trusted him enough to share them with him, but he didn't blame her.

Audrey and Charlotte skipped along in front of Daniel and Macie, continuing whatever game they had been playing.

"Thank you for taking care of her," Daniel said. His voice was a bit gruff, and he swallowed and blinked back the threatening tears. He didn't want Macie to think his emotions were anything negative.

Macie looked up at him. "I hope I didn't overstep. She was shaking, and I was worried—"

Daniel held up a hand. "You didn't do anything wrong." He opened his mouth, tempted to say more, but closed his mouth instead, not ready to bare his soul completely.

They walked on in silence. When they got to the fence, Daniel helped both Charlotte and Audrey climb over, then he held Evelyn until Macie was on the other side, then he handed the toddler over.

"Thank you," Macie blurted, obviously needing to say something to break the silence. Daniel hadn't thought it was awkward, but he supposed Macie was still embarrassed.

Daniel didn't want what he felt was an intimate moment to end. He had a strong desire to see her again.

"Come to the corrals tomorrow afternoon," he called out to her. "I'll teach you to ride."

Macie tipped her head in acknowledgment, but her eyes moistened. He wondered if he had misread her excitement about the horses when he picked her up from the airport, but Macie hurried to catch up to Charlotte and Audrey before he could ask if she wanted to learn. He hadn't told her a time, so he figured he'd better hang out near the barn after lunch the next day.

CHAPTER 28

THE NEXT MORNING, MACIE couldn't get Daniel out of her mind. She couldn't understand what was happening. No boy had ever paid attention to her. With Daniel, she felt like he was really seeing her, not through her.

After Macie put Evelyn down for a nap, Macie was about to suggest they go ride, when Audrey piped up.

"Can we play hide-and-seek?"

"Don't you want to go horseback-riding?" Macie said softly, glancing down the hall to make sure Mrs. Bailey hadn't wandered out of her room.

Charlotte nodded enthusiastically.

"But you said we could play hide-and-seek sometime," Audrey complained. "If we go riding now, Evelyn will miss it. She likes the horses."

Macie cringed at her loud voice. She put up her hands to placate her. "Okay, okay."

Then, before she could set some parameters for the game, they ran off.

"Don't peek!" Audrey called over her shoulder as they raced downstairs.

At least that would narrow the possibilities of hiding places. She would stay here for a few seconds and then follow after them.

She didn't even make it ten seconds. Her anxiety rose immediately, her chest tightening so much she couldn't take a breath. She nearly tripped running down the servant's staircase, hoping they wouldn't sneak back up the stairs. She forced herself to appear to be having fun, pulling open doors and looking in cupboards.

Macie ran to each room as she searched the house, being careful to keep quiet as she returned to the second floor to be sure the girls hadn't backtracked. They wouldn't have gone outside, would they? Why hadn't she called them back to give them the rules? She couldn't blame them for their excitement, but her heart thumped hard in her chest, and she couldn't breathe properly. She felt near hyperventilating.

Her heart raced, and sweat made her palms clammy. She didn't want Gladys to see her panicked, so she forced a smile on her lips as she went through the kitchen, but Gladys wasn't there. Macie checked the garage and mudroom, then stood outside the garage door leading to the backyard. Pausing to listen, Macie couldn't hear anything but the pounding of her heart.

Her legs moved her into a sprint, and she tore through the orchard, thinking the girls might hide in the trees. They were nowhere to be seen.

No, no, no! She'd lost them. She shouldn't have let them talk her into playing this dumb game. Mrs. Bailey was sure to find out.

She sprinted across the back of the house to see if they'd hidden around Gladys's car, then peeked around the corner to the front yard. Still no sign of them.

Memories flooded her brain, making it hard to concentrate on the present. She felt fifteen again, shouting Sammy's name over and over, but he wouldn't make a peep. Guilt had nearly consumed her. Hide-and-seek had been her way to get a break from his incessant chatter and demands to play the same game over and over. She bet she could find him, but after she counted, she took her time. Then she realized that he really was good at hiding.

His parents had found her calling his name and thought he had run away from her. She tried to explain they were playing hide-and-seek, but they must have sensed her panic because she didn't think they believed her. In fact, they told her mom she'd lied to cover up her irresponsibility.

Irresponsible. She hated that word.

Macie blinked back tears as she sprinted for the barn. It was the only place she hadn't looked. Maybe Daniel had seen them.

Her vision blurred as she approached the barn, and tears finally spilled onto her cheeks. Her breath was coming in ragged gasps. Her chest felt tight. Then she thought of the horse thief, and her legs nearly gave way before she found the strength to keep running. *Please, don't let the thief be here today.* What would the thief do to the little girls? Kidnap them? She ran past the opening in the middle of the barn, but movement in there stopped her short. Her shoes slid on the gravel, and she fell back on her bottom.

***

Daniel nearly jumped when Macie passed the barn's front opening as he made his way to where the girls were hiding to check on them. He had expected her to show up but hadn't expected to see her running if she were playing hide-and-seek. He wouldn't ruin the game by telling Macie where the girls were, though. A thump sounded outside the door, and he hurried to the door to see what happened.

Macie was on the ground, her knees pulled up to her chest.

Daniel rushed to her side.

"Macie. Are you okay?"

She turned her tear-soaked face toward him.

"I've lost them," she whispered. "I never should have agreed to play this stupid game. I can't find them. Mrs. Bailey will find out and send me packing." She put her head against her knees. "Why don't I ever learn?"

Why was she so worked up about not finding them? She hadn't even searched the barns yet. True, the girls weren't supposed to be in them in the first place, but he had made sure they were safe while he saddled the horse he planned to let them ride. He had left the area momentarily to check on the pregnant mare they were housing.

He gripped Macie's shoulders. "Charlotte and Audrey are fine. They hid in the barn. I made sure they were safe." He tugged slightly, coaxing her to stand.

She covered her face with her hands and turned into him, sobbing. Not wanting Mrs. Bailey to look out the window and see the scene, he led Macie into the barn before he wrapped his arms around her. He still had no idea why she was being so emotional, but he had a feeling some sort of insecurity had risen inside her. Warmth spread through his body as he held her close, breathing in the scent of her shampoo, which was a pleasant contrast to the manure in the barn. She was turning to him for comfort. It was exactly what he had wished for the day before. Even if she wasn't baring her soul, she was letting him comfort her. Her hands covering her face created a barrier between them he did not like.

He stepped back and lightly gripped her arms, then rubbed his hands up and down. She calmed down some, but her hands remained on her face.

He leaned forward and whispered, "They are still waiting for you to find them."

Macie's hands slowly dropped, and she raised her large brown eyes to meet his. He took her face in his hands. He had a sudden desire to kiss her, but he resisted and wiped the remaining tears off her cheeks.

Her eyes widened, then she glanced around the barn before returning her gaze to him. He nodded to let her know they were in the barn, then dropped his hands before he gave in to the desire to kiss her senseless. He went to Gypsy's stall to get her ready for the ride and nodded toward the storage room.

Macie's breaths still came in gasps, like she was trying to fight off a panic attack, but she found Audrey in the tack room. He gave her strict instructions to sit on the floor until Macie came. Charlotte's hiding place was a little harder. Macie wouldn't know the box underneath the pile of blankets had a lid.

After a few more minutes of searching, Macie's eyes filled with panic, and tears made her brown eyes glisten. Charlotte shifted. He put a finger to his mouth and another finger to his ears. Macie stopped and listened, closing her eyes. He wasn't sure if she was really listening or calming herself down. Charlotte shifted again. Macie's eyes popped open, and her attention went to the area where the box was. She looked questioningly at Daniel, and he took pity on her and made the shape of a box with his hands when Audrey was busy pulling on Macie's arm, but Macie had a tight grip on her hand.

Her relief was evident, and she pulled the blankets off the box and lifted the lid. Charlotte smiled up at her. Macie gathered them into her arms.

"You girls are good hiders." Macie's voice shook, and Charlotte looked at her curiously.

"Are you ready for your ride?" Daniel asked, not wanting Macie to have to explain her anxiety, even if he was more than a little curious.

Macie cocked her head at him before understanding dawned. "Oh, I completely forgot." She led the girls out of the barn. "Let me go get Evelyn and we'll be right back."

Daniel smiled as she walked away with the girls, then frowned.

CHAPTER 29

MACIE TOOK DEEP BREATHS as she made her way to the house with the girls. She was mortified Daniel had witnessed her panic attack, but her arms still tingled where he had rubbed them. Every part of her was aware of his touches, and she took great comfort in the compassion he showed without even knowing the reason for her meltdown.

She got Evelyn out of her crib and took the girls down the servant's staircase. She didn't want to risk seeing Mrs. Bailey and having the girls tell her where they were going. Mrs. Bailey didn't want the girls riding. But Daniel hadn't said anything about the girls riding, so she figured it would be okay for them to watch her.

Macie and the girls made their way out to the barn. They found Daniel in the corral next to the barn, a horse already saddled. The horse had a beautiful long mane and tail with black and brown patches on white.

"It's beautiful," Charlotte breathed. "What kind of horse is it?"

"He's a Gypsy Vanner. I thought you might like riding him." He smiled at Charlotte. "His name is Gypsy."

"Gypsy is a girl's name, not a boy's name," Audrey pointed out.

Daniel shrugged. "Your grandfather named him."

"That isn't one you are training, is it?" Macie asked, suddenly wary.

He laughed. "I'm not that mean. No, Thomas bought this guy seven years ago. My dad trained him. He's a gentle beast." He pulled the horse closer to them. "Pet him."

Macie clung to Audrey's hands, telling herself she wanted to make sure they were safe as they made their way forward. Charlotte and Audrey patted the horse's front shoulder, and Macie went to the head and rubbed his nose and let Evelyn pet him as well.

"Do you girls want to go for a little ride?" Daniel asked.

They both turned to Macie in unison. "Can we?"

"Well..." she hedged.

Would Mrs. Bailey know? Maybe.

Would Macie get fired for it? Probably.

She could feign ignorance, like she'd forgotten Mrs. Bailey had said anything, but that would be lying. Macie couldn't do that. She came out thinking she would be riding and they would be watching.

Daniel grasped her elbow lightly. "They'll be fine. I'll take them in a circle around the training corral."

He had obviously misread her reluctance, but Macie stared at his hand cradling her elbow. She couldn't get her brain to think anymore. "I guess."

Macie grabbed Audrey's hand and led her to the gate out of the corral. Charlotte stayed with Daniel to be the first rider.

She eyed Macie for a moment before calling. "It'll be okay, Macie. Mom doesn't pay attention to what we do, anyway."

That comment shot a sharp pain across Macie's chest. She couldn't leave these girls. They needed someone who paid attention to them. And if she was being truthful, Macie needed them.

"Ready, Charlotte?" Daniel held his hands out to her.

Charlotte jumped into his arms, and Daniel swung her into the saddle. "Hang on to his mane." He pointed to the hair that stuck out at the front of the saddle. Charlotte leaned forward and grasped it. The saddle didn't look like the ones Macie had seen in movies. There was nothing at the front to hold onto. Macie feared she would not be able to stay on the horse without that piece of saddle to hang on to, but told herself she would be fine if Daniel led the horse around. The horse started walking, and Macie felt her heart lurch when Charlotte leaned farther back than Macie expected.

After a couple of times around the corral, Macie's stomach unclenched. Charlotte would be okay. Charlotte talked nonstop while Daniel listened, replying once in a while. Then he stopped and looked at Macie. He said something, but she couldn't hear what. Charlotte replied, and Daniel's gaze found Macie's again. Macie averted her eyes, embarrassed that she was trying to eavesdrop, but the curiosity burning inside of her would not go away.

When it was Audrey's turn to ride, Macie asked Charlotte, "What were you and Daniel talking about?"

"Oh, lots of things." She put her hands up to show how many topics they covered in her short ride. "We talked about Aunt Jessie and how nice you are and how I wish you would stay forever. How I'm afraid Mum will send you away soon, and I asked if he was going to marry you and if he did marry you if I could live with you instead of Mum."

Macie gasped. Charlotte had actually asked Daniel if he was going to marry Macie?

"What did Daniel say?" Macie pressed.

"Well, he said Mum probably wouldn't want me to live with you instead of her, but I told him Mum didn't care where I lived as long as I was safe and out of her way."

Macie's throat clenched, but she forced words past the tightness. "I mean, if he was going to marry me." The words sounded breathy, and Charlotte looked at Macie with her head cocked and an eyebrow raised.

"Why wouldn't he want to marry you?" she asked.

Macie shrugged. Did eight-year-olds always ask such personal questions?

"He said he wasn't sure you would want to marry him. I told him I was sure. You're always watching him when you think no one knows."

Macie's cheeks were on fire. She put her hands over them, hoping that would hide her embarrassment from Charlotte and Daniel. She needed to stop. She didn't need any more eight-year-old information on the topic.

Daniel walked up with the horse, Audrey still on its back.

Evelyn clapped. "Me. Me."

Daniel smiled. "I wouldn't dare forget your turn, Evelyn."

He helped Audrey off and climbed on the horse, then gestured for Evelyn. "Hand her to me."

Macie looked up at him. The horse wasn't tall, but Daniel still seemed so high. Would Evelyn be okay?

"She'll be fine," Daniel said. "I promise."

Macie lifted Evelyn, and Daniel took her and set her in front of him. He let Evelyn hold one of the reins while he held the other. Macie had no idea how he steered the horse with only one rein. After a couple of times around the corral, he stopped, and Macie helped her down.

Daniel tied the horse and then turned to Macie. "Your turn."

"I... uh. Are you sure?" Macie glanced at Charlotte, Audrey, and Evelyn. They would be a good excuse not to get on the horse. She had to keep an eye on them. She had wanted this in the first place, but now she wasn't so sure.

"They'll be safe with me," he said. He reached out his hand.

Macie stared at it for a moment. She did want to ride the horse. She had always been fascinated with horses, even though she never had the opportunity to ride, but the fear coursing through her veins nearly paralyzed her.

"You'll be safe." Daniel thrust his hand a fraction closer to Macie.

She looked at Charlotte and Audrey.

"Go on, Macie," Audrey said. "We did it."

That did it. Macie couldn't let the girls outdo her. She gave Evelyn to Charlotte and climbed into the corral. She put her foot in the foothold as Daniel directed, calling it a stirrup. When she was settled in the saddle, he handed her the reins.

"You're not going to lead me around?"

He coughed, but it sounded more like a laugh to Macie, then shook his head. "Hold one rein in each hand. Pull on this one"—he grabbed her left arm—"To turn left and that one"—he pointed to the rein in her right hand—"to turn right."

Macie scrunched her forehead. "That's not the way they do it in the movies."

"That's because in the United States they hold the reins in one hand."

"Why can't I do that?"

He let out another breath that sounded like a laugh. "This horse was trained to follow the lead this way. He'll cooperate better if you hold the reins like I told you."

"But then I can't hold on to his mane." Macie pointed out, wishing again that this saddle had the horn thing in front.

"You're right. But you'll be fine. Give him a little nudge with your heels and he'll walk."

Macie didn't believe him, and her face probably showed it, but he winked and untied the horse. Macie took a deep breath and pulled with her right arm. The horse's head turned, but the horse didn't move.

"Put your heels into his side."

Macie kicked her heels as she'd seen cowboys do in western movies. The horse lurched, and her legs flew up into the air. Luckily, she grabbed the front of the saddle and a handful of hair before she toppled over the back of the horse. Somehow the reins stayed wrapped around her fingers. The horse took a few more steps and then stopped suddenly. She lurched forward, and her nose hit his mane.

Macie turned an accusing glare at Daniel. Charlotte and Audrey howled with laughter. Macie thought it was a good thing Daniel was now holding Evelyn.

He grinned, leaning against the fence. "Don't kick him. Just press your heels into his side."

Macie nodded but kept her hands firmly on the saddle and mane. She pressed her heels into the beast below her. He started walking. Macie's hips swayed back and forth, and her knuckles were white as she gripped the saddle leather and mane in front of her. She got to where the corral fence turned slightly to the right. The horse walked to the fence, and Macie lifted her leg to keep it from getting squished.

The horse stopped, and Macie swiveled in the saddle to glare at Daniel.

He was smiling, and both Audrey and Charlotte were laughing hysterically.

"You need to be the boss. Tell him where you want to go using the reins. You need to let go of the saddle."

"I might fall off."

He nodded. "You might."

"That's not very reassuring," Macie growled, even though she was sure Daniel didn't hear her.

Macie pushed off the fence with her foot, and the horse sidestepped. Macie gasped and squeezed her legs to keep her on the horse as she let go of the saddle and held the reins the way Daniel had shown her. The horse moved forward, and Macie pulled on the reins to turn the horse right, but he turned almost all the way around.

"You don't need to pull that hard," Daniel called.

Macie gritted her teeth and pulled left. The horse didn't turn as much. Her first lap around the corral was more of a zigzag. When she got to Daniel, he waved her on. "Keep going. You need some practice."

"Thanks," Macie said sarcastically.

She tried to forget Daniel and the girls were watching her, and, after the third pass, she was starting to get the hang of it.

"You can go faster if you want," Daniel suggested after the eighth pass.

"No, thank you," she said. "I'm good."

A few rounds after the fifteenth round, Macie relaxed into the soothing rhythm of the horse.

"It's probably time to head inside," Daniel called out.

Macie sighed but knew he was right. She steered the horse to him and waited for him to come take the reins.

He hooked the reins around his thumb and then reached up. Macie placed her hands on his shoulders and slid off while he supported her weight. Her legs nearly buckled when her feet hit the ground. Daniel hooked his arm around her waist to catch her.

"Sore?" Daniel asked with a twinkle in his eyes that told Macie he knew the answer already.

Macie opened her mouth to give him a piece of her mind, but it went blank when he pulled her closer to him, his face a breath away from hers.

"That's normal. Don't worry." His voice was low and husky, making Macie want to melt into his arms.

The hardness of his chest next to Macie's and his arm strong around her waist had her heart hammering in her chest.

He leaned toward Macie slightly, then stopped and shook his head as he let her go and stepped back. "You can come back and practice another day."

Macie nodded. She didn't know why she felt as if she had been deflated. She ached to reach for him again but forced her hands to stay at her side. She had no reason to feel so secure in Daniel's arms or so exposed now that he let her go.

CHAPTER 30

CALLUM STARED AT CLAY. He had come to Vin's house to talk to Vin. Why was Clay here?

"He's getting what belongs to him." Clay smirked. "Or will. He wouldn't have told you what he was doing. He doesn't trust you, you know." Clay climbed into his truck.

Callum figured as much, but having it pointed out by the smug kid standing in front of him hurt more than he liked to admit. He was family after all. He had stuck by Vin's side from the time they were small boys. Vin had been his idol and always seemed to know exactly what to do. Until Vin convinced, well blackmailed, Callum into setting up Thomas Martin's accident.

Callum knew Clay wouldn't tell him exactly where Vin had gone. Callum didn't know how many other things Vin was stealing, but he figured he better get to the Bailey Estate to see if he was there causing trouble. He wasn't going to stand by anymore and let Vin use him. If Vin gave the police all the details about his involvement in Thomas Martin's death, Callum would do all he could to see Vin join him in prison.

If he could convince Vin to let it go without getting him too angry, that would be best. Then, neither of them would have to go to prison.

Callum spun on his heel without another word to Clay, who was still staring at him with that irritating smirk, and jumped in his truck. He would have to play this cool. Vin would use the old road that wound into the back of the Bailey's property. Callum had told him about it and knew Vin had used it with his earlier visit.

Sure enough, when he pulled down the dirt road, he saw his cousin's truck blocking the road, with a trailer attached. Callum parked behind him, climbed over the fence, and made his way to the barn. He didn't know what kind of head start Vin had on him, but was grateful to see his cousin crouching behind the corral fence. He didn't even turn to look behind him before he sprang over the fence toward the barn. Callum ran after him.

***

Macie stood at the counter, chopping potatoes for Gladys. Gladys tired easily, and Macie and the girls had made it a habit of helping her as much as they could. Charlotte was peeling carrots, and Audrey was folding napkins. Evelyn clung to Macie's leg but chattered away and wasn't fussy, so Macie did what she could.

"Once you are done with the potatoes, we'll get them in the roaster with the meat." Gladys put a hand on Charlotte's shoulder. "Are you almost done with those carrots?"

Charlotte bobbed her head.

The door to the backyard slammed open. Macie jumped, and Evelyn started crying. Macie scooped her up and comforted her, murmuring nonsense with her eyes fixed on Nate, who was standing in the open door, his chest heaving.

He waved wildly toward the barn, and Macie's heart seized. Was Daniel hurt? She clutched Evelyn closer to her. Gladys stalked to her son and put both hands on his shoulders.

"What is it?" Gladys shook him slightly, as if trying to get the words to come out of him.

Nate took a deep breath. "There are two men arguing near the barn."

Gladys wiped her hands as she searched for the men out the window. "Oh, my." Fear flashed in her eyes.

"Did they see you?" she asked Nate.

Nate nodded, his eyes widening. "The one with the black hat charged after me, but the other man stopped him."

Nate was visibly shaking, so Gladys led him to a chair.

"Should I go get Mr. Bailey?" Macie asked, grateful it was the weekend, and he was home.

Gladys nodded, glancing out the door again before firmly shutting and locking it. Macie handed Evelyn to Gladys and ran to the study.

Mr. Bailey wasn't in there, so she sprinted to his room, hoping Mrs. Bailey wouldn't stall her too long.

She banged on the door in her haste and winced as the sound reverberated down the hall.

"What?" came Mrs. Bailey's voice. Macie could tell she had startled her, but didn't have time to worry about it too much. She opened the door.

"Is Mr. Bailey here?"

"No," Mrs. Bailey said. "Why?"

"Some men are here arguing near the barns."

"Then go get Daniel. He's in charge out there, not Mr. Bailey."

Macie didn't take the time to argue about who was in charge of what. Nate wouldn't have come to the house if Daniel had been available. Was he hurt? No, Nate would have mentioned it, surely. Maybe he had been called away to do some vet work.

Without another word to Mrs. Bailey, Macie shut the door and sprinted to the kitchen.

***

Daniel approached Joseph Roberts' house with long strides. He didn't know what the problem was, but couldn't shake that something was wrong, besides a sick horse.

"What is it?" Daniel extended his hand and shook Joseph's as the man ran out of the house to meet him.

"My hired help says the colt I bought last week is sick. He's sweating and pacing."

"You saw it, too?"

Joseph shook his head. "No. I called you right away."

Unease punched Daniel in the gut. Something wasn't right, but he wouldn't know for sure unless he checked the horse.

Joseph Roberts was wringing his hands as he led Daniel down the front stairs. Daniel knew he had recently bought some colts and horses to train and then breed, but he was new to the business. His panic had been evident over the phone.

He wished he had brought his own truck, but he hadn't wanted to waste the time running home so had brought the Bailey's truck.

As he followed Joseph around the house, his mind raced through every possible problem that would cause him to feel that something was off. Maybe the horse thief was at it again, now that he was away. Nate was on high alert, though, so even if the thief tried, he would be caught. Daniel was sure of it.

When they got to the barn, he stopped short at the familiar face. Clay. Daniel gritted his teeth and fished his phone out of his pocket. He dialed Mr. Bailey's number. No answer. He tried Macie's number with the same result.

"Where is the horse?" Daniel asked Joseph.

"Clay!" Joseph called. "Which horse is sick?"

"Clarabel."

Joseph stalked to the barn and showed Daniel inside, pointing to a sleek bay. Daniel's first guess was a thoroughbred, but he thought it might be a thoroughbred-Arab cross.

Daniel talked softly as he approached the horse and started checking her. Clay left the barn while Joseph paced.

"She seems fine," Daniel said after he did a cursory exam. In fact, with Clay involved, he was sure this was another ruse to get him away from the estate.

"Are you sure?" Joseph asked. "Clay said it was an emergency. I can't lose this colt."

"I'm sure." Daniel tried to keep his tone polite, but he was out of patience, and his sense that something was very wrong pulled at him, urging him to return to the Baileys.

Daniel peeked out of the barn. Clay was leaning over the company truck, the bonnet up.

Daniel's anger flared inside of him, but instead of yelling, he walked silently up to Clay. The gravel crunched under his boots before Daniel reached the truck. Clay swung around, and Daniel grabbed his shirt with both hands and threw him to the ground.

"What do you think you're doing?"

Clay glared at Daniel but backed away from him. Clay may have been arrogant, but he was outmatched physically.

"What's going on?" Joseph's voice came from behind him.

"Clay was tampering with my truck." Daniel gestured to the open bonnet.

Joseph's flitted from the truck to Clay on the ground and then to Daniel.

"I need to go." Daniel tried to start the truck before he closed the bonnet. It started right up, so he must have caught Clay before he could do any damage.

Daniel shut the bonnet and pointed at Clay. "As long as he is working here, I will not make house calls. You will have to bring your horses to me."

Joseph Roberts looked bewildered. Daniel didn't care what Joseph thought about him, didn't care if he thought he was being petty, but he was sure Clay was helping the horse thief and would not go to any farm where he was employed.

Daniel climbed in his truck and pushed the accelerator to the floor after he backed out of the drive. The truck spun out for a moment on the gravel before it caught traction and he flew down the road.

His phone rang. It was Nate. Not a good sign.

***

Macie marched through the kitchen and unlocked the door. "I'll go see what this is all about." She checked her pocket, but her phone wasn't there. She must have left it in the nursery. It was the place she set it since the phone didn't fit into her pants pocket. There was no time to go fetch it now. A suspicion that maybe one of the men was the thief lodged into her thoughts, and she didn't want him to get another horse without seeing who it was.

"I'll go with you," Nate said from behind her.

Macie took in his appearance. He seemed mostly recovered, and a steely determination had entered his brown eyes. Macie flung the door open and raced outside with Nate right behind her.

Macie spotted the men as soon as she stepped through the kitchen door. They were near the side of the barn closest to the corrals. She slowed her steps to a determined walk. It would not do to let her panic show.

"Can I help you, gentlemen?" Macie called when she could see them clearly. Both men were tall. Macie tried to think back to the day she saw the guy with Shadow. She couldn't remember anything but the tattoo. But he had been tall.

Both men stared at her, so she continued.

"I'm Macie Call. Do Mr. or Mrs. Bailey know you are here?"

Neither man said anything, but they glared at each other.

The blond guy turned to the dark-haired guy. "You need to leave."

That voice. It had been this guy who had been talking to Mr. Bailey in his study when the last horse was stolen. Callum Davies.

The guy with dark hair turned to Macie. The tattoo was clearly visible. Macie gasped. Her tongue felt like lead, making it difficult to talk.

"Macie," Nate asked. "Are you okay?"

Macie coughed, hoping it sounded real. Blackness enclosed around her, creating tunnel vision, and she couldn't think. She had expected this. She needed to get in control. Callum asked the tattoo guy to leave. Were they working against each other, competing to steal the horses?

Tattoo Man clapped Callum on the back. "Come on, cousin! There's got to be a way to work this out where we all win."

Macie's head was spinning. Callum was a cousin of the horse thief? She knew Tattoo Man by sight but still didn't know his name. Macie tried to study his face, searching for anything that would help her identify him later. Gray eyes. Sharp nose. No facial hair.

Nate was still staring at Macie while his hand flitted as if he wanted to touch Macie to be sure she was okay, but wasn't sure if he should. She met his gaze and flicked her head toward Daniel's place, even though she couldn't see the house. Nate's eyebrows scrunched together in confusion.

Tattoo Man glared at Macie, then led Callum into the barn.

"Daniel," Macie whispered. "Do you have his number? I don't have my phone with me."

Nate's eyes went wide. He nodded and sprinted for the house, pulling out his phone as he went. Macie followed the men to the door of the barn and listened.

"You've ruined it for today," Tattoo Man said. Macie stepped into the barn, and Tattoo Man glared at her. "You again. Don't you know how to mind your own business?"

Macie glared back at him. "This estate is part of my business since it employs me."

Tattoo Man smirked. "You've got spunk for such a little girl." He took a step toward Macie. She stumbled back a couple of steps, and Callum grabbed Tattoo Man's shoulder.

"Leave her alone."

Tattoo Man swung his fist around, but Callum ducked easily.

"You will pay for this. I could have been out of here if you hadn't intervened," Tattoo Man said.

"In broad daylight?" Callum sounded incredulous.

Tattoo Man rolled his eyes.

Macie turned to run.

Tattoo Man moved so fast Macie didn't know what was happening until his arm wrapped around her, pinning her arms to her sides.

"I said leave her alone."

Macie felt more than saw Callum's body as it slammed against her and Tattoo Man and wrenched her free.

Tattoo Man's eyes were full of hatred. Macie scrambled to her feet and backed up a few steps.

"You will regret this, cousin," Tattoo Man spat, then stalked out of the barn and hurried away.

Macie ran to see which way he went, determined to give the police as much information as possible.

Callum grabbed her arm. Macie tried to wrench it free, but his grip didn't loosen.

"Let me go!" she shrieked. "I need to see which way he is going."

The meeting Callum had with Mr. Bailey sprang to mind. The horse was stolen not thirty minutes after he was there.

"Where did you take the horse?"

Callum's eyebrows shot up. "*I* haven't stolen anything."

"But you were meeting with Mr. Bailey. A half an hour later, a horse was stolen. How could it not have been you?"

Callum let go of her arm and cursed. He stalked out the door. Macie followed him, doing her best to catch up. He was not going to leave without giving her some answers.

"Tell me his name."

Callum continued walking toward the middle of the barn, not looking back.

Macie held back a scream of frustration. Callum had information, and she wanted answers, but Callum was a lot bigger than she was. There was no way she could force him to talk.

Callum turned out the center opening in the barn. It dawned on Macie that he had turned toward the pastures. Where had he come from?

"Callum, you have to help us." Macie ran to catch up to him, desperate to get him to talk.

He swiveled around to face her, his eyebrows high. "No, I don't."

Macie stopped. He took three big steps to the fence that led to the pastures behind the barn. He swung himself over the fence and then, turned halfway back so she could see his profile.

"I would suggest asking Mr. Bailey about Thomas Martin's will," he said, then ran through the pasture.

Macie nearly sat in the gravel next to the gate to the pasture. Instead, she staggered to the barn wall and fell against it. What did Callum know about Thomas Martin's will? And what did it have to do with stealing horses?

Daniel needed to hurry back soon. She had to talk to him. Callum had worked on the estate before, so Daniel knew him. Daniel might have an idea why Callum mentioned Thomas's will, but she hoped Daniel would have some knowledge of it.

Macie backed into the barn, and Nate almost ran into her. Macie sidestepped just in time. He slid to a halt and stared at her, relief on his face. His chest heaved.

"Oh, Macie. I'm so glad you're all right. When I couldn't see you or those men, I thought maybe they had taken you."

"I'm fine, Nate. Did you call Daniel?"

"Yes. He should be here soon."

"Let me know the minute he arrives. I've got to go help with dinner."

"Okay."

Macie jogged to the house to see the girls happily helping Gladys in the kitchen.

***

Callum drove straight to his cousin's estate after he left the Baileys. He wanted to know why his cousin had made it look like he was the one stealing the horses. Vin was furious with him, but he wouldn't kill him for spoiling his plan.

Callum found his cousin in the back with Clay.

"You have nerve showing up here after what you pulled," Vin growled.

"You have nerve going there in broad daylight." Callum's temper flared, and he took a breath to calm himself. It wouldn't do to push Vin. Vin could use the information he knew to keep Callum doing what he wanted or send him to jail.

Callum took another breath. "That isn't why I came over."

"I hope it's to apologize."

Callum glared. "No. The nanny said you took the last horse not long after I was there. Was that a coincidence, or did you plan to set me up for the thefts?"

Vin pretended surprise, but Callum wasn't fooled. "Was that the same time you were there?"

"Don't play games with me. I told you I was going over there."

Vin shrugged. "Well, make up your mind. Do you want me to go at night or during the day?"

Callum curled his fingers into fists and relaxed them, fighting for calm. Vin grinned. He had the upper hand, and he knew it.

"Choose a night you know I won't be there," Callum said through clenched teeth.

"I might think about it if you don't interrupt me again. You pull a stunt like that again, I'll give the detective all the evidence you killed Thomas Martin so you could get the inheritance."

Callum glanced at Clay. Vin grinned. "Clay's on my side. He won't say anything against me."

CHAPTER 31

MACIE HAD JUST FINISHED drying the dishes used to make dinner when Nate found her. "Daniel's back."

Macie gathered Evelyn in her arms. "Do you girls want to come with me?"

Charlotte nodded vigorously, her braids flopping over her shoulders.

Daniel came out of the barn as they exited the house, Nate following them. He jogged up to them. "Nate will you show the girls the new mare." He kneeled down in front of the girls. "She should be having a baby soon."

"Me too?" Evelyn asked, reaching for Nate.

Nate held out his hands, and Evelyn went to him. He took them into the barn and turned right.

Daniel grabbed Macie's hand, and her whole arm tingled from his touch. He led her into the barn, turning away from the girls.

"No horses are missing. What happened?" Daniel didn't let go of her hand. Macie wondered if he realized he was still holding it.

Macie told him everything.

Daniel didn't say anything for a moment. He studied her as if he were going to find answers somewhere on her face. She didn't have any answers. Callum stopped Tattoo Man from stealing a horse again, but Callum also wanted to buy the estate. She guessed that made sense if the horses the Baileys owned went with the estate.

Macie endured Daniel's careful study of her face for a few more seconds before she broke eye contact. She didn't like that he seemed to be reading her mind.

"You could have been hurt or kidnapped," he said.

Macie brought her head up sharply. "I was not in any danger once Tattoo Man left." She tried to bore her eyes into his the way he did to her. "Why is Callum asking for the estate? Does he have a right to it?"

"Callum Davies just worked here. I'm not sure why he wants this estate so badly. He helped out around the estate for a couple days here and there for about six months before Thomas died. He's been after the Baileys to sell since the funeral."

"He was here asking to buy the estate the night the second horse was stolen."

"But how did he know 'Tattoo Man'"—Daniel put up finger quotes and Macie blushed at his emphasis of the nickname—"was going to be here?"

"Tattoo Man..." Macie paused, heat creeping into her face, but then she shrugged. It was the best she could do since she didn't know his name. "He called Callum cousin."

"Cousin?" Daniel asked. He let go of her hand, and her skin went cold. He took off his hat and ran his hand through his hair, a gesture Macie was starting to find endearing. "Should we go visit Callum?"

"We? Why do you want me to go with you?"

"I like your company." He winked. Macie was pretty sure she would have fainted, but she was so shocked her body froze instead. Then it went warm, all the way to the top of her head.

Macie found her feet and tried to keep her voice from shaking. "I don't think he'll tell us anything. The only help he gave was to find Thomas's will. I don't know what that has to do with catching the horse thief."

Daniel gripped her arm. "Mrs. Bailey said something about her lawyer warning her I might try to take over the estate. I need to find it."

Macie nodded. The awareness of his touch rendered her speechless until she finally managed to say, "Where do you think it would be?"

"I think I know. I'll let you know what I find." Daniel's hand moved up and down Macie's arm, sending shivers through her.

They stood in silence for a minute while she tried to get her body to do anything but stand there, thinking about all the possibilities with the will. What did it have to do with the horse thief?

She made her way to the other side of the barn to collect the girls, Daniel following close behind. The sensation of his hands on her arms lingering on her skin.

***

The next day, Daniel returned to the house after feeding the horses. Sundays were the best days. Today was even better since the girls seemed to have awakened his mother, and she was actually having conversations with him. He and his mother sat for a long time after lunch and just talked, but he couldn't get his mind off what Macie had told him. Why would Callum mention Thomas's will? Did his cousin know something about the will that made him think he had a right to the horses? But Daniel didn't know anybody with a large tattoo on his chest, and Callum never introduced any of his family.

The only place Daniel could think of that Thomas would keep a copy of his will was the small safe he found hidden behind the horse breeding books. He would access the safe, if only to find out whether or not it was there. If Callum was right, that would answer most of their questions.

Daniel didn't know if he could get into the safe, but the possibility of finding answers pushed him to try. Daniel knew the safe hadn't been there for long, or he would have noticed it one of the many times he met with Thomas in that study, talking business. Dinner would be the best time. He checked the time. The Baileys served dinner at six-thirty. It was five-thirty now. If he hurried, he could eat and take care of the horses afterwards.

He hopped up.

His mother put a hand to her chest. "What's the hurry?"

"I have to get back to the estate to bring in the horses. Do you mind if I start dinner now?"

His mother smiled. "It's already in the oven."

Daniel stopped. He must have been more in his thoughts than he had thought if that were the case.

He tried to keep from pacing while his mother finished dinner, but she kept glancing at him with raised eyebrows, so he decided to shower before she asked any questions. He might as well clean up and make a good impression on Macie, if he found anything to tell her. He wasn't sure if she had ever been with him when he didn't smell of horsehide and sweat. Maybe he would see her even if he didn't find anything. He found he craved her presence more and more.

It was a quarter to seven when he slid in the side door next to the servant's stairs. He would have to bring in the horses after he searched the study. He hurried down the hall and stopped next to the door to the dining room. He could hear Macie and the girls but didn't hear Mr. or Mrs. Bailey. The study door was open, but the light was off. He entered the room and quietly shut the door before he made his way to the lamp. It was light enough outside to see his way around, but the extra light from the lamp eased his conscience a little and helped him not feel like a thief.

He went straight to the bookshelf behind the desk and removed the books, searching the wood around it for the combination. It had to be written down if Thomas installed it, but he didn't find any hidden passcodes.

Where would Thomas leave the code, assuming Thomas set it? Thomas was never one to do things in what others would call the normal way. He studied the books. Nothing was out of the ordinary there. He rifled through the drawers, hoping to find a false bottom, but no such luck.

Daniel didn't dare stay much longer. He picked up the books to re-shelve them when he noticed a small black mark on the spine of one. He opened the book and flipped through the pages, wondering if Thomas had written it on a random page. On the copyright page, he noticed five numbers underlined.

Daniel sighed. Of course. Thomas would have to remove this book to get to the safe. It would make sense in his mind to have the book contain the code. But only five numbers meant that one of the numbers was a single digit. What would Thomas do? Daniel had known the man his whole life. He didn't do anything more complicated than it had to be. If that were the case, he would do the single digit first. Daniel tried that, and the safe swung silently open. Inside, a copy of the Last Will and Testament of Thomas Martin sat on top of a stack of papers.

Daniel picked up the will. He had never seen it. He wondered if it contained any directions on how to run the business, and Mrs. Bailey was simply ignoring his requests. Daniel scanned the legal jargon as quickly as possible. Then, his name jumped off the page. Why was he in the will?

A door closed. He quickly took a picture of the page with his name on it and of the last page with the lawyer's name on it, set the will back where it had been, and shut the safe. He re-shelved the books, hoping they hadn't been in a certain order that Mrs. Bailey or Mr. Bailey would notice.

He hurried to the door, swung it open, searched the entry hall, and hurried out the front door.

He had more than an hour before he could text Macie and tell her what he found, but figured he better take care of the horses and figure out why his name was in the will. She put the girls down at 8:00. He would have to wait until at least 8:30 to text her. He took care of the horses, doing his best not to get too dirty since he still wanted to make an impression on Macie. Afterward, he went to the fence where he could wait. He searched the area around him to make sure he was alone, then pulled out his phone. He hoped the picture of the one page was enough to give him an idea of why he was mentioned in Thomas Martin's will.

He found his name and read slowly, then he read it again, unable to believe what he'd read the first time.

Thomas had given him care and ownership of all of his horses. He also dictated that Daniel was to be deeded the pastures, barns, and corrals in the event that Mrs. Bailey decided to sell the house. She had no rights to the horses or the business. Daniel was to split profits from training and breeding with the Baileys as long as they lived in the house, but from what he understood, the business was his.

He returned the phone to his pocket. Was Mrs. Bailey aware of all of this, or had she not cared? Why hadn't he been notified by the executor?

Mrs. Bailey probably *was* the executor.

CHAPTER 32

COME TO THE SERVANT'S door.

The text came from Daniel at 9:00. Macie checked the girls, grateful they were all asleep.

Macie grabbed her jacket to ward off the chill in the evening air and quietly made her way down the servant's stairs to the side entrance. Daniel stood outside the door. He grabbed her hand and led her through the orchard. He smelled of cologne, which she had never noticed before, but she liked it. It almost covered up the smell of horse on his clothes. When they reached the fence that separated his property from the Baileys, he turned and grabbed both of her shoulders and pulled her close to him. Almost involuntarily, Macie's hands came up to rest on his chest. But was it to keep him at bay or to feel his closeness?

Macie swallowed and pushed away from him so she could see his face in the fading light. "Did you find it?"

"Yeah. I opened a safe in the study."

"You just opened the safe? Wasn't it locked?"

Daniel grinned. "I figured out the combination easily enough."

Daniel pulled out his phone and gave it to her. "Read that."

Macie zoomed in closer so she could read the words. When she had finished, she stared at the phone in stunned silence.

"Do you think Mrs. Bailey was keeping you in the dark?"

"It seems like it." Daniel shoved his hand through his hair.

Macie wanted to wrap her arms around him and comfort him, but held herself back. It must be infuriating to discover he actually owned the business part of the estate and the horses, but had never been given leave to run it as he saw fit.

After a moment, he turned. "I have to meet with Thomas's lawyer."

"That might be a good idea." Macie could see a war of emotions on Daniel's face, but none stuck for long. It must be a shock to find out he was the one being robbed and not his employers.

"I just wanted to show you. I'll walk you back."

The night sky had faded to nearly black, and Macie wasn't sure she would get through the trees without running into one. He grabbed her hand. Her heart did a little flutter. The night felt extra dark as they made their way to the house, and at first she wondered if it was just her own anxiety until she realized the clouds were completely blocking the moon and stars. Daniel seemed to be able to see in the dark as he moved through the trees. Macie didn't possess this skill, and her hair caught in a tree.

"Ow." Macie tugged on Daniel's hand, urging him to stop so she could get her hair untangled.

"Sorry. Are you okay?"

Macie nodded, rubbing her head after getting her hair loose.

Daniel pulled her closer and wrapped his arms around her. Macie returned his embrace, and they stood in the dark holding each other. Macie hoped he was taking the comfort she was attempting to give.

He gave her one last squeeze before pulling away. Macie could barely see Daniel's face, but she could tell he was studying her. She marveled at his uncanny ability to make her feel seen.

"Are you ready?"

Macie tried to make her voice sound normal so Daniel wouldn't know how much their embrace had affected her. "Yeah. I'm ready."

When they got to the servant's entrance, Daniel put his arm around her waist and pulled her close. Macie was grateful for the darkness since it would hide the warmth creeping into her cheeks.

"Thanks for meeting me, Macie," Daniel murmured into her hair.

Daniel's gaze became intense. Macie's stomach flipped in anticipation. Of what, she wasn't sure. He pushed a loose hair behind her ear, and her breath caught.

His smile, which was becoming more familiar, lit his face, and he moved his hand and gave her shoulders a light squeeze. "You'd better get up to bed. You're on call."

"Yeah," Macie whispered.

Daniel opened the door for her with a whispered, "Good night" and shut the door behind her, enfolding her in complete blackness. Macie slowly made her way up the stairs as she tried to make sense of her racing heartbeat. Was he as affected by her as she was by him? Macie let herself hope so, just for a moment.

CHAPTER 33

THE NEXT MORNING, DANIEL called Nate and gave him instructions. Daniel looked at the picture he had taken of the last page of the will with the lawyer's name—Calvin Willard—and found his number. His office in the city was about an hour away, but he had to find out why he hadn't been notified about the will. He called. Luckily, the lawyer could meet with him right after lunch. He had stayed up late the night before, trying to put the pieces together, but nothing made sense. The more he thought about it, the more he was sure Callum was involved more than he let on.

***

Daniel opened the door to the law office and told the receptionist who he was. While he waited for her to relay the message to the lawyer, Daniel took in the décor of the office. Potted plants were strategically placed and magazines were stacked neatly on a table next to the chairs. But it was the pictures in the reception area that caught his attention. He didn't know what kind of pictures he expected, but he hadn't expected pictures of horses. Several of them were racehorses, but there were a few larger prints of large herds, probably from America.

"Mr. Willard will see you now."

Daniel whirled around at the sound of the receptionist's voice. He followed the woman into an office down the hall. Mr. Willard stood and offered his hand. The lawyer was casually dressed in a polo with the buttons undone. His dark brown hair was cut a little shorter than Daniel's, but it was still long enough that the ends curled slightly. Daniel shook his hand.

"Have a seat." Mr. Willard leaned over to sit, and Daniel glimpsed a tattoo on his chest. Daniel froze momentarily before making himself sit.

He tried to act casual, but his mind was racing. A lot of people had tattoos. Macie had said the tattoo looked like a snake, but Daniel hadn't seen enough to know what it was. But no matter what he told himself, he felt that he could no longer ask this man about the will. If he played it cool, he might even be able to glean some information from the lawyer and find out for sure if he was the same man who stole his horse.

"Lacy said you wanted to talk about Thomas Martin's will?" Mr. Willard prompted.

"Uh, yeah." He had forgotten he had told the receptionist why he wanted to talk. He had to ask about the will, or it would raise his suspicions.

"How did you know Mr. Martin? Are you family?"

"Umm, no," Daniel said. Then inspiration hit him. If it wasn't inspiration, this meeting would end abruptly. Either way, Daniel hoped it would confirm his suspicion. "I worked for him for years, and before he died, he had said something about leaving me something, but I was never notified..."

Daniel trailed off, not knowing where to go from there.

"Why are you coming to me about this now?" Mr. Willard sounded skeptical. "He died, what, seven months ago?"

Why now, indeed? Daniel knew he had to get out of there quickly. "A friend mentioned Thomas's will, and it reminded me of what Thomas had said."

"How would your friend know?"

Daniel shrugged. He couldn't say who had mentioned it since Macie had told him Tattoo Man had called Callum cousin.

"Everything was left to Emma Bailey," the lawyer said. "Is that all?"

"Yes, sir." Daniel stood and offered his hand.

Mr. Willard shook his hand and walked him to the door before shutting it. Daniel was still close enough that it hit the backs of his boots. Daniel made a show of fixing his coat even though he was not visible to the receptionist.

"Callum?" Mr. Willard's voice came though the door. "I had an interesting visit. A"—he paused for a moment—"Daniel Evans was here to see me."

Daniel swore softly and hurried to the door. If Daniel was right and Mr. Willard stole the horses, then he may have started a chain reaction that might not end well.

***

Callum silently cursed Daniel. Yes, he had been the one to mention the will, but he didn't think he would go to the lawyer. In fact, he hadn't expected Daniel to find the original will. Thomas was the only one who had it. He didn't even know if Vin had kept a copy of the original. But if Daniel had found the will, it made sense that Daniel would want to know why he hadn't known about his inheritance.

"You blew it, Callum. Now I have to take care of business. Expect a detective to come to your house. I hope you enjoy prison."

"You'll go down with me, Vin," Callum replied evenly. "I promise you that." Callum ended the call.

He jumped in his truck and drove to the Martin Estate. His hand gripped the steering wheel so tightly his fingers were numb by the time he pulled up to the estate. His first step would be to take Daniel to get his horses back. He may not be able to right all the wrongs he had done and knew he would go to prison, but Callum vowed that Calvin Willard would be there with him.

***

Sleep had evaded Macie for another hour after she talked to Daniel, so when she woke up, it felt like she had barely fallen asleep. Evelyn wasn't crying, but Macie could hear her chattering over the baby monitor. Macie dragged herself out of bed and dressed as quickly as possible.

The memory of Daniel holding her made her heart skip a beat. She shook her head. She couldn't let Daniel know he affected her this way until she knew what his feelings for her were.

Macie's insides were tight and her nerves taut all morning.

After Macie put Evelyn down for a nap, she headed to the stairs to find out if the girls would be willing to wander to the barn. Charlotte and Audrey were already at the bottom of the stairs with their shoes on. They had learned that Macie preferred to go outdoors during Evelyn's nap if it wasn't raining. A door creaked open before she descended. Macie jumped and grasped the handrail to keep from falling.

"Ah, Macie," Mrs. Bailey said as she came down the hall from her bedroom. "I was hoping that was you. I'm sorry, but you won't work out. You'll be going home by the end of next week."

Macie's heart dropped. Charlotte's voice rang out before she could think of a response.

"No, Mum. If Macie leaves, I want to leave, too."

Mrs. Bailey's face went white, and her face pinched up. "What have you done to my girls?"

Macie's eyes opened even wider—a feat she didn't know was possible. "Nothing."

Little footsteps echoed up the stairs as Audrey and Charlotte came to face their mom. Charlotte folded her arms. "You can't make her leave."

Mrs. Bailey sighed. "I can. I don't think she'll work for low pay forever."

Charlotte's eye's met Macie's at the same time Macie was ready to insist that she would, but Mrs. Bailey went on. "Besides, we won't be here much longer."

Charlotte gaped at her mother. "Why not?"

"We're moving back to London," she said simply.

Audrey screwed up her face like she was going to cry. "We like it here better," Audrey said, sniffing. "We want to see Aunt Jessie."

Mrs. Bailey's eyes darkened, and she looked sharply at Macie. "Have you taken them to see her again?"

Unable to lie, Macie nodded, but she stared her down. She would not be ashamed of her decision. "She needs the company."

"She needs the company?" Mrs. Bailey shrieked. "What about me?"

Macie's eyebrows shot up. Mrs. Bailey had hidden in her bedroom. How was Macie supposed to know she wanted company?

"Mum. You've been staying in your bedroom. If you wanted to talk to us, you could come say hi." Charlotte's voice was soft but held a note of defiance. Her chin stuck out slightly.

This was not going to go well, but Macie didn't know how to temper the situation. She would not back down and say they would no longer visit Jessie.

"Mum has more important things to worry about," Mrs. Bailey said. The acid was still in her voice, but she also looked apologetic.

"More important than us, Mum?" Audrey's lower lip quivered, and Macie almost cried herself. These girls were telling their mother they wanted some of her time. They were much braver than Macie.

Mrs. Bailey glanced at Audrey, then at Charlotte. Her jaw clenched, but Macie didn't know which emotion she was trying to control.

"Fine. You can still visit Jessie. But we will be moving soon." She stalked back to her room and slammed the door before either girl could respond.

Macie flinched at the sound of the door hitting the door jam and stood silently, listening to see if the sound woke Evelyn. No cries echoed across the hallway, just the sniffles next to her. Macie grabbed Audrey and Charlotte's hands and led them down the stairs. "Let's go find Daniel. We'll go see Jessie tomorrow."

"You can't leave us!" Audrey wailed when they got to the bottom of the steps.

"Hush now," Macie whispered. "If your parents decide to move and send me home, there's nothing we can do about it."

Macie was lying to the girls. She felt bad about it, but she refused to go home without knowing the reason. Mrs. Bailey was too volatile to speak rationally. Macie would talk to Mr. Bailey when he came home. But for now, they walked out the kitchen door and made their way to the barns. She almost pulled her phone out to tell Katie she had failed, but resisted. She needed to convince Mrs. Bailey to change her mind, and she wouldn't accomplish that by breaking the rules.

CHAPTER 34

MACIE AND THE GIRLS didn't find Daniel in the barn, so they went to the training corrals where they'd had their riding lesson. Daniel was riding a horse, the reins tight, and Macie could see his muscles flexing under his shirt. Her breath caught, and she reminded herself to breathe. Macie had never seen Daniel training. His face was determined, but he was at ease. It was apparent he'd been doing this for a long time.

He rode for another five minutes before he noticed them. The girls were standing on the fence so they could rest their arms on the top rail. They watched Daniel in silence. When he noticed them, he nodded in greeting. The girls beckoned him over frantically.

Daniel dismounted and led the horse into the barn. After only a few minutes, he came out of the barn and hurried over to where they stood waiting.

Audrey burst into tears. Daniel looked at Macie in alarm and then put a hand on Audrey's shoulder. "What's wrong?"

"Macie!" But that was all she could get out as sobs wracked her body.

Daniel looked at Macie and then at Charlotte before resting his gaze back on Macie.

Daniel carried Audrey into the barn and found a box and sat.

"Now, tell me what's going on."

Macie yearned to feel his arms around her. She needed his steady presence. Audrey hid her face in his shirt, so Charlotte took charge.

"Mum says we have to move back to London soon, and Macie has to leave," Charlotte wailed, standing right in front of Daniel as if she was afraid he wouldn't understand the tragedy she was a part of. Daniel put his arm around her and shushed her while patting her back. He turned his green questioning eyes to Macie, and she nodded, not sure what else to do.

"Did she say why?" he asked. Though the question was innocent enough and his voice was steady, she could see the pain as it flashed in his eyes.

Macie shook her head. "Not really. The only reason she gave was that they were moving back to London."

Daniel cocked his head to one side. "She's going to take care of the kids herself? That doesn't make sense. Why would she need a nanny here and not in London?"

Macie wanted to suggest Mrs. Bailey realized her girls needed her, but she didn't believe that.

Daniel studied her for so long she distracted herself by playing with Audrey's hair. Finally he cleared his throat. "Are you ready to go home?"

A pain Macie had never felt stabbed her chest. She couldn't explain that she felt needed here. It felt like home. Macie stared at the ground, not wanting Daniel to see the pain in her eyes.

Daniel helped Audrey stand. His finger gently lifted Macie's chin, forcing her to look at him. His eyebrows were raised in question. Macie shook her head, and tears sprang to her eyes before she could blink them away. Macie wanted to sob like Audrey, but both girls needed her to be strong.

"Come on," Daniel said, grabbing Macie's hand, then Charlotte's. Audrey grabbed Macie's free hand. "Let's go for a little walk."

They followed Daniel out of the barn but were stopped short when Gladys ran from the house. Her breathing was labored. Macie was worried the exertion would be too much for her recovery.

"Daniel. Callum Davies is here to see you," she gasped, leaning over to rest her hands on her thighs.

Daniel's face went white.

Charlotte took a sharp intake of breath. "Callum Davies? Mum says he's a very bad man who is trying to rob us."

Daniel and Macie exchanged a look. He pulled Macie close and leaned over so his mouth was right next to her ear. "Should we bring the girls with us or send them inside with Gladys?"

Macie was glad that sending her inside with the girls was not an option he was considering.

Macie made a split-second decision. She was going home anyway. She determined the girls would not see Callum as a thief. In her mind he was innocent until proven guilty, even if all the evidence pointed to him.

"Come on, girls. Let's go say hi." Macie tugged on Audrey's hand.

"I'll tell him to head back here," Gladys said. "Mrs. Bailey won't take kindly to him being in the house."

Daniel nodded his assent, and Gladys went running off. They wandered toward the front of the house, and Callum came striding around the corner. Audrey pressed her body into Macie's leg, making it difficult to walk. Charlotte did the same to Daniel.

Daniel reached his hand out, and Callum shook it.

"Well, you started a stampede?" Callum asked, his anger evident.

Macie had no idea what was going on. She glanced from Callum's resigned face to Daniel's determined one.

Callum took a deep breath. "Now he thinks I've teamed up with you." He turned as if to walk away. "So, I might as well prove him right. Get the trailer. We're getting those horses back."

"You're not the horse thief?" Audrey peeked around Macie.

Callum raised an eyebrow. "Has your mum warned you about me?"

Charlotte came out from behind Macie and stood next to her sister, shaking her head adamantly. "We heard her talking after the first horse disappeared. She said it was 'probably that thieving Callum Davies. He was always jealous of me.'"

Macie couldn't stop the smile that spread across her lips. She was impressed with Charlotte's memory.

"So, is Mr. Willard your cousin?" Daniel asked. "It explains how you knew about the will."

Callum's jaw tightened. "Yes." His fists clenched. "His goal was to have Emma sell to me, but he also made it possible for him to take over the estate if it went bankrupt."

Daniel rubbed his hand through his hair. "Which is pretty much happening with the last horse he stole The owners gave up to two weeks to find the horse before the demanded payment to replace it."

"That was the goal, I believe." Callum shrugged. "Vin stopped telling me his plans a while ago. Just told me what to do, and I was a fool and did what he said."

"You knew I was in the will?" Daniel asked.

Callum took a deep breath. "He didn't tell me the particulars. I knew he had changed it. Vin said he would call the police on me, so now is the time to act."

"Why?" Macie asked.

"Nothing you need to know," Callum growled. "But if I'm going to prison, Vin is going to go down with me. I'll take you to his place to see if we can get your horses back. Maybe that will give me some leeway with the law."

Daniel nodded. "Meet me at the road in front of my house. I'll get my truck and hook up the horse trailer. I'll call the detective."

Callum hesitated, but then nodded at Macie before backing away. "Keep an eye on things. He's gone crazy. No telling what he might do, or when he'll be back."

Daniel waved at him. "Thanks, Callum."

Callum turned and ran around the house.

"Girls, can you help Gladys with dinner?" Macie needed to get the girls out of there so she could talk more openly.

Charlotte's lip jutted out.

"Please, Charlotte. I'll be right in." Macie squatted so she was eye level with Charlotte. "I need to talk to Daniel for a moment."

Charlotte looked from Macie to Daniel. Finally, she nodded and took her sister's hand. Macie watched until they were in the house, then turned to Daniel.

"Who is Mr. Willard?" she asked.

"Calvin Willard. The lawyer in charge of Thomas Martin's will."

Macie's hand flew to her mouth.

"I went to see him, since his name is on the will, and noticed a tattoo on his chest."

"Are you going to tell Mr. Bailey?"

Daniel nodded. "I'll call him after I call the detective to have him meet us wherever the horses are."

"You're not going to tell Mrs. Bailey?"

Daniel grunted. "That woman never wants to talk to me."

"I can't imagine why not," Macie said drily. "You're so personable."

Daniel's lips twitched. "You like me."

"I do." She smiled. "What's wrong with me?"

Daniel stepped closer to her and put his hand on her waist. "Nothing's wrong with you. I think I'm a likable guy."

Macie couldn't breathe. His closeness was suffocating, but she wanted him to take her in his arms. She suddenly couldn't remember what they were talking about. All her senses focused on his nearness. Macie snorted to cover up how he was affecting her. "You would."

His eyebrows raised a fraction of an inch. "You don't agree?"

"Once you get past the rough exterior, you're pleasant enough." She was forcing the words out. Her heart was pounding in her ears, and she was afraid Daniel could hear it.

Daniel took a step closer, and Macie put her hand on his chest to keep him at bay and was gratified to feel his heart hammering under her touch. He pulled Macie close and whispered in her ear, "Do you think you'll get fired if Mrs. Bailey sees me kiss you?"

Macie's knees buckled, and she clung to his shirt to keep from falling. His hand around her waist also helped. "I already am," she reminded him, but the words didn't register the pain from before as Daniel lowered his lips to hers.

His lips were soft and warm as he softly explored her mouth. Macie wrapped her arms around his neck and deepened the kiss.

After a breathless moment, Daniel backed away slightly and smiled at her. "Don't tell my mom," he whispered. "She'll probably have a heart attack."

The severity of their situation came back to her. "What are you doing, kissing me when you should be getting your truck? Get out of here."

"I'll get the horses and call the police." Daniel gave her a quick kiss and then sprinted to the orchard with the phone up to his ear.

Macie rushed into the kitchen and found the girls with Gladys. Gladys smiled at Macie and raised her eyebrows. Had she seen the kiss? Macie's face heated, but she couldn't help the smile that tug on her lips. She took the girls into the playroom until Daisy came to get them for dinner. Macie took in the empty house as they made their way to the dining room. Had the police found Calvin? Would they come here or call when they caught him?

CHAPTER 35

DANIEL'S STOMACH TIGHTENED AS he followed Callum. He had told the detective the address when he met up with Callum at his house. Did he really trust Callum? Was he driving right into a trap? He tried not to think of it but had to be prepared for the possibility. The detective would probably be there before them, so it would be fine. Unless Callum had given him the wrong address. He pushed that thought away. He would deal with that if it happened.

He was on high alert as Callum pulled into a driveway featuring a huge mansion that rivaled the Bailey's. He parked for a moment to call the detective. He wasn't completely sure he should be trusting Callum.

"We're right behind you," Detective Clark said.

Daniel sighed and continued past the mansion and down a road until they reached a large barn not visible from the house.

Callum stepped out of his truck and motioned for Daniel. Daniel checked the area around him but saw no threats, so he stepped out.

"Let's go find your horses," Callum said.

"What are you doing here?"

Daniel and Callum both turned to see Clay stalking toward them from the barn.

"Change of plans," Callum said.

"I don't think so." Clay stepped forward. "Vin said you had turned."

Callum continued to walk forward but looked over his shoulder at Daniel. "See what I mean?"

Callum's fist moved before he even finished his sentence, hitting Clay in the jaw. Clay fell back, stunned.

Callum flipped Clay onto his belly and pulled his hands behind his back.

"Let us take it from here," Detective Clark called out.

Callum backed off. Detective Clark ordered a few men to hand cuff Clay. Callum waved Daniel forward. Detective Clark followed them.

"Be quick," Callum said. "If Vin left Clay to watch things, I'm afraid he might be heading to the Baileys."

Fear shot through Daniel, and he sprinted to the barn, glancing in each stall until he found the two horses taken from the Martin Estate penned together at the back stall. He showed them to Detective Clark, who quickly took pictures. He rushed to put lead ropes on them and jogged with them toward the trailer.

"I'll drive ahead," Callum said from his truck. "I can drive faster than you with that trailer."

"I'll follow behind after getting some of my men to check the area for more evidence of Mr. Willard's wrongdoing," Detective Clark said.

Daniel nodded. Callum jumped into his truck.

"You'd better park at your place," Callum yelled out the open window. "Who knows what Vin will do if he knows you're there."

Callum's tires spun in the dirt for a moment before they caught traction, and he sped up the dirt road to the main highway. Daniel got the horses settled in the trailer, nervousness humming through his body.

He slammed the door and dialed Nate to warn him. Another thirty minutes back to the Baileys. He only hoped Callum was wrong.

***

Daisy slipped Macie a note as Mrs. Bailey came into the dining room followed by Mr. Bailey. Macie couldn't hide her shock at seeing Mr. Bailey.

Mr. Bailey's lips formed a thin line that Macie thought was trying to be a smile. "I came home early to help with things here."

Macie nodded, unsure what to say. Everything was happening so fast. Maybe they wouldn't have to move when they had the horses. Had Daniel called Mr. Bailey as he had said? Macie didn't dare ask with Mrs. Bailey present. She had a feeling she might be angry.

Macie got Evelyn settled and quickly read the note. *Daniel called to say Calvin was not at home. I'm going to keep an eye out at the stables until he comes back, hopefully with the police. Daniel says to stay inside. You'll be safer. ~Nate*

Macie quickly folded the note and stuffed it in her pocket as she put a bib on Evelyn. Macie didn't know how to act with Mrs. Bailey present.

Macie chatted with the girls and asked them what they were excited to do for summer vacation since she couldn't think of anything else.

"I'm hoping to learn to ride," Charlotte announced.

Macie sucked in a breath and held it for a moment. Mrs. Bailey would not approve of that, and her reaction to the statement was not surprising.

Mrs. Bailey's head whipped around to stare at Charlotte. "You are never to ride those beasts."

"They aren't beasts. Daniel said he would teach me."

"That's another reason to move back to London. You girls are starting to act like country bumpkins." Mrs. Bailey turned her sharp gaze to Macie. "A good nanny would never encourage such behavior."

Macie only gave a small nod so Mrs. Bailey wouldn't think she was ignoring her, then she continued to feed Evelyn silently. Macie might as well stay in her good graces and until they moved.

"I don't want to move to London. I like it here, and I like Macie." Charlotte slammed her fork onto the table and stood.

"Sit down, young lady!" Mrs. Bailey yelled, but Charlotte stalked out of the dining room.

***

Daniel parked his truck at his mother's house. Leaving the horses in the trailer, he crept to the orchard. He stopped when movement across the lawn caught his attention. Calvin strode from the trees lining the property on the other side of the house. Where was Callum? He should be here.

Calvin slowly opened the front door and then stopped short. Someone screamed, and Calvin rushed inside, leaving the door open.

The scream sent adrenaline shooting through Daniel's veins. Macie's face filled his mind, and he had to fight to urge to barge into the house behind Calvin. He didn't want to startle Calvin into doing something drastic.

He scrambled to the corner of the house and made his way carefully along the wall. Where were the police? They should have been right behind him. He paused beside some shrubs near the door when voices drifted through the open front door. He slid behind the shrubs, being as silent as he could, hoping the conversation would cover any sounds he made.

"Calvin, please. I'll help you escape," Mrs. Bailey was sobbing.

"We had a deal, Emma. I need that money now." Calvin's voice was strained and almost manic.

"I won't have any money; the house will go bankrupt," Mrs. Bailey said. "I need to sell the horses. You said I would get a fair price for the estate if I helped you know which horses to steal, but then you stole one that was not ours."

Mrs. Bailey's voice was frantic.

"I lied and this is where it ends now that the police are after me."

Daniel forced himself not to move, even though he wanted to run inside the house and confront both Calvin and Mrs. Bailey. She could sell the house, but she had no rights to the entire estate, which included the horses, pastures, and barn. But he had no idea who had screamed. He had no idea if Calvin had someone or not.

"Please!" Mrs. Bailey shouted.

"There's no time," Calvin said. "Callum turned on me. The police are going to be here soon. You said that as soon as you could, you would sell the property. What has taken so long?"

"I told you that before you told me Callum got first choice of buying. I would rather die than see my father's property in that bloke's hands," Mrs. Bailey shouted, her fear obviously turned to anger.

"I can take care of that."

CHAPTER 36

TWO GUNSHOTS FIRED IN rapid succession. Daniel gasped, flattened himself on the ground, and covered his ears. Another scream followed. Daniel's mind raced. *Not Macie, please not Macie.* His breathing was ragged, and he didn't know what to do. Daniel had no way to protect anyone against a gun.

Calvin exited through the front door, carrying a kicking and screaming Charlotte.

Daniel almost surged forward to grab the girl from Calvin. He stopped himself as he saw the glint of the setting sun reflect off the gun in Calvin's hand. His fingers dug into the dirt as he helplessly watched Calvin carry Charlotte away. Where was Macie?

"Macie!" Charlotte screamed.

Then Charlotte's flailing feet caught Calvin between the legs, and his hold faltered enough for Charlotte to fall the the ground. She was up and running before Calvin could catch his breath. He raised his gun.

"No!" Daniel yelled.

The yell had been automatic, but it had the desired effect. Calvin swiveled to the source of the noise, but Daniel knew he was hidden. Calvin watched Charlotte crouch behind Gladys's car and strode toward Daniel.

Daniel held his breath, but his muscles were ready to fight. Calvin marched past him and around the house. Daniel let out a sigh. Calvin must have thought the shout came from the side of the house.

Daniel waited until he turned the corner of the house before sprinting to where Charlotte had hidden.

Charlotte's face was streaked with tears as she curled up in a ball. Daniel crouched in front of her.

"He shot them," Charlotte screamed.

"Shot who?" Daniel asked. "Macie?"

His stomach clenched as he said it. His eyes flicked back at the house, every part of him wanting to run through that door to save Macie if there was still a chance.

"Mum and Papa," Charlotte said.

Daniel let out his breath with a woosh. It wasn't Macie, but sadness shot through him at what Charlotte had just witnessed. What a horrible thing to see.

"Charlotte, listen to me," Daniel spoke. "You need to hide." Daniel tried to think of a place where Calvin wouldn't find her. And Daniel was sure he would come back for her. He had to protect Charlotte now, then he would go find Macie.

"I can hide where I did when we played hide-and-seek." Charlotte's voice trembled, and her body shook.

"No. He might go there." Daniel's gaze fell on the trees that lined the pasture. "Hide in those trees. Don't move until I call for you and say it is okay. Don't believe anyone else." Charlotte nodded. He watched as she ran for the trees.

Daniel called an ambulance as he made his way around the front of the house. He followed Calvin's path. If Calvin wanted to get rid of witnesses, he would want to find Macie.

***

Macie hurried toward the orchard with Evelyn and Audrey, hoping that would at least make it harder to shoot them.

Nate jogged around the barn and sprinted to meet them. "Macie. What's going on?"

"Nate! Calvin shot someone, and Charlotte is in trouble. Take Audrey and Evelyn to Jessie's house. I'll distract Calvin, so he doesn't follow."

Nate reached for Evelyn, but her grip was tight around Macie's neck.

"Nate will take you to see Aunt Jessie." Macie prayed the trick would work. She rubbed the girl's back. "You need to go, so I can help Charlotte. Aunt Jessie will keep you safe."

Evelyn whimpered, but she went to Nate. Macie watched as they disappeared over the fence, down the hill, and into some trees.

"Macie!" Charlotte's cry jolted Macie.

She crept through the orchard and got a glimpse of Calvin striding across the front of the house. She turned and sprinted toward the barn.

"Macie. I know you are out here!" The shout came from the other side of the orchard.

Macie wrenched open the barn door and shut it, before finding a box she could slide across the floor. Macie searched frantically for a place to hide. Her eyes landed on the large crate covered in blankets—the same one Charlotte successfully used to hide from her when they played hide-and-seek. Not that she had looked very hard. Macie hoped it would fool Calvin.

Macie hefted the box lid, keeping the blankets on top, and slid inside just as the door jiggled. Calvin swore, and she heard his footsteps pound around the barn. She concentrated on taking slow, silent breaths and prayed Calvin hadn't seen her hide. His footsteps echoed as he entered the barn, probably through the front opening. A small slit under the blankets gave Macie a view of the entrance, and he stood, looking around.

"I know you're in here, Macie. You're the last one who can identify me. The others are dead."

He's lying. Macie told herself. *He's listening for your reaction.* The girls couldn't lose their parents. Even if Mrs. Bailey was a cold and distant mom, no one deserved to lose a parent. Macie sucked in a breath and forced the emotion threatening to overwhelm her back. She had to keep it together, to keep Calvin looking for her and not the girls. Her chest tightened, and she struggled to calm herself. Macie took a deep, quiet breath and focused on what she knew. She had heard only two gunshots. Three people had been with him. He didn't have Charlotte with him, but that didn't mean she wasn't dead. But she had heard her yell. Macie should have told Audrey to tell Jessie to call the police. Why wasn't Daniel back yet?

"No one's around to save you."

Calvin stepped closer. He turned in a circle, looking at the ceiling. He thought she was in the loft.

"Vin, put the gun down," Callum's voice rang from the back of the barn.

"Well, if it isn't my traitor cousin." Calvin lifted his gun, aimed at the door where she assumed Callum was, and shot.

Macie bit her tongue to keep from screaming as the sound of the gunshot reverberated off the barn walls. Macie shifted to cover her ears but froze at the small rustling sound. Everything inside of her wanted to scream, but the fear kept her frozen in place, which was a good thing since Calvin would most certainly shoot her. Calvin didn't seem to notice the sound as he continued to speak. Tears rolled down Macie's face, and she blinked more away, determined to stay focused for when her chance to escape came.

"Stay out of this, Callum."

"I can't let you hurt anyone else." Callum didn't sound hurt. Calvin must have missed.

Macie held her breath as Calvin continued to search the barn, then he stared directly at her hiding place. Macie held her breath as Calvin took a slow step toward her. Macie knew he hadn't seen her since his face held curiosity, but in a few minutes, he would find her.

"The police are already looking for you. I told them all about your plot against Thomas and your horse thieving and your plan to get the estate," Callum said.

"That's fine, Callum, but you're coming down with me." Calvin raised the gun, aiming at the back opening.

Calvin returned his gaze to her hiding spot. "As soon as I get rid of all the witnesses, I'm out of here. You can come with me or be arrested. I left plenty of evidence at my office for the police to find that will incriminate you."

"And you have my witness against you for not telling Daniel he inherited the horses, and not Mrs. Bailey. Did Mrs. Bailey even know that?"

Calvin's face turned hard. "No, she didn't, and I guess I will have to get rid of you, too. I might have regretted that a week ago." Calvin swung his arm around to aim at Macie's hiding spot. Macie flinched at the movement.

Someone appeared behind Calvin and rammed into him as he pulled the trigger. Wood splintered above Macie's head as the shot rattled the wall behind the box. Macie shrieked.

She peered through the crack in the crate. Daniel wrestled with Calvin. Macie spotted the gun a few feet away from them. Panic shot through her when Calvin dove toward the gun. Her eyes were riveted to the scuffle. She was terrified Calvin would get the upper hand and shoot Daniel, but she couldn't do anything but watch in horrified fascination.

Daniel tackled Calvin, but Calvin flipped Daniel over his head. Daniel grunted, swiveled, and kicked Calvin's chest. Calvin flew backward, hitting the wall. Callum rushed into her view and dove for the gun.

"Keep your hands where I can see them!" The shout came from the front of the barn.

Daniel's head whipped toward the front opening and kept his hands where they could be seen. Callum copied the gesture.

Detective Clark came into view, and Macie let out a breath. Calvin kneeled and put his hands in the air. He glanced at the gun as another officer kicked it farther away. Calvin glared at Daniel.

Calvin was handcuffed and dragged away.

"That's Callum Davies," Calvin yelled. "He's responsible for Thomas Martin's death."

Daniel's head jerked to stare at Callum.

"I told you I'd take you down with me," Callum said as he stood calmly and waited for the police to also handcuff him.

"Take them both to the police station," Detective Clark said. Daniel scrambled to Macie's hiding place and lifted the lid.

Macie crawled out, her arms shaking. Once she was clear of the crate, she nearly collapsed on the ground.

Daniel dropped the lid and caught her in his arms. He held her close for a moment before loosening his grip ever so slightly.

"Come on," Detective Clark said. "You both better come with me."

CHAPTER 37

Daniel's eyes had a sort of glazed look about them as if in shock, but he took in every part of Macie before returning his gaze to meet hers.

"Are you okay?" he asked as he helped her follow Detective Clark.

Macie shook her head; she wasn't okay. Then she remembered Charlotte. "Charlotte! What did he do to Charlotte?"

"Charlotte's safe. I helped her hide," Daniel said. "But I need to call to her to tell her it is safe."

"The ambulance is here," an officer called across the lawn as they emerged from the barn, and Detective Clark motioned for Daniel and Macie to follow him.

Macie remembered why an ambulance was needed. "Are they...?"

"I'm afraid Emma is," Detective Clark said as they stepped toward the door. "We went into the house first before the maid ran up and said he had gone to the barn."

Macie struggled against Daniel's grip. "We have to get Charlotte." She turned to Daniel. "And make sure Audrey and Evelyn made it to your mom's with Nate."

Detective Clark held up a hand. "You have to come with me to the house. I'll question you there." He turned to Daniel. "Where is the girl?"

"In the trees by the garage, but I told her not to come unless I said it was safe."

Detective Clark nodded. "You better get her quickly, then bring her to the study."

"Can I at least call my mum to check on the other girls?" Daniel asked.

Detective nodded. "Go into the study." He paused and pursed his lips. "Actually. I'll question you in the kitchen. You can check in with your mum, then we'll see if we can figure out what went on here."

Macie followed the detective to the house while Daniel ran to the trees to get Charlotte. Moments later, she came running into his waiting arms. He carried her to meet Macie and the detective at the kitchen door. Macie entered the kitchen in a sort of numb haze. She hadn't been fond of Mrs. Bailey, but she never thought Mrs. Bailey deserved to die.

Daniel helped Macie sit, handed Charlotte to her, then called his mom. Macie held her breath until Daniel nodded, indicating Jessie had Audrey and Evelyn.

"I shouldn't have gotten so mad at Mum. It's all my fault," Charlotte mumbled, her face buried in Macie's shoulder.

"It isn't your fault, Charlotte." Macie rubbed the girl's back as she sobbed into Macie's shirt.

Macie's own tears mingled with Charlotte's cries.

Detective Clark cleared his throat. "We need to talk to each of you alone."

Macie opened her mouth to argue, but Detective Clark held up his hand to stall her.

"After I talk to you and Daniel, I will allow you to sit with Charlotte as she tells me what she can."

Macie wanted to argue. Charlotte wasn't in any kind of condition to talk to the police, but at least she would be there to comfort Charlotte as needed.

Daniel led Charlotte outside accompanied by the police officer, and Detective Clark took the seat Daniel had vacated. Macie relayed everything she could remember, but already felt like she was remembering things in a haze. The tears she had tried so hard to fight flowed down her cheeks, and she didn't bother stopping them. She didn't care who saw her cry now.

"Detective, can you tell me if Mr. Bailey is okay? I know Mrs. Bailey is..." Macie's throat tightened, and the words cut off.

"Mrs. Bailey was pronounced dead at the scene. I'm sorry. We are waiting for updates about Mr. Bailey. You're the nanny, right?"

Macie nodded, her stomach roiling, even though it was empty. She was suddenly glad the detective had the presence of mind to meet with them here in the kitchen instead of the study. Since right outside the study was the scene of the murder.

Murder. Macie nearly choked. How had she got caught up in a murder investigation? She had only wanted to figure out who had taken the horses.

"Can you watch the girls until we know Mr. Bailey's wishes?"

Macie brought her attention to the detective. "Of course."

Macie didn't know what to think or feel. She felt numb.

Charlotte ran to Macie as soon as she exited the kitchen to the backyard. Daniel left to tell his side of the story. Macie sat on the grass, nestling Charlotte into her lap. Charlotte and Macie held each other in silence, tears running down their faces until Daniel reemerged.

Daniel kneeled beside Macie, placing one hand on Charlotte's back and one on Macie's shoulder. "Will you be okay?"

Macie wasn't sure if he was talking to her or Charlotte, but she nodded.

Daniel patted Charlotte's shoulder and stood. "The detective gave me leave to go. I need to get the horses out of the trailer and check on mum and the girls."

Macie stood and brought Charlotte to her feet with her. "Come on, Charlotte."

Charlotte's brown eyes searched Macie, fear evident in their depths. "You won't leave me?"

Macie pulled her close as they walked into the kitchen. "No, Charlotte. I won't leave you."

Detective Clark indicated the seat across the table from where he was sitting. The other police officer stood in the corner next to the door that led to the entry hall. Macie was grateful she didn't have to go there. Macie sat and pulled Charlotte onto her lap.

Detective Clark stood and walked around the table, kneeling so he was eye level with Charlotte. "I know this has been hard for you. I just want to hear what happened from you. You don't have to worry about it being exactly right. Just tell me what you remember. Can you do that for me?"

Charlotte sniffed and nodded.

The detective patted her hand. "That's a good lass."

He made his way around the table and sat with his pen poised.

Charlotte was silent for a moment before she blurted, "I was really mad at Mum because she was going to make Macie leave, so I left the dining room."

She started sobbing. "It's all my fault."

Macie rubbed her back and murmured to her. After a few moments, her tears subsided again.

"Can you tell me what happened after you left the dining room?" the detective asked, his voice soft.

"The front door swung open and a strange man I've never seen came in and grabbed me. I screamed."

Charlotte shuddered, and Macie tightened her hold on her.

"Mum and Papa came running out, and the man pointed something at them. It looked like a gun, but I've never seen one in person. Mum was crying and saying things that didn't make sense, but I could tell Papa was surprised by what she said. Then the gun made two very loud noises. I tried to cover my ears, but the man trapped my arms, and I couldn't." She paused and then whispered. "It was so loud."

She opened her mouth to continue, but then she paled and the tears started anew. Macie rocked her gently on her lap, wishing the detective would say she didn't need to go on.

"Then they both fell," she wailed.

"Your mum and papa?" the detective clarified.

Charlotte nodded. "There was so much blood, but then the man carried me out of the house. I tried to get away." Her voice was tight and tears streamed down her face.

She turned to looked Macie in the face. "Maybe if I didn't yell, Mum and Papa would be okay."

Macie shushed her. "No, sweetheart, you didn't do anything wrong."

"I was kicking with all my might, and my foot hit him. He dropped me, then I heard someone yell 'No!'. It didn't sound like the man who had me, but I ran faster since I didn't see anyone else. I hid behind Gladys's car, and the man walked away. Then Daniel came and told me to hide in the trees until he called for me and not to come out for anyone else. Gladys called for me, but I stayed hidden because I thought maybe the guy had her call for me to trick me. I was so scared Daniel wouldn't come back. What if the man shot him, too? I was afraid I would have to stay in the trees forever."

Macie's chest squeezed as the girls words died down. She hugged the little girl tighter and waited for the detective to tell them Charlotte was free to go. He wrote notes in his notebook and took the time to read through them again. Charlotte had her face pressed into Macie's shoulder, and her quiet sobs continued as Macie rubbed her back gently.

The detective stood up. "We are done for now. Don't go too far in case we have questions. Here's my card in case you think of anything else that will be useful."

Macie took the card, but didn't relinquish her hold on Charlotte. Detective Clark left with the police officer, and the house went quiet. It seemed to Macie they sat forever. Eventually, Charlotte fell asleep in Macie's lap, and soon after, Macie's legs started going numb. Macie wasn't about to move and wake her, though.

"Can she lie in your bed for now?" Macie asked Gladys when she came in. She must have seen the police leave and figured she was safe to come into the kitchen.

Gladys nodded and lifted the girl out of her arms. Charlotte opened her eyes and searched frantically around until she spotted Macie. She reached out to Macie, so Macie stood up and took Charlotte's hand and followed Gladys into her room.

Macie sat on the bed, holding Charlotte's hand until she fell asleep again.

Macie carefully extracted her hand. Charlotte stirred, so Macie rested her hand on the girl's head to comfort her until she settled into a deeper slumber.

When she entered the kitchen, she found Gladys cleaning up dinner. How could she think about cleaning at a time like this? Macie watched her for a moment. Gladys's movements were sharper than needed, and Macie understood that Gladys probably felt the need to keep busy. Macie's heart ached for her friend. Gladys probably wondered what would become of her since her employers were shot.

Macie caught sight of the leftovers and remembered she hadn't eaten, but the thought of food made her stomach turn.

She laid a hand on Gladys's shoulder, bringing the woman's attention to her. "It will be okay," she whispered.

Gladys threw her arms around Macie and held her tight. Her body shook, breaking Macie's determination to keep her emotions in check until she was alone. She and Gladys stood hugging each other for a long moment before Macie broke away. She had to check on Audrey and Evelyn. "Keep an eye on Charlotte, will you?"

"Of course. The police said Daisy, Nate, and I needed to find a hotel by tonight. They will come back in a bit with everyone they need but said it could take a while. They are concentrating on booking Calvin and Callum first."

"Okay. I'll go check on Evelyn and Audrey, but it sounds like I'll need to come back to get Charlotte. We'll need to sleep somewhere else as well." Macie took a deep breath. She needed to tell the girls the bad news, and her heart was already breaking for them.

***

An hour later, Macie was still holding Audrey in her lap, running her hand down Audrey's hair and her back in an effort to comfort her.

Finally, Audrey took a deep breath. "I don't think Mum wanted us, anyway."

Tears sprang to Macie's eyes, knowing that thought hurt more than her mom being taken away. "Why do you say that?"

"She never played with us. If we didn't have a nanny, she would get Daisy to watch us most of the day. When we did have a nanny, we wouldn't see her for days."

Macie held the girl tighter. Audrey would never know her mother's motives for avoiding them. Even Macie didn't understand it. Macie felt that pain with Audrey. Evelyn wiggled out of Jessie's lap and put her small hand on Audrey's. Then she gazed up at Macie.

"Mummy gone?" she asked.

Macie nodded as a rush of tears fell down her cheeks.

"Macie stay?"

Macie's throat tightened, but she forced herself to answer honestly. "I don't know."

Evelyn's lower lip trembled, and she started to cry.

"I'll stay until we know what your dad wants," Macie rushed to add. "I won't leave for a while."

Tears spilled onto Evelyn's cheeks, and Macie picked her up and set Evelyn on her other leg.

"I don't want you to leave," Audrey said.

"I know," Macie whispered into her hair.

Macie had to get to the house but didn't really want to take the girls there. Charlotte might wake up at any time.

"Leave them with me for now," Jessie said softly, as if reading her mind. "In fact, you can bring Charlotte, and you can sleep here."

Macie let out a breath of relief. At least she wouldn't have to find a hotel for them to stay in. Especially since she didn't have a lot of money saved from the five weeks she had been there.

"Thank you," Macie whispered.

Macie hoped Charlotte would eventually be able to stay in the house again without nightmares. Macie made a mental note to call a therapist or counselor for Charlotte. And maybe for herself. She rushed to the house and through the back door.

Charlotte was sitting on a barstool, staring out the window. Her eyes flitted to Macie for a second before returning to cast a blank look over the backyard.

"Gladys, we're going to stay at Jessie's house until the police clear us to come back."

Gladys nodded, and Macie could see the worry in her eyes. "I'll bring over some tarts in an hour, and we can have a little treat before bedtime." She gazed at Charlotte, obviously waiting for a reaction to the mention of her favorite treat. "How does that sound, Charlotte?"

Charlotte shrugged.

Macie held out her hand. "Come on, Charlotte. Let's go see Jessie."

They walked in silence until they got to the bench next to the flower garden in Jessie's backyard. "Why would Mum do that?"

Macie sat on the bench and pulled Charlotte down next to her. "Do what?"

"She wanted to go back to London so bad; she paid someone to steal our horses."

Macie had wondered how much of the talk Charlotte had understood or even absorbed. She hadn't mentioned it to the detective, but maybe in the stress of the moment she had forgotten.

"Do you want to talk to someone about what you saw today? Maybe in a week?"

Her brown, glistening eyes met Macie's. "Would you come with me?"

Macie wrapped both arms around her. "Of course I will. As long as I'm still here."

"You can't go!" Charlotte cried. "Who would take care of us?"

"Hopefully, your dad will pull through and be as good as new."

Charlotte scrunched her nose. "But he doesn't know anything about taking care of us. He's never done anything with us besides eat."

"Maybe we can convince him to let me stay." Macie's voice clogged, and she cleared it. "I want to stay."

Macie needed them as much as they needed her. And not only them. Macie needed Daniel. She needed his strong presence and his acknowledgment of her efforts.

"Macie?" Daniel's voice rang from the house.

Macie turned. Daniel's body was silhouetted in the light from the house behind him. Her heartbeat quickened at the sight of him. Macie took Charlotte's hand. "Are you ready to go inside? We're going to have a sleepover here."

Charlotte gave Macie a tentative smile, but Macie could see in Charlotte's eyes she wasn't as excited as she would have been under different circumstances. Macie grabbed her hand, understanding that she might never be the same.

"Did you get the horses taken care of?" Macie asked when they passed Daniel as he held the door open for them.

Daniel nodded. His eyes took in Charlotte's state, and then he looked back up at Macie with his eyebrows raised.

Macie shook her head. If he was asking if Charlotte was okay, she wasn't. But it was understandable that she wouldn't be.

When they joined Jessie and the girls in the front room, Macie let go of Charlotte's hand. Jessie put up her arms, and Charlotte barreled into Jessie's hug and sobbed. It was clear she felt she had to hold it together for Macie, but she was free to show her emotions with Jessie.

"Gladys said she will bring tarts in an hour," Macie announced softly, more to let Jessie and Daniel know.

Daniel put an arm around Macie's waist. "Mum tells me you guys are sleeping over today. I figured the girls would want to sleep in the same room as you, so I moved some mattresses from the guest rooms into the biggest one."

Macie nodded. She didn't want to meet his eyes, knowing sympathy would be evident in their green depths, and it would undo her. The events of this night were fresh, and she needed to be strong for the girls. They didn't need to see her break down as well.

"I called the hospital," Daniel whispered in her ear. "They are hopeful Jack will pull through."

A sob escaped Macie's lips, but she swallowed and nodded. "I'm glad. I would hate for the girls to be orphaned."

He put his arm around her waist, pulling her closer to him. "They won't be."

CHAPTER 38

LATER, AFTER THE GIRLS fell asleep, Macie sat on the settee in the large guest room. She texted Katie to let her know what had happened. She wished she could call, but knew it was in the middle of the night for her sister still, so she was surprised when her phone began buzzing.

Grateful she had kept the sound off, she answered, whispering, "Hi, Katie."

"You need to tell me the whole story, now." Even though Katie sounded frantic, she kept her voice quiet as well, probably to keep from waking her own family.

Macie quietly told her what happened, letting herself cry as she relived it.

"You know I have to tell Mom and Dad."

"No, let me. I'll call them."

"So, will you be coming back to the States after that?"

"I hope not," Macie whispered. "These girls need me."

Katie sighed. "It sounds like you found your place there. I'll miss you dreadfully, but I understand. Plus, now I can come visit you, and you can show me England."

"I'll be seeing most of it for the first time with you." Macie laughed, but one of the girls stirred so she immediately quieted again.

"I better get more sleep," her sister said through a yawn. "I just happened to be up putting a kid back to bed when you texted."

"Sorry to keep you up."

"Take care, Macie."

"I will."

She sat on the settee, gazing out the window. She couldn't even think about sleep yet. Even though she was exhausted. She stared out the window over the pond and into the distance. If she put her face right against the glass, Macie could see the back porch light still on. The police must still be there working.

The bedroom door clicked open. Daniel stood in the doorway, a light down the hallway filtering into the room. He made his way to Macie and sat down.

"Why aren't you sleeping?"

"I'm not sure I can," Macie admitted. The shots ringing out through the house, the tense moments in the barn... Macie was afraid if she closed her eyes, she would relive those moments much too vividly.

"Are you okay? I mean, from the barn. I didn't get a chance to check on you. Everything happened so fast."

Macie nodded, trying to lie, but then she shook her head. Her body started shaking, and Daniel lifted her and set her on his lap while she sobbed as silently as she could but still let the tears run freely. Daniel rubbed Macie's back while holding her tight against him. Her sobs finally subsided, and Daniel handed her a tissue. She wiped her nose and eyes, but tears continued to flow down her cheeks.

"He was going to shoot me," Macie whispered, finally voicing aloud what she had known and feared. "How did you know where I was?"

"I didn't at first. I was outside the front opening, listening to Callum try to talk reason into Calvin. I snuck in under the gate and made my way closer. When Calvin walked toward where you were hiding, I remembered that was where Charlotte hid. When Calvin aimed at the crate, I just reacted."

He lifted Macie's chin, forcing her to meet his gaze. "My heart nearly stopped when he aimed his gun at you. I was so sure he would check first."

He lowered his lips to meet Macie's, not seeming to care about the tears on her cheeks. He kissed her softly, then kissed her tear-soaked eyes, and her cheeks, before his lips found hers again. Macie broke away.

"What's going to happen to me?" she asked. She had been truthful with the girls. She might have to go home.

"I'm sure Jack will keep you on as the nanny."

"How can you be sure?"

Daniel wiped her tears away with his thumb and rested his forehead against hers. "He knows those girls love you." He slid his hands down her arms, sending shivers through her body. "If he isn't as smart as I think he is, you can stay here and help my mum until I can convince you to marry me."

Macie inhaled sharply. "Marry you? We've only known each other for two months."

Daniel moved his lips next to her ear. "And I was a fool for the first while and wasted a lot of time thinking it would be better to keep my distance."

Macie leaned back to stare into his face. "I thought you thought I was incapable of taking care of myself. And if I remember right, you assumed I was a horse thief."

Daniel pulled her closer so their faces were almost touching. "Can you forgive me for being an idiot?"

"I did a long time ago," Macie whispered as her breath caught, and Daniel kissed her again. His kiss grew hungry, his arms tight around her waist. Macie clutched her arms around his neck, deepening the kiss, afraid that if she let go, this would all end up being a dream. Her whole body trembled as he rubbed her back softly before his grip tightened. When Macie felt she couldn't breathe anymore, she pulled away. Her breath came in rasps. Daniel's eyes were dark with passion. Macie had never had anyone look at her that way before, and she wished he wouldn't stop, but it had to end.

Macie stood up to put some distance between them.

Daniel stood, stepped toward her, and kissed her one more time, so lightly her lips barely registered the touch. "Good night." He glanced at the girls. "Let me know if you need help dealing with nightmares. We'll call CAMHS tomorrow. We can find help for you as well."

"Call who?"

"Child and Adolescent Mental Health Services."

"Oh, yes. Charlotte needs that. What she said she saw..." Macie shuddered. "Probably the other girls, too."

"We can find some help for you as well," Daniel added.

Macie nodded, unable to speak. He moved his hand to her arm and lightly squeezed before making his way around the sleeping girls. He lifted his hand in a goodbye gesture and shut the door before Macie could think of a response.

After the buzzing in her body slowed, Macie remembered what he said. He wanted to marry her. But that was crazy. Why would he want to marry her? Macie sighed and crawled under the covers. She could figure all that out later. First, she had to get the girls to a counselor and hope that Jack survived his gunshot wound.

***

The next morning, Daniel was sitting at the breakfast table when Macie walked in. Her eyes were red, and her hair was still mussed from sleeping on it. Her cheeks reddened when she made eye contact with him, so he winked at her and was gratified when the blush deepened. He stood and pulled out the chair next to him.

"Are you hungry?"

Macie shrugged. "Not really, but I better eat."

Daniel dished her up a plate. "I made enough for the girls and Mum, too. Will you make sure they all eat?"

Macie nodded. "Where are you going?"

"To check on Gladys and Nate and Daisy. The horses still all need tending. I can't do much more than that until the police clear the crime scene, but I also need to show the detective the original will. Until the police clear the place, I can work on what I want to do to start breeding. I called the owners of the other horse that was stolen, and they want to come get it soon, so I need to finish up. He was almost ready to be returned, anyway."

Macie's face reflected confusion, so he went on.

"Sorry. I have to do something. The memories are going to overwhelm me if I don't." He hadn't slept at all the night before. Dreams haunted him. He had witnessed his dad's death, had found Thomas dead, and had found out that it wasn't an accident. He was sure he would go crazy if he didn't do something to distract him. It may not be the healthiest option. He mentally added making an appointment at the health services for him and Macie to the list of things to occupy his time and his mind.

Macie sighed, bringing his attention back to the moment.

"What is it?" Daniel set his fork down.

"I can't help thinking that none of this would have happened if you had been aware of what was in the will."

Daniel's jaw twitched.

"Sorry." Macie stared at her plate, blinking away tears.

Daniel rested his hand on top of hers. Macie met his gaze. He stared at her for a moment, willing her to tell him everything she was feeling, but she looked away. He understood. It might be too soon to relive the last twenty-four hours. Daniel had a feeling that if he had been aware of his part of the will, Mrs. Bailey would have packed up and left long before Macie came. He couldn't wish that away. He needed Macie.

"Do you want to stay here?" Daniel forced himself to voice his fears. He wouldn't blame Macie if she wanted to go back home after what happened.

Macie snapped her head up. "I've never felt more at home than I do here with you and the girls. I'm actually needed here." Macie's voice cracked, and she cleared her throat.

Daniel's grip on her hand tightened. "I want you to stay, but purely for selfish reasons."

Macie's lips twitched slightly, and Daniel couldn't help but smile at the red blotches creeping up her neck. He knew she was thinking of last night. The thought was enough to make him want to take her into his arms again and kiss her senseless.

"I need you probably as much as the girls need you," Daniel said, rubbing his thumb over her knuckles. "I'm not sure when you turned from a cute but frightened young lady to the woman I would give my life for, but I can't stand the thought of you going back across the pond." His lips curved up. "That's a long commute. I'd have to move to the States." He wrinkled his nose to show how distasteful the thought was to him.

"I'm sure it wouldn't be that bad," Macie teased.

"Not as long as you were with me. I could endure anything."

Macie pushed his hand away. "Stop. You're making me blush."

And her cheeks were indeed becoming a light shade of red that mingled so perfectly with her olive skin. She picked up her fork and focused steadfastly on her breakfast.

Daniel chuckled, but immediately sobered. "My mum said you would stay here until the police clear you to go back to the mansion. We have plenty of room for you all to have your own room, but I have a feeling the girls will want to sleep in the same room as you for now. Is that okay?"

Macie met his eyes again, her smile softening the stress lines on her face. "That would be great."

CHAPTER 39

ALMOST A WEEK LATER, Jessie walked with Macie and the girls to the fence that separated the two properties. Charlotte was gripping Macie's hand so tightly her fingers tingled slightly, but Macie didn't complain. She needed support. She had to let go long enough to climb the fence, but as soon as they were both over, Charlotte staked her claim next to Macie.

They walked to the back of the house and entered the kitchen. Gladys and Daisy were both sitting at the kitchen table.

Gladys spoke before she was able to voice a question. "It's all cleaned up. The police cleared us to clean it and called us at the hotel yesterday. We came here first thing this morning to make it look like new."

Macie shuddered and started forward into the kitchen, but Charlotte refused to move. Gladys got up and went to Macie since Charlotte still refused to step into the house. Gladys wrapped her arms around Macie, enveloping her in a warm hug.

Gladys nodded toward the girls. "I hope you got them into a counselor."

"Yes." It had been a nightmare to do so since Macie wasn't their legal guardian. They had to hope Mr. Bailey would be able to sign a paper that said she had permission to take them.

"Should we go welcome Shadow back?" Macie said to the girls. They couldn't stand in the doorway with the door wide open. Charlotte loved the horses. Maybe a minute with them would have Charlotte ready to enter the house.

Evelyn reached up to Macie. She swung the little girl onto her hip. Audrey grabbed onto her hand, and Charlotte bolted out the door. Macie wished she knew how to help her, but she understood her aversion to being in the house since she had witnessed her mother's murder there. Jessie stayed in the house to help Gladys.

Macie walked to the barn. Macie immediately recognized the horse when they reached his stall. The black sheen in his coat was as beautiful as ever. The girls walked to his stall and rubbed his nose.

A few minutes later, Macie jumped when a hand rested on her shoulder. Daniel stood next to her. His solemn face wasn't studying her, but Charlotte. He jerked his head toward the door.

"Can you girls keep Shadow company while I talk to Daniel for a minute?" Macie did a visual sweep of the barn to be sure there was nothing that would harm them. The horses were safely locked in their stalls.

Charlotte looked around nervously.

"Nate will stay here with you," Daniel assured her.

Charlotte nodded and turned her attention to Shadow, but her movements were stiff and robotic, and her eyes continued to dart around the barn.

Once they were out of earshot but could still see the girls petting the horse, Daniel grabbed both of Macie's arms.

Macie studied Charlotte. "I don't know how she'll get back to normal."

"Give her time. Meeting with the counselor will help. I'm sure of it."

Macie shivered, even though it was warm. "I can't imagine how she could move on after seeing something so horrific."

Daniel gathered her in his arms and kissed the top of her head. "She'll always have the memories, but I'm sure she will cope with them. I know it is different, but I witnessed my dad killed in his riding accident. I thought I'd never get over it."

Macie gasped. "I didn't know you saw your dad's accident."

His lips formed a grim line. "My mum doesn't even know. I didn't dare tell her. She had me meet with a counselor, and he was the only one I ever told until you."

Macie didn't know what to say, so she leaned her head against his chest and put her arms around his waist. "I hope Charlotte doesn't have to testify," Macie murmured into his shirt.

Daniel's grip tightened around her. "Me too," he whispered softly, then he pulled back. "Last I heard, Jack is still stable. They are hopeful he will wake soon. I do have some good news."

Macie tilted her head. "I could use some good news."

"Thomas Martin had a list of contacts to start his breeding business. I called a few of them, and they were all excited to work something out."

"That's great."

Daniel moved his hand up and down Macie's arm, and Macie leaned into him.

"It will only be great if you get to stay and be my support." Daniel kissed her forehead, and Macie's cheeks warmed slightly.

"Macie, Daniel!" Gladys yelled as she entered the barn.

"What is it, Gladys?" Macie asked.

"Hospital called. Mr. Bailey is awake."

Macie spun around and bumped into Daniel in her rush to get to the girls. He caught her as she bounced off him. She craned her neck to see behind him, grateful to see Nate hurrying toward them with the girls in tow. Macie grinned at Daniel and snuck under his arm to get to the girls.

"Your dad's awake. Should we go visit him?"

Audrey and Evelyn both nodded. Charlotte shook her head.

Macie put her hand out to her. "Come with us. You don't have to go into the room if you don't want to."

"Promise?" she asked.

"I promise."

"I'll drive you," Daniel said and turned to Nate. "Keep an eye out here, will you?"

"Yes, sir."

They collected Jessie from the house so she could stay with Charlotte if she decided to stay away from her dad's room. Macie was grateful the Bailey car was big enough to hold six.

It took a good half hour to get to the hospital, and by then both Audrey and Evelyn were asleep. Charlotte was so pale; Macie worried she was going to pass out.

"Do you want to stay out here?" Macie asked her.

She nodded.

"I'll stay with her," Jessie said.

Macie smiled her thanks and collected Evelyn, while Daniel got Audrey out of her booster seat and carried her into the hospital. She was awake, but clung to Daniel, hiding her face in his shoulder.

"I'm sorry, only family is allowed," the nurse informed them when they asked where Jack Bailey was.

"These are his kids," Macie explained.

The nurse hesitated a moment more before nodding. "Come with me."

Macie halted at the door of Mr. Bailey's room, unsure if she should send the girls in, but Audrey grabbed her hand and hauled her inside, waving at Daniel to follow. Mr. Bailey had obviously fallen asleep, but Audrey went up to him and grabbed his hand, standing on her toes to see.

"Papa?" Her voice was tremulous, but strong at the same time.

Mr. Bailey's hand tightened around Audrey's, and she broke down. Daniel picked her up and set her next to her father. Mr. Bailey winced as he moved to give her room, but wrapped his arms around her as she curled up next to him and sobbed.

Evelyn wiggled in Macie's arms, and Macie set her down on the other side of her father. "Papa okay?"

Mr. Bailey's lips lifted slightly at the corners, tears forming in his blue eyes. "Papa's okay."

He looked at Macie. "They tell me Emma..." His voice caught, and tears formed in his eyes. Macie bit back her own tears as he struggled against his emotions.

Macie took a few steps toward him. "We don't need to talk about it now."

He lifted his hand that had settled on his stomach. "We do. I need someone to care for my girls. I know Emma wanted to send you home, but I need you. I know the girls love you." He paused and took some slow breaths.

"You may need to be there by yourself during the week until I can get permission to work from home more." He looked away as more tears formed in his tired eyes.

"I'm happy to stay." Macie stepped forward and put her hand on his arm, unsure where he was injured.

"You may not need to work at the same job if you want to help me with the business." Daniel stepped up and put an arm on Macie's shoulder. "I found Thomas's will, and I actually own the horses and business. I am required to share a part of the profits with you as long as you live in the house."

Mr. Bailey's eyes went wide for a moment before he looked away, staring out the window in his room.

"I should have known how miserable she was. It's all my fault."

"Shhh," Macie whispered. It was all she could say. She wanted to say that it wasn't his fault that his wife chose to do what she did, but Macie knew that wouldn't bring any measure of comfort.

"Come on, girls." Macie tugged at Audrey's shoulder and scooped up Evelyn.

"Papa?"

Macie whirled around at the sound of Charlotte's voice.

"Charlotte?" Mr. Bailey's voice sounded pinched.

"Oh, Papa!" Charlotte lurched forward and clung to Mr. Bailey's arm as she sobbed.

Macie finally couldn't hold her tears back, and they slid down her cheeks. Her heart broke for Charlotte. Daniel tightened his hold on her. Mr. Bailey winced as he moved his arm across his chest to rest his hand on Charlotte's shaking shoulders.

Once Charlotte's sobs quieted, Mr. Bailey spoke. "Charlotte. I want you to remember that none of this is your fault. What happened had nothing to do with you. You were in the wrong place at the wrong time. Mum didn't know his plans. It isn't your fault."

When Charlotte continued to hide her face, he spoke a little more firmly. "Promise me, Charlotte."

Charlotte looked up, confusion clouding her wet, shimmering eyes.

"Promise me you won't blame yourself for what happened. You are much too young to take on such a burden."

"I don't know if I can, Papa." Charlotte's voice caught. "If I wouldn't have stomped out from dinner, none of this would have happened."

"Hush now," Mr. Bailey said. "It would have happened one way or another. Calvin was desperate."

Daniel stepped forward and put his hand on Charlotte's shoulder. "If anything, Charlotte, it's my fault for investigating him. He was in trouble, which drove him to desperate measures."

Charlotte's lips lifted into a small smile. "I could never blame you."

Daniel kneeled in front of her, turning Charlotte so his hands were on both of her shoulders, even though she still clutched Mr. Bailey's arm with one hand. "Then don't blame yourself. None of this was your fault."

Charlotte averted her gaze and stared at the floor. "I guess I can try," she finally whispered. Then she let go of her father and threw both arms around Daniel and cried.

Epilogue

Mr. Bailey had taken the girls to visit their mother's grave. It had been three months since the horrific night Mrs. Bailey had lost her life, but Mr. Bailey took the three girls to visit the gravesite every week. From what Charlotte told Macie, he shared the happy memories when Mrs. Bailey was content with her life.

Macie appreciated his efforts to keep her memory happy. Macie also loved the few hours she had to herself. Since it was Sunday, the stable yard was empty. Daniel and Nate didn't work on Sundays and instead let the horses out to pasture. Macie wandered out to watch the horses.

She thought over the last few months. The weeks of therapy had been hard for Charlotte. She didn't talk about it much, but she always came out with a tear-stained face and a calm spirit about her. Macie knew she was healing, but it would probably take years before she fully let go of any responsibility she felt for what happened.

They had all gone to some therapy, but the counselor suggested he keep working with Charlotte even after he said Audrey and Evelyn would be okay, and to continue practicing the tools he gave them to help them cope when memories surfaced.

Macie's parents had flown in to visit shortly after their first visit to Jack in the hospital. They tried to talk Macie into coming home with them, but she told them she belonged here.

"Enjoying your time alone?" Daniel's voice right behind her made her jump, but she wrapped her arms around his waist as he pulled her close.

"I was," Macie teased.

"You don't mind if I interrupt you for a minute?"

Macie grinned. "I guess not, as long as it's for a good reason."

"Then I better get to the point." He kneeled on one knee next to her, opening a ring box to reveal a small teardrop-shaped diamond ring.

Macie's hand flew to her mouth at the same time tears sprang to her eyes.

"Macie Call. Will you marry me?"

"You don't mince words, do you?" Macie asked, laughing. Her chest swelled, making her feel as if nothing could ever be wrong again.

Daniel stood. "You want me to say more?"

Macie tilted her head to see his green eyes dancing. "Maybe."

"Macie. You make my world go round. I thought I knew what I wanted before you came, but now, any future without you feels bleak and unwelcoming. I want you by my side as we run the business, take care of Charlotte, Audrey, and Evelyn, and"—he winked—"maybe have a family of our own."

Macie's breath caught. She couldn't believe this was happening. She had dreamed about this day for as long as she could remember, but to have that dream turned into reality was something else. She could never have imagined such love would course through her when she listened to the man she adored talk about how much she meant to him. She stood on her tiptoes and brushed the lightest of kisses on his lips.

"Daniel, I would love nothing more than to be your wife."

He grinned, but Macie didn't miss how he blinked tears away rapidly. He put the ring on her finger and kissed that hand. Then he lifted her and swung her around once before setting her back on the ground, his eyes lighting in a way she hadn't seen yet.

"Should we go tell your mom?" Macie asked.

"I thought you wanted your alone time?" he asked as he leaned down to kiss her nose.

"Alone time with you sounds even better."

"Yeah?" he asked.

"Maybe we can go tell your mom in a minute," Macie suggested.

"Or two." Daniel kissed both eyelids and traced light kisses along Macie's jawline.

Macie sighed in response and clutched her arms around his neck, pulling him closer.

His lips finally found hers, and she let his kisses express his feelings for her and cement in her mind that she had made the right choice. She belonged here, wrapped in the arms of this amazing man who had shown her what it felt like to be seen for who she was.

To SIGN UP FOR Sharolyn's newsletter and learn of new releases, go to sharolynrichard swriter.com.

ABOUT THE AUTHOR

Sharolyn Richards graduated with a B.A
. from BYU-Idaho in English, emphasis in Creative Writing, and with her M.S. in Literature and Writing from Utah State University. Sharolyn has been published in two nonfiction essay anthology entitled *Wanderlust: a collection of travel tales* and *Faithful Hearts*. *Secrets Beneath the Saddle* is her third novel. Her other novels, *Arlington's Treasure* and *Betrayed in Taiwan,* are available in major bookstores online. When she is not writing or teaching college classes, she likes to spend time with her husband and three kids, cook yummy food, and have dance parties in the kitchen with her kids. She currently resides in Utah. You can find Sharolyn online at sharolyrichardswriter.com and on Instagram @sharolynrichards_writer.